DARK CROSSINGS

KAREN HARPER

MARTA PERRY   PATRICIA DAVIDS

DARK CROSSINGS

ISBN-13: 978-1-62090-168-7

DARK CROSSINGS

Copyright © 2012 by Harlequin Books S.A.

The publisher acknowledges the copyright holders
of the individual works as follows:

THE COVERED BRIDGE
Copyright © 2012 by Karen Harper

FALLEN IN PLAIN SIGHT
Copyright © 2012 by Martha Johnson

OUTSIDE THE CIRCLE
Copyright © 2012 by Patricia MacDonald

CONTENTS

To my husband, Don,
who loves Amish country as much as I do.
And to the helpful and generous Plain People of
Holmes County, Ohio, who prefer not to be named.

THE COVERED BRIDGE

KAREN HARPER

CHAPTER ONE

A STRANGE, SHRILL VOICE dragged Abigail from deep sleep. No, it was two voices, one low-pitched, one high. She huddled under her sheet and quilt, then thrashed against them. Dreams had haunted her again—of a couple running through a cornfield, whooping in delight, with Ben leading the way. Ben laughing, knocking over the stalks...running in crazy circles... Had she been dreaming of Ben and Liddy? No. The voices were real. She could hear them right now.

Clutching the covers, Abby sat bolt upright. At least the people weren't outside her house. Maybe down by the creek, or on the covered bridge. That often funneled sounds her way. Probably *rumspringa* kids, maybe some she knew. Drinking beer, staying out late, just as she had during her running-around time. Or maybe it was outsiders telling ghost tales on the old bridge where, if you shouted loud enough, your voice echoed. *Ja,* scaring someone about the Amish girl and *Englische* boy who hanged themselves there years ago because their love was forbidden.

Despite the fact she was sweating, Abby shivered. She didn't believe in ghosts but she knew the story: the Amish girl had argued with her lover, saying it was wrong to take a life, but he had convinced her to put the noose around her neck and jump with him into the darkness....

Abby stopped breathing and strained to listen to the high-pitched voice again. *Ja,* it was a woman's, strong and strident. Land sakes, couldn't they quiet down and let a body sleep?

Trying to keep calm, Abby fumbled on her bedside table for her flashlight, clicked it on and shot its beam toward her battery-run clock. It was 4:14 a.m.! Now she'd never get back to sleep. She had to get up before dawn to make more mushroom chutney and relish for the Saturday farmers' market. And she wanted to take a loaf of friendship bread over to her new neighbors across the creek, plus harvest more mushrooms.

Her feet hit the rag rug on the floor, and she found her slippers by feel. Though her place was six miles out of town, and the nearest Amish farm was two miles away, she'd lived here for years, first with both grand-parents and then just with *Grossmamm.* She'd never felt afraid here, she told herself, and she didn't now. She knew Wild Run Woods behind the house, Killibuck Creek—really a river—and the old bridge better than anyone. And people had better learn to be quiet at night!

As she wrapped a shawl around her flannel night-gown, another thought hit her. Maybe the folks who had taken over the old Hostetler house across the creek had gone down to the bridge and were arguing. If she were the woman who had just moved into that run-down place, she might be shouting, too.

By now her curiosity was as awake as she was. In the front room, she knelt by the window she'd left cracked in the crisp September air, and raised the sash a bit higher. The woman's voice wasn't Amish in tone or rhythm. Abby couldn't be sure, but the man must be a modern, too. This part of Eden County had folks who weren't Amish, but they all had the good sense not to be disturbing the peace this time of night.

A light shone from one of the windows on the bridge everyone called "the Hanging Bridge," partly because it was suspended from the rocks above the rapids but also because of the double suicide that had happened there. She couldn't imagine taking one's own life for love. Sad that two young folks couldn't see there was so much to live for, even apart. Why, she'd turned down Elam Garber's proposal a few months ago, and she felt she had plenty to live for.

It wasn't that she didn't sympathize about true love, Abby told herself. She'd seen her older sister, Liddy, as well as friends and cousins, fall in love and get married. But she'd given up on passion and desire ever since she'd been silly and stupid enough to have a huge crush on Liddy's eighteen-year-old come-calling friend, their neighbor Ben Kline. That had been about ten years ago, when she was a mere kid of fourteen. Thanks to Ben messing up his life, he hadn't married Liddy, and had left here for good, jumped the Amish fence to the big city of Cincinnati. Until she found someone who swayed her head and heart like he had, she was content to run her business and her life, Amish to the core and yet a bit on her own, too.

"You're an idiot!" she heard the woman screech, followed by something she couldn't catch. Despite the constant rustle of white water over rocks below the bridge, the female voice carried.

That's all she could take, Abby decided. She was

going to go out, shine a light their way, then hustle back
here and lock herself in.

She hurried into her kitchen, banging her shin on a
log plugged with oyster mushroom spawn, and got her
big flashlight. She'd needed both lights to gather the
mushrooms after dark last night, then pack and store
them in the cellar for sale at the market. She went out
the back door, which faced her mushroom beds and the
forest beyond, then hurried around the side of the house
onto the river path. She knew each step in the dark, so
she'd wait to use the large flashlight until she was on
the old, now-deserted road that led to the bridge.

Once she was there, she aimed at the black throat of
the bridge and turned on the big beam.

Ach! Even pointed away, the brilliance almost
blinded her. The shaft of light illuminated a woman
dressed in black and wearing an Amish prayer *kapp,*
so it must be one of her people. The figure turned toward the light, threw up a hand to shield her eyes and
hissed, "Someone's coming. Get down!"

The voice was *Englische!*

And get down from what? Surely someone wasn't
drunk enough to jump out a window into the rapids,
even though the river was up with all the rain. They'd
be smashed on the rocks below, maybe drowned.

Abby heard something clatter, then a man's low
voice. Not wanting a confrontation, she clicked off her
flashlight, turned and fled, losing one slipper, but not
turning back. In the house, she locked the door and
peered out the kitchen window. Nothing now. No light,
no sound. About ten minutes later she saw red taillights
on the far side of the bridge disappear, as if a wild animal were backing away into the blackness.

AFTER BREAKFAST, Abby searched hard for her lost slipper and couldn't find it. So she fed her buggy horse, Fern, let her out to graze in the small meadow, then had a hearty breakfast of a honey mushroom frittata and herbal tea before going to work.

Her wood ear mushrooms—"They are listening!" *Grossmamm* always used to say since they looked like human ears—seemed perfect as she used her sharpest harvesting knife to cut them from the stacked logs she'd inoculated with their spawn last year. After she finished, she'd take that loaf of bread over to the new couple she'd caught a glimpse of moving in. She couldn't see them that well through the autumn trees, but she could tell they were *Englische*.

Abby prayed they would be good neighbors, as she intended to be. A shame they were moderns, but she didn't mind her half-hour buggy rides into town for market and church on her own. Unlike most Amish *maidals* with many siblings, Abigail Baughman had only one sister, who now lived in Pennsylvania. A baby brother born too early in a bad birth had taken their mother with him. Because her parents were forty when she was born, and Liddy seemed so much older, more like a second mother, Abby had always felt like an only child. She had lots of friends from her school days, and many cousins, but she had to admit she'd become a bit of a loner, especially after her *mamm* died and *daad* still traveled so much with his construction team.

Many Amish girls were married by twenty-four, Abby's age. She knew she'd find the right Amish man one day and rear her own family. But he'd have to live out here where she could pursue the wildcrafting, gathering and overseeing of the mushroom crops that were, as *Grossmamm* also used to say, "Our bread and butter."

About ten o'clock, after making a kettle of mushroom chutney, left on the stove to cool, Abby changed her work apron and shoes, donned her bonnet over her prayer *kapp* and packed up the loaf of friendship bread. It wasn't quite hunting season yet for deer or wild turkey, only for squirrel, but she locked the door behind her. Last year two *Englische* hunters had scared her to death. She'd come back from gathering precious morels in the woods and walked into her kitchen to find them getting drinks of water.

As she set out, still skimming her gaze across the ground for her lost slipper, she jerked to a stop. Two sets of tracks—and hers—marred the mud by the path where she'd watered her ever-thirsty shaggy mane mushrooms yesterday. One print was smaller than the other, but they could have belonged to either sex. The mud was so wet that only the shape of the shoe was there, not tread marks.

Abby followed the footprints toward her house and around the edge of the bed of wood chips that boasted her big parasol mushrooms, then lost them where the sawdust trail began. In the meadow behind the fence, Fern was cropping grass. The gentle mare looked up at Abby as if to ask, "What? What's wrong?"

"Nothing," Abby answered, and headed down the path toward the bridge again. Just someone passing through? Squirrel hunters? She'd heard some distant rifle shots yesterday. Had Elam come to pester her again, maybe with Ruth Yutzy, the new girlfriend he'd been showing off? Or maybe the tracks belonged to the people who had been on the bridge? But she hadn't seen or heard anyone follow her last night. Keeping an eye on the woods, she continued down the path.

Several covered bridges in this area drew occasional visitors, but none were used much anymore. The Hanging Bridge, once called the Homestead Bridge after the nearby town, had been built of white oak in the 1870s. It was wearing well, partly because its roof and some support beams had been restored about a decade ago. The foundations were planted firmly in the bedrock ledges above Killibuck Creek, and a web of trusses supported the plank flooring and roof. Six square openings were cut into each side of the 140-foot span to let in light, but they weren't big enough that horses could see out and get spooked by the rushing water beneath.

A weight limit on motor vehicles was posted at each entrance. Once painted red, the weathered boards had now faded to a soft, pinkish gray. Years ago when *Mamm* and *Daad* used to bring her and Liddy out to help *Grossmamm* harvest her crops, Abby had thought the bridge looked like a big old barn hung right over the river. It must also look like that to the barn swallows that flew in and out and suspended their cup-shaped, mud pellet nests from the beams and rafters.

As she passed the point on the bridge where she'd seen the woman last night, she noted nothing unusual. At least whoever it was hadn't made a campfire, like some careless kids last year. The char marks from the flames that could have caught the entire bridge on fire still showed. Abby pictured again how the woman's white *kapp* had glowed and her white palm caught the light when she'd thrown her hand up. Of course she could not have been wearing a prayer *kapp,* Abby realized now, because something had glittered on her wrist.

No Amish woman ever wore gold or jewels, not even a wedding band.

Abby breathed in the clear, crisp air as she headed down the path on the other side of the river. The neighbors' house was not directly across from hers, but almost. When the leaves dropped, she'd be able to see in their windows, as they would hers. Then it hit her: could the new couple have been walking around her house after they'd argued on the bridge last night? It was obvious she was the one who had shone the light on them. Maybe they'd picked up her slipper... But it would be rude and unkind to ask.

She shook her head to clear it, and sent up a silent prayer for peace of spirit and good relations with her new neighbors. Besides, this close, the long-abandoned house didn't look as forbidding. A curl of sweet-smelling smoke wafted from the chimney. A well-kept black truck with large pieces of wood stacked neatly in its bed sat in the gravel driveway. The windows she'd seen the woman washing yesterday gleamed in the sun. If it wasn't farm market day tomorrow, Abby would volunteer to help her get settled. Maybe she would later.

She walked up on the porch, which creaked, but a new-looking swing for two, painted a fresh white, was hanging from two shiny chains. She noted that from the swing the couple could see her house and mushroom patches through the yellow and orange leaves.

Before she could knock, the door opened. Abby stumbled back a step and drew in a sharp breath. Her heartbeat kicked up and her pulse began to pound. A tall man stood there, broad-shouldered, blond with intense eyes as green as grass. He was dressed modern, in jeans and a bright blue flannel shirt, but she knew instantly who he was. Though he'd been gone ten years, he was still under the *bann,* ostracized by and forbidden to the Amish.

Before her stood the man of her girlhood dreams, who now tormented her in nightmares. Ben Kline, her sister's come-calling friend. A man Abby had once silently, sinfully adored.

CHAPTER TWO

"ABIGAIL BAUGHMAN! Abby?" Ben asked when she stared up at him a minute too long, almost as if she'd seen a ghost. He bent his knees a bit to see under her bonnet, and came out onto the porch. "I never figured you'd still be living with your *grossmamm* almost next door. You've sure changed! You're looking beau— Looking great."

"I'm not. I mean, I'm not living with *Grossmamm*. She's moved to Pennsylvania and left me the mushroom farm." Abby started to gesture with her hand, although he obviously knew where she lived. She felt a fool when she realized she was waving the loaf of bread in the air.

Abby had never spoken to a shunned person before, and Ben had chosen to use English, not the familiar *Deutsch,* so didn't that hint he was content with worldly ways? When someone was under the dreaded *meidung,* or *bann,* the Amish were not to seek him or her out in hopes that shame and loneliness would return that person to the fold. It was permissible to give them gifts, but not to accept things from their hands or eat with them—or, if wed to the shunned person, to sleep with them. But since Ben had chosen the world, his worldly wife would hardly heed those rules.

"Abby, you okay? I didn't mean to startle you. You want to sit down in the swing?"

"No—I'm fine."

"How's Liddy?"

"Oh, fine," she blurted a bit too loudly, realizing she sounded like an echo of herself. "She wed Adam Miller five years ago this fall, lives in Union County, Pennsylvania, near where *Grossmamm* lives now, because she—*Grossmamm*—had arthritis bad, so I took over for her. Liddy's wedding was here, and I haven't seen her for two years since I went to another big Miller wedding there...." Realizing she was rambling, she thrust the bread at him, careful their hands didn't touch. "Here, for you and your wife. You understand I won't be able to mix with you, but tell Mrs. Kline she's welcome to come over anytime."

Ben's eyes bored into hers. She felt pinned to the porch, like a butterfly in a collection. Benjamin Kline was tall for an Amish man; she had to look up at him. His hair was cut close and mussed. Unlike the married brethren, he had no beard, though a golden stubble gilded his tanned cheeks and square jaw. His nose was a bit crooked, maybe from the brawl that had got him shunned. His shoulders and chest muscles were bigger than she recalled. *Ja,* he'd put on some weight from the lanky boy he'd been, but he carried it well. As ever, it was his eyes that unsettled her. They always reminded her of a deep pond she and her friends used to swim in, even though it was forbidden.

Ben took the loaf of bread in one big hand. There were nicks and cuts on it and a single, flesh-colored bandage. "I understand about your treatment of someone still under the *bann,* Abby. But I'm not married."

"Oh! Well, me, neither. But I saw—I mean, when I glanced over yesterday..."

"The woman here? Maybe you didn't see her husband. They're friends from Cincinnati who owned the place I rented there. They helped me move my stuff in, lots of wooden boxes and carved chests. I'm a carpenter of sorts, not an artist, but an artisan. I design and carve the boxes, mostly for jewelry, and lately I've been doing hope chests, too—since I knew I was coming back home."

Back home. His words echoed in her head. She realized she was gaping at him again. An Amish man—former Amish—making boxes for fancy, prideful things like jewelry. Her people did not approve of adorning themselves with anything.

"I see," was all she could say to that admission.

"I don't think you do. The boxes can be used for other things or sold outside the community, just like the Amish-built gazebos, where worldly folk might have their parties with liquor, or like that porch swing where someone cheating on his wife could sit with another woman. The things themselves aren't evil, and how they are used is the choice we all make. Abby, if you talk to others, you can tell them I've come back to see if the old life is for me. And if not, this is a great place to get hardwood and make a living—though if I don't ask to rejoin the church, the Amish won't be buying a thing from me. But I had to try to bridge the gap, come on home."

Abby's thoughts raced. Ben Kline was unburdening himself to her. Treating her like someone who could be trusted, not like the young girl who'd tried to tag along with him and Liddy and their buddy group. Best yet, he was considering returning to the church. He'd have to atone, of course, for his display of violence and his defiance when he'd left, though it had happened long ago. Folks said he'd always been a troublemaker, even before he'd beaten up the man who had assaulted his sister, and then told the bishop and elders that he could not repent for what he'd done.

"I surely hope and pray you can find your way back to the church," she said, "to us, just as you've found your new house." She began to back away. "So it's all right to let others know, *ja?*"

"Word's gonna get out fast, anyway. I'm planning to set up a booth at the farmers' market tomorrow, so maybe I'll see you there."

"That's good," she said, remembering just in time to turn and not tumble backward down the porch steps. "So, see you there." *And everywhere else now,* she thought, *not just in my crazy dreams.*

BEN COULD NOT BELIEVE the transformation in Abigail Baughman. Ten years ago, she'd been a gawky girl, skinny, all legs and pretty much a pest. But she'd become a beauty with her shapely form and expressive face. He was now used to seeing women with flyaway bangs and long, loose styles—or one in particular with short, sculpted silver hair. Yet Abby's long blond hair, parted simply in the middle and pulled back, seemed so natural. Sure, she'd been shocked to find him here, and nervous. He tried to remember why he'd always wanted to ditch her years ago when she'd hung around, staring at him with those big blue eyes. He hadn't thought of her sister, Lydia, in a long time, but he bet she couldn't hold a candle to her kid sister now.

He realized he was just standing there, staring at the sway of her hips and swing of her ankle-length, dark green skirt as she walked away. He hurried after her, his big strides easily catching up. She must have heard him coming because she spun around.

"Forgot to tell you," he said, "the bread's much appreciated."

"It's called friendship bread. Maybe someday you'll be friends with your people again."

He nodded. They stopped about six feet apart. His eyes trailed over her once again.

"Oh, I meant to ask," she said abruptly. "Did you hear voices on the bridge last night—I mean in the morning, around 4:00 a.m.? A man's and a woman's? They had their car parked somewhere on the road on this side."

He didn't let on, but the possibility that someone could have been sneaking around really annoyed him— scared him even. What if it was that Cincinnati detective or the pushy female investigator from the insurance company again? "No," he told her. "I was so exhausted I fell asleep with my headphones on. You know, listening to music," he added when she frowned. He hoped she believed him.

"They just woke me up, that's all. See you," she called back as she hurried away.

He had more he wanted to say, but he had to let her leave, so he just called after her, "Right. See you!"

ON HER WAY HOME, with her head and heart full of long-buried memories of her secret crush on Ben, the morning sun was slanting sideways into the bridge through the eastern windows. Abby had come here once with Liddy and Ben to make plans about creating circles in the Stutzman cornfield, a prank that got them all in trouble. Well, not exactly, since no one knew who was to blame. She felt embarrassed now that she'd almost blackmailed the two of them into letting her go along.

Ben had thought it would be funny to make everyone guess what had caused the two large circles they themselves had made after dark with boards, pushing the half-grown corn flat in one direction. After all, he had argued, his laughter and voice echoing right here on this bridge, the Plain People loved a good joke.

But everything had gotten blown out of proportion, kind of the way her feelings for Ben always had. The local paper had featured the circles, and the story was picked up worldwide. *Ja,* even over the ocean! Aliens Visit Amish Farm, Leave Crop Circles! one headline in the grocery stores had screamed, and people had trampled a lot more corn coming to see for themselves.

Ben had felt guilty enough to leave fifty dollars of his hard-earned money from his job at the sawmill for Noah Stutzman, who had lost some of his crop. No one ever knew who was to blame. Ben had made Abby and Liddy take an oath—those were *verboten,* too—not to tell by pricking fingers and mingling blood drops. Besides, Ben had said to them, all the outsiders coming into town had boosted sales in the local stores and restaurants, so something good had come of his idea.

Land sakes, Abby thought now, heaving a huge sigh. Life with Ben was probably always like that, exciting and amazing and—and entirely forbidden.

Something on the planked bridge floor caught her eye, a glitter, a tiny pinpoint dancing in a shaft of sunlight. Then it was gone, so she backed up a bit. There it was again, sparkling in the crack between two floorboards.

Expecting to find a drop of water or a piece of cel-

lophane, she bent closer. A jewel! A diamond, set in a
circle of gold with a tiny spike out the back of it. A piece
of a pin? Part of a ring, or maybe an earring worldly
women wore through a hole in their earlobes? Last summer at the farmers' market, Abby had seen a woman
who wore something like this stuck right through her
nose.

She cradled the jewel in her palm in the patch of sunlight, examining it, turning it. Glorious colors, glinting,
flashing. And since the woman on the bridge last night
must have worn a sparkly bracelet, could this be hers,
too? It was no doubt dear and precious, so maybe she
would come looking for it. But Abby dared not leave a
sign saying she'd found it, or anyone could come and
claim it. She would keep it safe, though, in case someone did ask about it.

As she walked home, for one moment she regretted
that her people never wore or possessed such beauty.
After all, God had made diamonds deep in the earth,
and they reflected his heavenly light. But thoughts
like that would only get her in trouble—and so would
thoughts of how much she still felt pulled to Ben Kline.
It was bad enough to dream about him at night, but now
with him living just across the bridge…

"Head home, Abby!" she scolded herself aloud.
"Hide this jewel and get busy, 'cause you have lots to
do, and Ben Kline's not any part of it."

CHAPTER THREE

ABBY LOVED THE farmers' market, which ran on Saturdays from May through October. The vendors' booths and tables stretched down both sides of the one-block downtown on Homestead's Main Street. She always set up tables for her Wild Run Woods Mushroom Products on the north side of the street at the edge of the sidewalk in front of the Homestead Hardware Store and across from the Citizens Bank.

On blue-and-white oilcloth, she displayed her array of fresh mushrooms and canned relishes and chutneys in gleaming glass jars. In the near future, she would also have walnuts gathered from the woods and bunches of bittersweet tied with pumpkin-colored ribbons.

Besides the money she made from sales to Amish and *Englische* alike, market day meant she got to see her buddy group friends and meet new people. She spent the whole day in town, stocking up on supplies, chatting, getting new books from the Eden County Public Library bookmobile parked down the street, and depositing some money in the bank, which also had the town's post office. First thing she always did was pick up her week's mail.

Today she was thrilled to find a circle letter from Sarah Weaver, one of her second cousins who had become special friends she'd made two years ago at the big Levi Miller–Lizzie Troyer wedding in Pennsylvania. Sarah had proposed this way to keep in touch— a round-robin letter, she'd called it, where each would write about her life and then pass it on in their circle of three. Though she was anxious to read the letter, Abby tucked it carefully away in her purse with the rest of her mail until she had time to savor it. Then she would add her news and pass it on to Lena Troyer.

It felt so strange to bond with long-distance cousins, both unwed and her age. Too bad they lived far apart because they had so much in common. Their conversations were deep and sharing. All three of them wanted to marry but had nothing definite on the horizon. How fast time had flown since those exciting days they had spent together. Sarah and Lena were the only two who knew about her girlhood crush on Ben. Wait until she wrote them that he was living in plain sight now and might even become plain again! *Ja,* that's exactly what she'd write.

The new circle letter almost burned a hole in her purse as she hurried back to her tables.

The traffic was always diverted on market day, so only pedestrians crowded the street. Homestead, the county seat, was made up of a variety of businesses, including a grocery, hardware, three fast-food places and one Amish country cooking restaurant, an antiques shop, volunteer fire department and county sheriff's office. A scattering of houses curled around each end of town before the hills and rolling farms began. The charm of the place and the large population of Amish living, working and selling their goods here made this a tourist stop. Two buses were already parked a couple blocks away and visitors, as usual, had poured out of them.

As she sat in her lawn chair behind her table, she saw that Ben Kline was doing what he'd said he would. From the back of his truck parked in a side alley, he was unloading several carved chests just the size to store linens and quilts for a future marriage and family. A hope chest—what a good name for that sort of big box. Someone she didn't recognize had stopped to help him unload.

Already he'd arranged a row of polished, smaller boxes on his two long, wooden tables. The hand-printed sign hanging above them read Storage or Gift Boxes. From across the increasingly crowded street, like it were a river of people between them, she saw curious folks already stopping to look at his goods. Worldly people pressed close to his table, and though some of the Plain People greeted him, they were obviously keeping back.

BEN WAS PLEASED to be making sales, all tourists so far. Even the non-Amish farm families from the area didn't approach his table, though some called out hi or waved his way.

Another tourist came up and stood staring at his boxes—and then he saw who it was. Melanie Campbell, the insurance investigator who had been watching him since the jewelry heist. He might have escaped to Amish country, but he hadn't escaped her.

"I suppose this is a coincidence and you're just another tourist, Ms. Campbell," he said. He'd found the best way to deal with her was to be straightforward. She usually wore imposing black pantsuits and starched white blouses, but she had actually dressed down for once. Yet even this setting had not softened her stiff, sour expression. She was probably in her fifties, but tried to look younger with long, dyed blond hair that just didn't fit the wrinkles and frown lines on her face.

"Right. Just a tourist," she said, glancing from him to his boxes and back again. "One who's real interested in how you've landed on your feet far from Cinci. You must have saved a lot of money to be able to buy a home here on the river."

"The place is a real fixer-upper. Maybe you haven't seen it."

"Actually, I have."

He squinted up at her in the morning sun. "I don't appreciate having anyone dog my steps."

"Are you calling me a dog, Benjamin Kline?" she said, crossing her arms over her chest. "A hound dog, maybe. Yeah, I like that. And I won't give up on your scent until you come clean, because you reek of guilt. Meanwhile, enjoy playing Amish!" She took a step away, then turned back. "Actually, I am here as a tourist today. My husband's with me and likes plain country cooking. See you. And I will see you." With a toss of her head, she was gone.

Ben took a few deep breaths, as if to clear the air. He could only hope the woman was as dedicated to keeping an eye on the other suspects who had worked at the store. Harassment must be her standard procedure. Maybe she and her husband were the ones bothering Abby. He'd heard Melanie Campbell would get a big cut of the value of Tornellis' stolen property if she could find it or the thief. The owners of the jewelry store where he'd worked were wealthy people.

At least he was pleased to have a clear view of Abby

from time to time. She was distracting him, but in a nice way. Since his life had blown up in his face, both personally and professionally, the last thing he needed right now was to get involved with a woman, especially someone Amish. But if it was Abby...

Maybe running back here had not been the right thing to do. He'd known it might make him look guilty, but the detective and that insurance hound dog that had been sicced on him could search all they wanted. They'd find nothing but a guy who had screwed up his life once and wasn't going to let it happen again, even if he was their main "person of interest."

As for a real person of interest, Abby was looking at him, too, and despite the crowd that flowed between them, it suddenly seemed as if they were the only two people here.

ABBY TRIED NOT TO FEEL prideful about the bounty of the farmers' market with its mostly Amish vendors. But who else could fill the laden tables and bright booths adorning the sidewalks with food and handmade items?

Open boxes boasted pyramids of shiny crimson and golden apples, squash and pumpkins. Stacks of fresh-picked sweet corn, globes of red and white onions and potatoes all smelled sweetly earthy, but they, too, seemed to shine in the sun. On beds of chipped ice, Swiss and Colby cheese and trail bologna awaited buyers. The Zook family booth offered honey, maple syrup, molasses and sorghum. Tables with bakery goods, from pies to cakes to breads, dotted both sides of the street. Amish cooks often shared their recipes and baking with each other, trading or giving them away. If one woman ran out of something or a pie was requested that she didn't have, she would send the buyer right over to another table. All the Plain People ignored the American hunger for competition and lived in cooperation.

Nonfood items included young Gabe Kauffman's birdhouses, and next to Ben's display were wooden puzzles, games and kids' wagons. Abby's friend Ella Lantz sold her lavender products, and beside her was a booth with late-blooming herbs. Hand-sewn, quilted wall hangings and table runners were displayed on dowels at another booth. Faceless Amish boy or girl dolls spilled from yet another table, and more than one plain child too young to understand Amish restraint and control wailed if they couldn't have one.

Restraint and control, restraint and control, Abby recited to herself as her former come-calling friend, Elam Garber, sauntered up to her table with Ruth Yutzy in tow.

"Still doing everything on your own," Elam said. "Just the way you like it, *ja.*"

"Hello, Elam. And Ruth," she said, ignoring his baiting tone. Elam had not taken it well when she'd turned down his marriage proposal and asked him not to come calling again—a request he'd ignored at first, appearing several nights in his new-bought, two-seat, open buggy, and pestering her to go for a ride. While they were courting, she hadn't been sure if he'd taken a liking to her or her property. More than once he'd said he could help her sell it to the gun club in town for a hunting lodge. Not that he belonged to that group, but he had worldly friends who did.

Besides, Elam thought messing around with mushrooms and compost piles made her look off her bean. Instead of fungi, he always said 'Fun? Gee!" and thought

"There's a fungus among us" was really funny. Elam worked at the buggy shop in town, but always turned his head when a fancy car went by, and his heart wasn't in any kind of farming. He was brown-haired and blue-eyed, thin and very ambitious. They'd had some fun together, but she told him he'd best spend his money and his time on someone who might marry him.

Obviously, from the adoring expression on her freckled face, the much younger Ruth was that girl. Sad to say, Abby recognized the look and feeling, but not from when Elam had come calling.

As Ruth started off ahead, Elam turned back and lowered his voice. "You have put me to shame. Folks keep asking about you, even when Ruth is right there."

"I didn't put you to shame. You know it's our way to keep courtships quiet. You're the one who spread the news before you asked, not me."

"Oh, no. Not you. In love with your mushrooms, not a man, that's you! You'll be sorry," he growled, then hurried off to catch up with Ruth.

Again, Abby marveled at his pent-up anger. Could Elam have been sneaking around her house, maybe with Ruth? Just two weeks ago he had suddenly appeared and scared her silly when she was working by lantern light after dark. But as for Ruth Yutzy raising her voice and arguing on a covered bridge or anywhere else—no way.

The morning swept by as customers bought her products. Abby kept trying to catch glimpses of Ben through the shifting parade of people—just to see how he was doing. After another quick glance at him, she dragged her gaze and mind back to business.

"Yes," she answered Ella, who had darted down from

her lavender booth. "The red in the chutney is chopped peppers. The spices are cloves and allspice."

"I think that's what I bought from you once before and really liked," Ella said, examining the preserve through the glass jar. "I'll take two and give one to *Mamm*. By the way, I can see you know who's back in town. Your sister's old and now forbidden friend."

"He's living out across the bridge from me and says he's here to examine his life and maybe rejoin our people."

"*Ja*? I'll have to tell Bishop Esh. If Ben's taken back, our people will do more than just say hello. From my booth, I can see he's only getting short greetings and nods so far. It's probably a good thing your sister doesn't live here now, 'cause she might still have a soft spot in her heart for him, and *Daad* said he was always trouble. Well, see you later if you're going to stay for supper at the restaurant." She turned as the owner of the Dutch Farm Table came up beside her. "Oh, hi, Mrs. Logan! Table for six of us buddy group friends when this is over!" With a wave Ella darted off with her jars of chutney.

"You all sure do love your eating and talking," Ray-Lynn Logan said with a smile. "What's that expression you use?"

"*Klatsche und schmatze,*" Abby told her. "Talking and eating. It's one of our secret rules," she added with a little smile.

Ray-Lynn, a middle-aged redhead with a Southern accent, usually sent one of her waitresses to the market to buy button mushrooms for breakfast omelets and soup. But word was that the owner of the popular restaurant was pretty sweet on the county sheriff, Jack Freeman, whose office was at the end of the street. He always walked the Saturday market, chatting with the locals. Maybe that's why Ray-Lynn had come out herself today, though the sheriff was over talking to Ben right now.

"What's the one that tastes like cashews, Abigail?" Ray-Lynn asked, looking over the array of fresh mushrooms, each with its hand-lettered label. "Not for the restaurant, but for me. I love the flavor of cashews, but if I overeat the nuts themselves, they send me to the ladies' room a bit too often, if you know what I mean."

"Better switch to the walnuts I'll have in a couple of weeks," Abby told her. "But these oyster mushrooms— that's what you're thinking of. Stir-fry them for about fifteen minutes or just garnish salads with them. And here are the sacks with your standing orders."

Ray-Lynn paid Abby and put her purchases in her cloth bag, chatting about how she'd love to decorate her restaurant at Thanksgiving with the turkey tail mushrooms, because they looked just like the bird. Abby tried to concentrate on everything this kindly woman was saying, but she kept darting looks across the street to see how Ben was doing. Sheriff Freeman hadn't been in office when Ben lived here before, so maybe he was checking Ben out.

Her next customer, a man she did not know, had bought one of Ben's boxes. He put it down while he paid for the mushrooms, and Abby had a chance to see it up close. Maple leaves were carved on the corners and scattered across the top. It was absolutely amazing, just as Ben had always been.

ABBY, ELLA AND FOUR OTHER friends met for a late-afternoon dinner at the Dutch Farm Table Restaurant each market day. Mrs. Logan gave them a big table in the back room and they chatted and laughed. As Abby tied Fern's reins to the long hitching post in front of the restaurant, she saw that Ben's black truck was parked nearby. When she went in, he was at the counter where singles often sat. She just said, "Hope you had a good day," as she went by toward the back room.

"Looking good right now," he said to her, keeping his voice low, too.

Now what did he mean by that? she thought, as a bolt of heat raced down her spine and curled in the pit of her belly. But she didn't glance back as she longed to do.

Abby and her friends ordered quickly—they all had the big menu memorized—and it didn't take long for Clara to mention Ben.

"I heard a rumor he's here to rejoin the church, and if he does, can't you just imagine the *maidals* who will be hoping he comes calling? He'll weigh an extra hundred pounds by the time their *mamms* and *grossmamms* get done feeding him up at their tables, he sure will!"

"And I bet you'll be first in line, Clara Hershberger!" Ella said with a pert grin. "But Abby used to know him, 'cause her sister went with him for a couple of years. And did you see those not-just-for-pretty hope chests he makes? I'm going to start saving for one, fill it with lavender and linens."

"I think," Barbara Yoder said with a smothered laugh and an elbow to Ella's ribs, "you two could go into business together—lavender sachets sold in his carved boxes. I saw one with butterflies all over it and another with tulips, so why not lavender outside—and in?"

Barbara Metzler, who was a bit older, sighed and rolled her brown eyes. She was the schoolteacher and always sounded like one. "Now, let's bow our heads and thank the good Lord for bringing Ben back, and hope he'll return to the fold. Then Abby can describe that old house he bought, since she's just a stone's throw away."

"That's right!" Clara said, looking up from her first attempt to bow her head. "He's really close to you."

"Living close," Abby corrected. "But if he's just a stone's throw," she went on, her pulse pounding hard for no reason except they were talking about her and Ben in the same breath, "it's like one of those throws where the stone just skips and skips over the water and doesn't land where you ever meant it to."

Ella frowned at her, and the others went silent. "Like what does that mean?" Ella asked. "Never mind. Are you sure you're not eating those kinds of mushrooms that mess up your head? Now, I'm just teasing. You can tell us how it was when he was close to your sister, and what you know about him beating up that *Englische* guy that tried to—" she dropped her voice to a whisper now, as if they were talking about a mass murderer "—put his hands all over Ben's sister. That's the way my brother Seth explained it. And then Ben refused to admit to the bishop and the elders he'd done wrong, and got put under the *bann*."

As the waitress placed their rolls and salads on the table and they finally bowed their heads for a moment of silent prayer, Abby admitted to herself and to the Lord that she and her friends gossiped too much. She also admitted—as she would never do to anyone else, ever—that she still cared for and wanted Ben Kline, no matter what he'd done wrong in the past or even if he did something bad now. That's just how much she was slipping into sinful thoughts about him again!

ABBY WAS STILL AGONIZING over Ben and that diamond she'd found when she got home just before sunset and unpacked her few unsold goods. As daylight faded, she unharnessed and fed Fern in the small barn she used for her gardening tools. Next she went down into the cellar where she hid her extra cash in a metal box, way back on the shelves. In front of it, she stacked the panes of glass held together with duct tape that kept her mushroom spore prints ready to be sown on prepared hosts.

But her lantern light wavered, and she felt a sudden cold draft down here. That was odd. The first thing she thought was that she didn't need her spores getting chilled or the buckets of water with spore slurry icing over.

She gasped. One of the cellar windows was lifted up—wide open, when she had left it barely cracked! It couldn't have slid up on its own! She grabbed her lantern and swung the light around the crowded room. Shadows leaped at her as the fungi growing on detached tree limbs seemed to sway.

She noticed muddy footprints on the floor under the open window. Someone had evidently jumped down into the basement. Her heart pounding, she thudded up the stairs. She wanted to search the rest of her house to be sure her spending money and that diamond she'd hidden under her stockings were still there, but instead she simply grabbed her purse, not even locking the door behind her, and ran outside.

Darkness was descending, but the sunset still silhouetted the Hanging Bridge in streaming reds. Not stopping to get Fern, she fled toward the bridge and Ben's house. *Bann* or not, she needed help, and he was it.

CHAPTER FOUR

ABBY'S INSTINCT WAS TO shout for Ben, but she kept quiet in case her intruder was nearby. At least she could see Ben's lights across the river. She'd noticed his truck in the driveway earlier, so he'd beat her home. The bridge loomed ahead, and she ran into its dark, cavernous depths.

Sounds outside muted instantly. Panic pounded in her ears as her feet thudded on the floorboards. Her bonnet bounced off, held by its strings around her neck, and she felt her heavy braid come loose from its hairpins under her prayer *kapp*. As she burst out the other side, an owl's hoot demanded *Who? Who?* as if echoing her own fears. Who would break into her house and why? All these years out here, so safe. Now everything had changed, since Ben came back.

Gasping for breath, she tore up onto his porch and knocked hard on the door. He peered out the closest window. Frowning, he yanked the door open.

"Abby, what hap—"

"Someone broke into my house, though the cellar. I don't know if he's still there or not!"

He came outside fast, stooped and squinted across the creek, but she could tell he couldn't see much. A breeze had come up, and the trees shed more leaves. "Did they steal anything?" he asked, taking her elbow.

A lightning bolt shot clear up her arm. Ben, forbidden.
Ben, touching her. *Verboten,* but what could she do?

"I don't know," she answered, panting for breath and
pulling slightly away. "I saw the open window and footprints and ran."

"Stay inside here while I go over to look around."

"No, I can't—shouldn't. I'll come with you."

"Wait right here."

He ducked inside and came out with a leather jacket
and a rifle.

"Ben—a gun. You can't—"

"It's my old hunting rifle, and I haven't used it since
I left here. It's not even loaded, but it could be useful,
even as a club."

"I don't mean for you to do violence—you know
what I'm saying," she insisted as he frowned at her.

"We'll just be sure your place is safe," he said.
"Come on then."

He locked his front door and started off at a jogging
pace, with Abby holding up her skirt a bit to run behind
him. He called back to her, "I'd like for you to put this
jacket on, but I know you can't take it from me. You're
sweating but shivering."

"I ran out so fast without a coat—just nerves."

"You have anything valuable over there? You had
any trouble with this kind of thing before?"

"Never. Never in all these years."

But he'd asked about something valuable. Her stomach cartwheeled. What if the person who lost that diamond had come back to look for it and broken into her
house? Should she tell Ben about shining the light on
that couple?

As soon as they entered the bridge, he threw his

leather jacket on the ground. He must mean for her to put it on, though she could not take it from his hand. He'd waited until they were hidden on the bridge.

She stooped to pick it up, and swirled it around her shoulders, then hurried to catch up with him again. Even in the dark—a half moon was now tilting over the treed horizon when they ran from the bridge—Ben seemed to know the trail to her house.

Did that mean he'd explored here before? Without breaking stride, he followed the sawdust path past her stacked logs and around the irregular mushroom patches. She saw now that, in her panic, she'd left the lantern in the cellar. Wan light shone from the two low, closed windows on this side of the house.

"Do you want to just peek down into the cellar first?" she whispered, out of breath. "I know the window the person used to get in."

"Okay. Show me."

She took him around the back of the house, which faced the forest. Dark now, with the wind up, the Wild Run Woods seemed a living, breathing thing, shifting, whispering, watching.

She stuck so close to Ben that she bumped into his back when he stopped and knelt to look in the open window. She stooped beside him.

"Mushrooms down there, too," he whispered. His mouth was so close to her ear that his breath heated her temple even in the chill breeze. "Let's go in, but you stick tight."

Holding his gun like a club, he led the way through the back door. "Sheriff Freeman here!" he bellowed, so loudly she jumped. Despite the fact it was a lie, it was

somehow a good one. Maybe there were shades of gray
in what this man said and did.

They stopped just inside the kitchen, barely breathing. Ben locked the door behind them. No sound came
from inside the six-room, single-story place but the familiar creak of its old bones.

"Light another lantern," he whispered. Nervous, but
feeling so much safer with Ben here, she fumbled with
the match, then blessed the gentle hiss as soft lantern
light enveloped them. His eyes gleamed as he looked
over at her, then nodded as if to give her courage. She'd
slipped her arms into his jacket now, and appreciated
its warmth. It felt cold in the house, as if the wind were
trying to break in, too.

After opening the pantry door to look inside, and
then checking under the sink while she held the lantern
for him, Ben started into the living room. With Abby
close behind, he peered into each nook and corner, in
closets, behind doors, under beds in both bedrooms.
Well, she had nothing to hide, though it felt strange to
have the man of her dreams in her bedroom. He seemed
to dwarf her bathroom as he pulled the shower curtain
aside and checked the tub. She wished she'd scrubbed
it better. They bumped into each other as he turned
around to head out.

Once he was sure no one was hiding anywhere, he
checked the front door, too. "Things look untouched,"
he told her, not whispering now. "You see anything
amiss?"

She shook her head. "I didn't look in my money
box, but I'll check that. And I have a few other things
hidden."

"Thieves can be clever. Some are neat, too, and until you do an inventory, you can't tell what's missing."

He looked as if he wanted to say more. A frown furrowed his forehead again, and he seemed suddenly angry. But he only said, "Now the cellar." He hesitated at the top of the stairs that led down from the kitchen. "Any cubbyholes or closets down there where someone could hide?"

"*Ja,* a root cellar that goes off from the main part, but it's pretty full of bags of compost."

"Point it out but stay back."

They tiptoed down into the cellar, where he immediately closed and latched the open window and examined the footprints on the concrete floor. "What's all that?" he whispered, pointing to her buckets of slurry.

"Virgin spawn to inoculate maple chips," she whispered back.

"Virgin spawn? To impregnate male what?"

"Maple chips! To inoculate them—to make more mushrooms."

"Oh," he said, staring at her, his mouth half-open.

Annoyed at herself for blushing over nothing, she pointed toward the root cellar, lifting her lantern higher. Ben hefted his gun again and, keeping her behind him, swung open the unlatched door—which shouldn't have been unlatched, she realized. When he said, "All clear," Abby peeked around him and gasped.

"What?" he asked. "Whew! If an intruder hid in here, he paid the price!" The dim, four-foot-square space with bags of mixed mulch and manure smelled like the stalls of the dairy farm where she'd gotten the compost. He dared to bite back a grin.

"It's not funny! Ben, someone was in here! He

shoved those bags aside and even sat on one. See that footprint in the mulch mix scattered there? I keep the floor swept—and the bags closed tight—so he somehow spilled that, then stepped in it. And maybe he was hiding while I was working down here!"

"At least he didn't mean to harm you then."

She nodded, but something else shook her. Either accidentally or deliberately, in the dim corner of the old, hand-dug root cellar lay her lost slipper.

As Ben looked around the rest of the room, she retrieved it, wishing it could talk. "What's that?" he asked, sinking wearily onto a stair step.

"It's the slipper I lost on the path the night I heard that arguing on the bridge. I found it missing the next morning. That doesn't mean the people I heard shouting are the ones who brought it here, but—"

"I'm going to get my sleeping bag and camp outside tonight in case your intruder comes back."

"Ben, it's cold. I can't ask you to do that."

"Would you rather get in my truck, and we'll drive to the sheriff's office, have him come look around?" he demanded, his voice rising. "I know as well as you do that our people don't like to get the law involved, and I sympathize with that, believe me, I do. Or we can drive to someone's house—one of your Amish girlfriends, who can move in with you for a while and get you in trouble for coming to me."

"You know I can't do any of that. I'll be more careful, lock up day and night. I'm the one who left that window ajar. I had hunters wander in for a drink last year and—"

"And you didn't learn from that? Abby, you could be a sitting duck out here for—for someone wanting... anything!"

"My family has had this place for decades and nothing has ever hap—"

"Even when you were just a kid, you always were too stubborn for your own good!"

"And you got in trouble protecting another woman. I'll be fine. I know I shouldn't have run to you, but I panicked."

"Oh, right. Don't call Ben, don't trust Ben Kline. Why, he committed violence once, beating up a drunkard who was going to rape his sister! You've still got my jacket on, so don't let anyone know about that, either."

"I really am grateful," she said, taking the coat off and handing it to him. He snatched it back and threw it on the step beside him. "You know how the rules are," she protested, "the *ordnung* about those under the *meidung.*"

"Yeah, I do, but do you think somebody who breaks in and leaves a slipper plays by rules? If you want me off your property, get in your buggy and ride for the sheriff or the bishop to charge me with trespassing or putting a hand on your arm. Otherwise, lock up tight here, I'll camp outside and we'll both get back to our separate lives tomorrow. Then I won't offer you any more advice—that is, maybe until I'm Amish again, if I ever am. Or have you got a come-calling friend who can ride to your rescue?"

"I had one, but I turned him down and—and for all I know, he might have done this."

"You're not kidding, are you? Who is it?"

"You can't have a word with him. If I see any signs it's him, I'll ask his parents or the bishop to deal with it."

"Any other candidates for your B and E—that's

worldly cop talk for breaking and entering—though I guess this was only entering?"

She thought about mentioning the people arguing on the bridge again, but she needed to calm him down, get him to leave now that it was late. He shouldn't be here in the first place. But she was so glad he was.

"Ben, I am regretful about our circumstances. We're really strangers and need to stay that way until you decide about your future. But *danki, danki* for your help. I'll be more careful now, really, but I'm sure I'll be fine."

He stood with a sigh, picked up his jacket and went up two steps before turning back and stooping to look down at her. "You are fine, Abigail Baughman. That's why, if you see anything else suspicious after tonight, you come to me, and it will be our secret. Come upstairs and lock up behind me then. I'm going to circle the house and make sure no one can lift any other window, so watch me from inside."

She did as he said, closing the curtains after he'd checked each window, following him around, watching him intently—kind of like she used to do years ago, she thought. He finally waved and walked away toward the bridge. Everything was closed and locked, so she felt safe now. Safe, except for her wild feelings for Ben Kline.

She felt even better when she saw the spending money kept in her bedside table untouched, and that things in her dresser looked completely undisturbed. Until, that is, she searched the back of the middle drawer under her neatly rolled stockings. Her grandmother's handkerchief was there, folded just the way she'd left it. But the diamond piece of jewelry she'd so carefully secreted inside was gone.

CHAPTER FIVE

BEN ROLLED OVER. His back hurt, his hip hurt. As he snuggled deeper into his sleeping bag, it took him a minute to recall where he was. He'd slept under a tree just off Abby's property, and he ached all over. This was the second night he'd spent here, without her knowing it. Let's see, this was Monday morning. He'd hurried away yesterday before she'd driven off to church in her buggy.

That stubborn woman thought she didn't need him, but he'd decided to camp out here to keep an eye on her place. He stretched stiff muscles. He'd slept only the last few hours. He had his own inner demons to worry about.

Dawn was breaking, coloring the eastern sky. He figured he'd better get up and cross the bridge before she saw him here.

He unzipped the bag, then realized it wasn't a tree root but his cell phone pressing against his shoulder. If he rejoined the Amish, it was one of the many things he would have to give up, but returning to his Amish roots would give him more important things back. His people's trust and support. So much to live for, and hope for in future. A family of his own. But to get all that, he'd have to not only atone for his past here, but level with the bishop and the elders about being under suspicion for a massive jewelry heist.

As Ben slid out of the bag and stretched, he heard a
voice coming from behind a large stack of wood that
sprouted layers of mushrooms.

"I see you didn't listen to me," Abby said as she hurried toward him, carrying a tray of food. She looked as
if she hadn't slept well, either, but she was still beautiful in that natural, windswept way of hers. She wore
an unbuttoned navy blue coat over her dark green dress
and work apron. Though she wore her prayer *kapp,* she
had not pinned her big braid up under it, and loose ten-
drils peeking from the starched linen blew against her
rosy cheeks. Gawky Abby, he thought, the little pain
in the neck he recalled from years ago, had turned into
a stunning, seductive vision. He half wondered if he
was still dreaming. He could almost imagine how she
would look with her honey-hued hair loose against her
bare shoulders....

He blinked and shook his head to clear it. The tray
was crowded with a glass of orange juice, a fat muffin,
two pitchers, a mug and covered plate. His nose told
him the larger of the two pitchers held steaming coffee.

"I'm sorry I can't ask you in, and should not have the
other night, but this is the least I can do," she said, putting the tray down on his sleeping bag. "You...you've
been out here two nights, haven't you? I hope you didn't
work yesterday on the day of rest. I'm going to have a
lot to do around here today."

She chattered on, no doubt nervous to be feeding
someone under the *bann.* It was a strange game they
played, he thought, giving each other things but not
touching. And he wanted to touch her. The time he had
merely taken her elbow had shaken him, which showed
how much he needed a woman.

"I hope you like mushroom fritters," Abby was saying. "There's maple syrup in the little pitcher. I'm assuming you still drink your coffee black, *ja?* Well, I have many chores, so I'll let you eat. I'll be right in the garden when you're done so I can get your tray. You shouldn't have stayed out all night—either night—but *danki* again. You look ravenous."

He was ravenous, all right, and not only for food. He realized he was staring at her, so he said, "This is a great surprise. *Ja, danki, mein freund* Abigail." He sat cross-legged on his sleeping bag and tucked into the delicious food, the best picnic he'd ever had. Under the covered plate he found not only fritters, but stewed apples with cinnamon and three thick strips of country bacon. Abby Baughman knew how to feed a man. And mushrooms had never tasted so good.

ABBY WAS CUTTING giant garden mushrooms off a patch of bark mulch when Ben came into the garden carrying his tray. "You're a great cook," he said, putting it on a wooden bench by the back door. "Man, those things are big," he observed. "A couple of those tops are about a foot across."

"You can grill or sauté the caps in butter. These were in your fritters. They taste good with corn, too."

"I have a lot to learn."

"*Ja,* I guess we all do about a lot of things—and each other. So, you said it didn't fret you to make ornate boxes for fancy jewels even though you were raised Amish?"

He looked a little confused at the sudden change of subject.

"I consider it honest work."

"So did you leave your life there just to come back for the good hardwood in the area, like you said, or the simple life? And did you bring any jewels back with you?"

He narrowed his eyes and tilted his head as if he wasn't sure what to say at her barrage of questions. His hair looked mussed, his usually clear blue eyes a bit bleary. His beard stubble gleamed in the sun again. She ached to stroke it, to flick her fingernails through the gold sheen. She forced herself to look away, to put another mushroom in the basket at her feet.

"You're curious about my jewel boxes," he said, as if she hadn't brought up the jewels themselves. "Since I can't invite you over to view my inventory, I'll leave a brochure on your porch from the Jeweled Treasures Store where I worked in Cincinnati. The company has a lot of my work displayed online, too—the internet. But not for the Amish, right? I know the internet's forbidden, unless the computer's owned by a boss at work, and I don't think your mushrooms have a website."

She smiled tautly at his attempted joke, then swept a cobweb away from the next big mushroom she cut. "A website—sounds like a spider at work to me," she said, trying to keep her voice light. But she knew there were two laptops in the library bookmobile, and she could take a look at his carved boxes there. She shouldn't, of course, but...

He wasn't leaving. He kept staring at her.

"So," he said, pointing at the mushroom in her hand, "is there such a thing as a 'dummies' guide to mushrooms' for someone like me?"

"I'll tell you my main observations—just to show you how much you can learn about people from them."

"About people?"

"About life," she said. Elam Garber had hated her work with the mushrooms, while Ben seemed sincerely interested. "Can you guess what I mean?"

"Okay, here's my first thought. This garden of mushrooms—" he swept his arm around her backyard "—makes me feel like I'm in a special place, maybe like walking on another planet, because they all look so exotic."

"Exotic? Not to me. I'm so used to them. Actually, native types do better than exotic ones—same as life around here, right? Real outsiders, *auslanders,* stand out, but once you're born and bred here, it's hard to leave, *ja?*"

"Ja," he whispered, staring into her eyes. He was so close she could see her reflection in them.

"But," she rushed on, "like people, mushrooms have so much hidden beneath the surface."

He frowned. "Big roots?"

"Masses of rhizomes. The real core is hidden, but the fruits show. Like the Bible says, people are truly known by their fruits, their actions."

"I hear you loud and clear. I'm going to see about returning to our people's life and ways. I'm planning to see the bishop soon, to learn what needs to be done. But you and I have been put together, here—almost together with Killibuck Creek and the bridge between us—so let's lean on each other from a distance."

He stepped even closer. *Lean on each other.* His words echoed in her head. And he was hardly keeping his distance. She did not give ground, but held the mushroom in one hand and her knife in the other, crossing her arms over her chest as if she could ward off his power over her. Yet she almost swayed toward him.

She didn't really know him now, however much she wanted to. Could she trust him? They were not allowed to be together, not this close. Her toes curled, her lips tingled and she felt as if little butterflies fluttered in her belly.

"I'd better go," he said, taking a step back. "But here's the thing. Each day we're losing more leaves off the trees, so I can see your side windows from my place, and you can see mine. If anything goes wrong and you need me, just open one of the dark green curtains in your main room and hang a white towel or sheet there with a lantern behind, and I'll rush over."

"And you'll do the same so I can rush over?"

She was teasing, almost flirting, but he didn't seem to notice. "I don't want you out at night," he said. "No working these mushroom beds after dark, either."

"But autumn is the time to harvest a lot of these. Daylight hours are getting shorter, so I sometimes get a lantern and—"

"No! No, or I'm going to get the sheriff involved or camp out on your doorstep again!"

"All right. I'll work in the light of day. But there's one thing I need to tell you, too."

He came closer again. She'd agonized last night whether to tell him about her slipper showing up and the diamond going missing. But since he'd worked for a jewelry store—Jeweled Treasures of Cincinnati, he'd said—he might have some good advice for her.

"As I was heading back from your house after I brought you the bread," she said, trying to choose her words carefully, "I found a diamond between two floorboards on the bridge. A round one, really pretty, set in a gold circle with a little spike, like one that would go through a rich lady's earlobe."

His eyes widened and he frowned through a long silence. Then he said, "Can I see it?"

"That's what my intruder must have taken—only that, as far as I can tell. But it was like a ghost stole it, because nothing was disturbed. The things around it in my drawer were just as I'd left them, a handkerchief I folded around it was the same—and don't say I just dropped the jewel, because I looked all through the drawer, on the floor...."

"Could someone have seen you picking it up on the bridge?"

"I don't know. Why wouldn't they just ask me about it if it was theirs? The previous night, I shone a light at those people in the dark, so they probably put two and two together and know who disturbed them—after they'd disturbed me. Maybe it's just the Lord telling me I should never have kept the diamond, but I thought if I put up a lost-and-found sign, anyone could say it was theirs, so I was waiting for someone to come asking."

Ben looked really upset. Did he think she was a thief for keeping the jewel? Should she have gone to the bishop or the elders with it, or even asked him earlier? A frown furrowed his brow, and he sucked in his lips as if to keep from talking. Finally he said, "Keep looking for it. I'd think a thief would have messed something up, but if your drawer is that neat, maybe you just—"

"I know where it was, Ben!"

"Okay, okay. Listen, thanks again for the great breakfast and for confiding in me. Keep your doors locked even in the day, and you can signal me anytime. If you need me during the day, just hang a sheet over that lattice there, because I can see it from my place. Gotta go, but be careful."

He was holding something in and something back. Funny how she could read his moods, but then, she'd studied him like crazy when he was younger. But he obviously didn't want to talk about it—or the diamond. Or maybe he wanted nothing to do with her now, for some reason she couldn't figure out. She'd forgotten to tell him about her slipper appearing, but she didn't want to upset him more. The mention of the stolen diamond had obviously riled him a lot for some reason.

He lifted a hand and backed away, bent to roll up his sleeping bag—he didn't seem to have his rifle—and strode toward the bridge. She saw him punching numbers into his cell phone, then pressing it to his ear, but he didn't seem to be talking to anyone.

Abby took his tray into the house and washed the dishes. Her stomach rumbled. She hadn't eaten breakfast but had taken her meal out to him without fixing more. Looking outside through the yellow and orange leaves on the trees bordering the creek, she saw him emerge from the bridge, no longer on the phone, and hurrying toward his house. She was drying his coffee mug when she noticed he had a visitor, a thin man in a ball cap, jeans and a sweatshirt who drove into Ben's driveway in a beat-up truck. Maybe Ben had an appointment with someone, and that's why he'd left in a hurry. She wondered if she'd recognize the man walking to meet him. He was gesturing wildly, as if Ben was late.

She gasped. The stranger shoved him, then took a swing at him, catching him on the jaw. Ben started to fall, but righted himself and backed away. He stopped the man's next blow with his rolled sleeping bag, using it as a shield. But the man—she could hear him shouting, but couldn't catch his words—kicked and swung at Ben again and again.

She took a second to lock her back door. She knew Ben was trying hard not to use violence again, so he could be forgiven and taken back among the Amish, and she wanted that with her whole heart. But she wasn't going to stand by and do nothing, no matter what he'd ordered.

Grabbing her spade and cutting knife, Abby tore toward the bridge.

ABBY RAN BREATHLESSLY onto Ben's property. She could hear the stranger shouting.

"You bastard! I heard you was back. You sent my brother to prison, just 'cause he was making it with your sister! She wanted it, the Amish slut! You shoulda gone to prison for beating him up!"

"Like you're doing to me now?" Ben yelled back, dodging most of the man's blows. He turned his head, shocked to see Abby. "Get away!" he shouted, but looked at her a second too long. The enraged man—it must be Burt Commons, the brother of Steve Commons, who'd attacked Ben's sister—landed a blow on his face. Ten years back Abby had followed every word of Steve's trial by sneaking copies of the *Wooster Daily Record*.

She was tempted to trip or hit Commons with her spade, but she realized she'd be doing exactly what Ben had done—explode in violence. But this wasn't fair. This was wrong.

"It's okay, Ben!" she shouted. "Thanks for loaning me your cell phone, because I called Sheriff Freeman, and he's on his way!" It was a lie, but, she figured, better than braining this beast.

For a moment, she thought Burt Commons would come after her. He turned her way, a snarl on his bearded face. She darted up onto the porch. If Ben came to her aid like he had his sister, it would be a replay of ten years ago.

She could see Commons waver. He wasn't sure whether to believe her or not. But at last he turned tail and ran back to his truck, got in, slammed the door and shouted out the window, "I'll be back! You're gonna pay for what you done!" As he sped away, he spun his wheels so hard they spit gravel.

Ben came up onto the porch, threw his sleeping bag down and collapsed onto the swing. Abby could see he was bleeding from the nose.

"We're both good at using Sheriff Freeman to ward off danger," he said. "Maybe the Amish are wrong to mistrust *Englische* law and its enforcers. At least you didn't smack him with that spade or use your knife. For a moment there, I wondered. Don't mess with Abby Baughman."

"This is no time to joke. You heard what he said. He could be dangerous. And for all we know, he's been hanging around before. Do you have ice in your freezer so I can get some for your nose?"

"I'll take care of my nose," he said. "Look, I'm sorry you got involved in that. I had no clue he was even in the area now. Even though, back then he was at his brother's trial every day." Ben heaved a huge sigh.

"What I'm thinking is, what if he and some woman were on that bridge arguing, planning to attack you, and they're the ones I overheard?"

"Listen, Abby," Ben said, wiping away blood with his sleeve. "I don't think he's a clever enough thief to sneak in and carefully steal a diamond. He's not the type to own a diamond in the first place. I'm pretty sure your invoking the sheriff's name will keep him away—like his brother, he's basically a sneak-attack coward. But when I go into town, I'll tell Sheriff Freeman and let him have a word with Commons."

"But you can't file charges. The bishop won't permit—"

"I know. I'm going to see Bishop Esh, too, so I'll level with him—about Burt Commons. Please head on back now and stay put. I guess we're partners in helping each other out, but we can't keep spending time together—not until later, at least. Not unless things change. I'll take care of this," he added, with another swipe at his nose. "Go on now, Abby—please."

She yearned to tend to him, but when she saw he meant to stay bleeding on his front porch until she was back across the bridge, she walked away. As she emerged on her side of the river, she felt his eyes on her and glanced back. She quickened her steps even more. She had a lot to do today and was getting a late start on her chores, but not a late start in loving Ben Kline.

CHAPTER SIX

THAT MORNING, Abby set about inoculating her maple chips with virgin spawn, remembering how Ben must have misheard her when they were whispering in the basement. Evidently the word *virgin* had got his attention. As she worked in her familiar mushroom patches, she felt good in the sun and brisk breeze, with the late hangers-on of richly colored leaves floating down around her. But when she went into the house for lunch, her once safe haven bothered her.

She hadn't slept well the past two nights, so would she be able to this night? Seeing Ben out there in his sleeping bag had helped, but she still felt uneasy that someone had been in her house and taken the diamond. It was almost as if she'd imagined its glittering beauty, as if she'd dreamed it or made it up.

But no. All this was real, much too real.

And how badly she wanted to see more of the jewelry boxes Ben made, maybe so she could understand him better. That one she'd looked at briefly on market day was so beautiful. She'd been thinking of getting out of here for a little while to clear her head, to stop looking across the river at Ben's house.

Besides, she had mushrooms to deliver by tomorrow to the Yoders' roadside stand, and that was close to where the Eden County Library bookmobile would be today. She could take just a few minutes, ask for help to find the Jeweled Treasures website of Cincinnati, and have a closer look at Ben's carved boxes. It wouldn't take long. Then she'd come back and do a bit of wildcrafting in the woods while the afternoon sun slanted in. No more after-dark work. She'd promised, and right now it was for the best.

She ate a grilled cheese sandwich with a slice of mushroom. When she saw Ben drive away, hopefully to see both the sheriff and the bishop, she harnessed Fern to her buggy, locked up carefully and set out. As much as she loved Killibuck Creek and her home there, it was good to get away.

BEN WALKED OUT OF the sheriff's office into the bright autumn sunshine. Jack Freeman had said he'd "talk some sense" into Burt Commons and would drive out after dark from time to time to the old Hanging Bridge to check on things. And he'd told Ben, even if he was thinking of returning to the Amish, to keep his cell phone for now and phone him day or night if anything "looked fishy." Ben hadn't explained about returning to the church, but the sheriff had guessed as much when Ben had refused to bring charges for assault and battery against Burt. The sheriff was used to forgiveness from the Amish, at any cost.

But Ben knew he'd held something back he should have told the sheriff—that Abby had found a diamond on the bridge and then someone had stolen it from her bedroom. Because Ben had to give his address to the Cincinnati police and the insurance investigators, they had already informed Freeman about the theft at Jeweled Treasures.

As he got in his truck, he wished he had a buggy instead, so he could drive to see Bishop Esh and talk about possibly returning to the church. Maybe he'd park out on the road and walk up the lane to the Esh farm. He did miss his horse and buggy sometimes. It slowed life down, made the world seem real and lovely, at a reasonable pace instead of rush, rush, rush.

He agonized, too, about whether his timing was right for atonement and reinstatement among the brethren. Things sure weren't settled in his life. Hundreds of thousands of dollars worth of unset gems and designer pieces had been carried out of the jewelry store either with or in his boxes. An inside job, the police and insurance agency had decided. The theft had happened after-hours and pointed to someone who knew his way around. Amish past or not, Ben was the newest staff member, still the outsider, clever enough with his hands and knives to jimmy locks. The theft had been so quick and clean, the paper had called it a "cat burglary."

And darn it, why didn't Triana Tornelli, the co-owner of the store, call him back so he could be certain that earring wasn't hers? He hit the steering wheel with a fist. Could she have driven out to see him? Cesar might have followed and caught up with her, and they'd argued, maybe struggled on the bridge? Triana had said Cesar sometimes played rough. Then when Abby's flashlight surprised them, Triana had lost an earring.... No, he was probably just getting paranoid. A lot of women had diamond stud earrings, but the way it had been taken from Abby's drawer made him think of a cat burglar. And that was Triana, sleek and smooth.

He tried to shake off the memory of the day she had come after dark to his apartment, saying she wanted to see how he was doing on his first seashell box, a special order for a rich customer who spent her winters in Florida. He'd seen from the first that Triana had more in mind than looking at his carving, which he would have brought in the next day.

It would have been so easy to sleep with her. But Cesar was his boss, too. It was wrong, and she was wrong, but her perfume and her red mouth...

He'd turned her down, literally held her off and talked her out of it. She'd pretended not to care, had shrugged and flipped her jacket over her shoulder and made a grand exit. But she'd treated him differently after that. Like Melanie Campbell, she was always watching him, as if waiting to pounce. Now, unlike Ms. Campbell, Triana seemed to be shunning him.

That was what Abby should be doing. Things were hardly settled between them, and couldn't be unless he returned to the church. Yeah, he admitted, that was another factor pushing him to come clean with Bishop Esh. Talk about a hidden gem—Abigail Baughman was that in the flesh. It might be a short distance across the covered bridge that separated them, but a long road stretched ahead before he could ever hope to court her openly.

Ben parked his truck in a pull-off on Oakridge Road about a half mile from Bishop Esh's farm, got out and locked up, then began the long walk toward his future.

"So you just type in the name of the store in this space," Nicole Anderson, the librarian in the bookmobile, said, pointing to the top of the screen. "And we'd better put a plus sign and the word *Cincinnati,* too, in case there are other stores by that name somewhere in the world."

"Oh. This covers the whole world?" Abby whispered as she slowly typed all that in. The front part of the bookmobile was fairly crowded with people she knew, and she didn't want to broadcast what she was doing. She shouldn't even be online.

Instantly, when she clicked on the scrolled words Visit Jeweled Treasures Here or In Person, a colored picture sprang onto the screen of jewels and pearl necklaces dripping from carved, half-open boxes, no doubt Ben's. Each one had something from nature carved on its top or handle—butterflies, leaves, even seashells. Off to the side was a close-up photograph of the owners of the store, Cesar and Triana Tornelli. They were both really trim. Obviously, they hadn't been anywhere near Amish food. Probably in his mid-fifties, Cesar was a silver-haired, tanned man in a worldly suit, with sharp gray eyes and a prominent nose. Triana Tornelli wore big, hanging emerald earrings and a matching necklace against her bare throat and upper chest. She was pretty despite her hair being chopped really short and slicked to her head and, Abby guessed, dyed that silvery-white shade. Both of them reeked of wealth and worldly power.

She was so intent on studying them that she jumped when Nicole spoke again. "You just click the cursor on those buttons on the left to find particular things on pages within this website. Let me know if you need help," she added, and moved away.

Oh, *ja,* she needed help, Abby thought. She was in love with a man who said he wanted to return to the Plain People, but had worked for a fancy, just-for-pretty jewelry store with amazing things for sale. She searched each page, astounded at the variety and prices of the jewelry. And then she saw what Nicole had called a button, labeled Custom Jewelry Boxes.

She clicked on it, and there was picture after picture of Ben's work, some with him doing the carving or holding up a particular box. But one thing gave her hope. In none of the pictures had he let the photographer show his face, so maybe he was truly, at least a little, still Amish at heart.

When she got off the website so the next person in line would not know what she'd been looking at, she saw something else listed, a kind of headline: Jeweled Treasures—Theft of Millions Worth of Jewelry Called Inside Job.

Wide-eyed, she skimmed the Cincinnati newspaper article that came up. Listed among the "persons of interest" in that huge theft was Ben's name!

ABBY ATE NEXT TO NOTHING for lunch. Since it was broad daylight and the falling leaves allowed a clear line of vision to the house, she locked up and, taking a big hemp wildcrafting bag from her pile, went on her familiar way to the edge of the forest. She had to do something besides brood and cry over what she'd read about the jewelry "heist," as they'd called it. She'd had to look the word up.

So had Ben come back to the Home Valley to find his Amish life, or escape his English one? Charges were pending; an investigation was still going on. Surely, he could not be guilty. What if he'd dropped a diamond from his stolen gems, and that's why he was upset she'd found it? Maybe he'd even figured out she had it—had seen her find it that night—and then stole it back. She felt sick to her stomach with fear, but she still believed in him. Didn't she?

She knew Ben was not back yet, and if—when—he was, would she confront him with what she'd learned? She hoped he'd talked to the sheriff, who maybe knew all about this. But she prayed he'd also taken time to see Bishop Esh. That was a conversation she would love to eavesdrop on.

Feeling depressed despite the pretty day, she gathered walnuts first. When her bag got heavy, she trudged back to the house, dumped her bounty in a bushel basket and returned to fill the sack again. With an edgy feeling she'd never had in Wild Run Woods before, she glanced around a lot and didn't go clear into the shaded ravine, despite the fact that there were two more good-size walnut trees there.

Abby felt not only sad, but nervous today in these woods she knew so well. She treasured happy memories of wildcrafting here with her mother and grandmother, but that hardly helped. She jumped when she startled a doe and fawn from the underbrush, where they must have been sleeping or grazing by a big hollow log that sported wild wood ear mushrooms she'd need to cut soon. She called after the fleeing animals, "Sorry! It's your home, too!" But the deer just ran faster, as if Abby was a danger to them.

She lugged her load of walnuts back once more. Now, where had she put those extra hemp sacks? Because this one had a tear in it. She saw Ben's truck was parked at his place now, but she didn't see him outside. At least if he glanced or came over—which she hoped for, but wasn't expecting—he'd surely see that she was out in the open and not taking risks. Even when she next cut the branches of bittersweet growing along the old road that led to the bridge, she would be in a clearing. *Ach, how she hated to have to fret for her safety now. Fret not,* it warned in the book of Psalms. That only causes harm.

The diamond thief had ruined everything, and she sure hoped it wasn't Ben. She couldn't believe he would steal. But he'd had enough money for his land, house and planned remodeling. And he'd suddenly fled back here when he was surely doing well away. She could see why he hadn't told her that people thought he might be guilty, though.

Toting two large, empty baskets on her next trip down the old road, Abby crunched through the carpet of leaves as others blew around her. After she was done, she'd be tempted to go back for those wood ears near the spot where she'd seen the deer. She took out her knife and began to cut bouquets of the red-orange berries along the narrow road. Foliage on both sides, including lots of tall weeds, choked the former route, almost making it a mere pathway.

Why was bittersweet given its name? she wondered, examining the vibrant berries close up. She'd never tasted them to see if they were bitter. Or maybe it was named for the time of year. The berries bloomed in a glorious burst, but soon dried. Bittersweet—that's how she thought of her relationship with Ben now.

The leaves rustled loudly in the breeze. Was the weather going to change?

She froze, the new-cut branches in her hand, a nearly full basket at her feet. The rhythmic sound grew closer. Footsteps? Hoping it was Ben, she spun around, only to scream in horror. A man, or a tall person at least, appeared wearing a big hempen bag—the one she'd left outside at the house?—like a loose garment. More hemp covered his head like a hood. There were slits for his eyes and nose, and the fabric was tied at his neck like a scarecrow. He was coming straight at her, with her own spade in his gloved hands. And he was swinging it before him as if he was reaping grain with a scythe.

Grasping only her small cutting knife, Abby ran. She tore down the road at first, but heard him behind her. Picking up her skirts to her knees, she veered into the forest for a shortcut home. Whoever it was, she had to know this area better than he did.

Thank heavens, she heard him fall and grunt. But still she was terrified she wasn't going to make it home in time. Someone was after her in broad daylight. But why? Who?

Even if she made it back into her yard, it would take her a while to get the key out from under the rock where she kept it. Her pursuer could easily catch her and hit her with that spade. There was no time to hang something in the trees—no time for Ben to come. Maybe it was Burt Commons. That looked like the spade she'd taken with her to confront him. Surely not Elam! And the diamond thief had what he wanted, didn't he?

She heard the person running again. If she beat this monster out of the forest, she could shout for Ben and run across the bridge. But would she make it? Her heart was pounding, she was nearly breathless, and she felt a stitch in her side. Daring a quick look back, hearing but not seeing her pursuer, Abby made a desperate decision.

When she neared the hollow log, she hit the ground and belly crawled into its depths, lying there, panting and praying. If he had seen her, she was trapped. The littlc knife she held would be useless against the blade of that spade.

She tried not to breathe so hard. It was filthy in here, with slugs and crawling things. She was so tensed up that her calf muscle cramped, and tears ran down her cheeks at the pain. But she stayed silent.

At first, her haven muted outside sounds, but then she heard his footsteps again in the dead leaves. Close. Very close. Then stopping.

She sucked in a big breath when he passed by the end of the log, hesitated, then turned, evidently looking around. She could see he wore old running shoes and worn jeans under the hemp sack. He must have taken that sack from her garden. Maybe he'd been watching her for a long time. She willed Ben to come looking for her before this man—he was pretty thin, like Burt Commons or Elam—could find her hiding place.

She jumped when something hit the log. The spade? Dust, dirt and bugs rained down on her. She shut her eyes and jammed her finger under her nose so she wouldn't sneeze. Had he figured out where she'd disappeared to? Was he going to chop into the wood to get to her? Maybe he'd peeked inside and seen her feet.

But, blessedly, he walked away. She couldn't see him, even peering out the little crack in the log, but she heard his footsteps scuffing through the leaves, then fading. Or was that a trick? Though she wanted to crawl out and bolt—if she could even run on her cramped leg— she stayed put, catching her breath, trying to build her courage.

But it was anger that roiled through her. How dare someone invade the places of her heart—her home, garden and woods, even the bridge the other night! Who hated her that much to make her want to cower and suffer? What had she done?

Trying to flex her sore leg, she lay there for what she judged was about a half hour before she crawled forward and stuck her head out. What if he was waiting for her near or even in her house? If she saw Ben's truck was still at his place, she was going to head straight for the bridge and run across it to him.

As she limped past her house, she saw her hemp sacks thrown atop the tall pile of logs with her crop of turkey tails, the spade thrust into them. Worst of all, a piece of paper had been punched over the handle and now flapped in the breeze. Abby could clearly make out the large, crudely printed words in *Deutsch* and English: *Raus Jetzt! Get out!*

CHAPTER SEVEN

ONCE AGAIN Abby ran to Ben. A fleeting thought crossed her mind—that the Lord kept throwing them together despite Amish law that they must keep apart. And she needed Ben now again, desperately.

She rushed to the rear door of his house so she couldn't be seen from across the river. Someone must have hiked into the woods behind her house. Getting a car over there was nearly impossible, and the bridge was too rickety to take such a heavy weight. The old road could be approached from behind only by a round-about drive from town.

Abby pounded on his back door with both fists. He opened it with a large, half-carved piece of wood in his hand. She threw herself into his arms.

Though she slammed into him, at first he didn't budge. Then he dropped the piece of wood. As she pressed herself against him, her cheek to his chest, he closed his arms hard around her. He pulled her inside and slammed the door, leaning back against it. She heard only her ragged breathing and his heart beating hard.

"What happened?" he whispered, his chin atop her head as he clamped her full length to him, her hips pressed to his, her breasts flattened against his chest.

"A man draped in a hemp sack with a hemp mask—

gloves—chasing me. Swinging my spade like he wanted to cut me down."

Ben's body tensed. "Did he follow you across the bridge?"

"No. Chased me down the road beyond the bridge and through the forest. I hid in a hollow log. When I ran home, I saw he'd left me a note in the garden that said get out. In *Deutsch* and English!"

Ben squeezed her tighter, then tipped her back to look down into her eyes. She realized she was smudged with dirt from the hollow log, but that hardly mattered. His intense gaze made her light-headed. Her knees nearly buckled, but his legs were strong and firm against her quaking ones as he propped her up.

"You stay here," he said. "I'll go over and look around. Is your house locked?"

"*Ja,* but who knows what he's done? Ben, I will not just leave my house and garden at harvest time and run like a rabbit, though I guess that's just what I did. I know I can't stay here, but—"

"We're going to lock you in right now. I'll just look around over there and bring the threatening note back for evidence. You've got to get help from the sheriff. He said he'd be away the rest of the day, but back tomorrow. First thing in the morning, I'll follow you into town. I have a meeting with Bishop Esh and the church elders set up then."

"That's great. But what about tonight?"

"When I get back from checking your place, we'll talk, decide whether this is aimed at you—or at me."

"At you? You think it might be Burt Commons? He threatened both of us. Maybe he's picking on me to get to you? Or it could be Elam Garber."

"So he was the one you turned down? If it's Elam, the bishop can deal with him better than the sheriff, though I don't want to see anyone put under the *bann*."

"But taking that diamond from my bedroom doesn't seem like something either Burt or Elam would or could do. Commons wasn't even around then. It has to be someone else."

"Would you just listen?" Ben demanded, suddenly sounding angry, almost desperate. "That's what we need to talk about. I'll be back in a couple of minutes."

But still he seemed to be clinging to her. She hugged him again, her arms around his back, his clasping her waist.

"Now you listen to me," she told him. "If there's someone over there, don't get into a fight—not for me."

He lifted one hand to tip her chin up so she was looking straight into his eyes. "I'm in a fight for you already, a fight with myself," he whispered. "Stay put now, make yourself at home, and I'll be right back."

She nodded, making the hand clasping her chin bounce. But he didn't pull away, didn't leave. Then it happened, just as she'd dreamed of so many times.

He lowered his lips to hers, slowly, as if to give her time to turn her head or back away. It was as if they were merely taking a taste of each other, but things turned crazy wild as he took her mouth, again and again. She tilted her head so their noses didn't bump. Their mouths fit perfectly, slanted sideways, open and so needy and natural. Nothing mattered but his touch and kiss. She clung to him to stop the swaying of the world.

He pulled back before she wanted him to, setting her away at arm's length as if she had burned him.

"My fault," he said, breathless. "I wanted that—and you. Lock yourself in and watch out the windows...."

He glanced through the kitchen window himself, as if he were being chased, then banged out the back door, picked up a piece of firewood and hurried toward the bridge.

FRIGHTENED FOR BEN'S SAFETY, Abby kept her nose glued to the side windows for at least a quarter of an hour. Only when she saw him striding back across the bridge did she think to wet a paper towel and wash her face and hands. She finally glanced around his large, wood-paneled living area with its dominating, raised stone hearth. This old place needed work, a woman's touch, but it suited his needs.

On the big table and two end tables, and on two of the three chairs, lay various types of wood, tools, sandpaper and jars of stains. And displayed in a corner cabinet were four completed boxes, with their satin finishes and creature carvings so real they looked as if they could take flight or swim through the waves....

She let him in the front door.

"You didn't bring the note back," she said.

"It wasn't there, nor your hemp sacks, or any kind of mask. Though I saw your spade leaning against the back door, neatly stowed next to your hoe and broom."

She stamped her foot in frustration. "In other words, things are just as if it never happened, as if I'd made it up."

"Abby, I didn't mean that. Though if I thought you were creating dangers just to run into my arms, that would be fine with me... I'm kidding. But this is no kidding matter."

"My enemy is very tidy," she mused as she looked back across the river through the side windows. "He arranges things nicely, whether he's making diamonds or pieces of paper disappear."

"Let's sit at the kitchen table. I need to explain some things before you go to the sheriff and I see the bishop. This has gone too far."

She nodded, but hoped he didn't mean too far between the two of them.

BEN FELT REALLY NERVOUS. He hoped he wasn't dooming Abby if the Amish learned she was in close contact with someone under the *meidung*. And he was finally going to tell her the truth about what had happened in Cincinnati. He had hoped to keep her admiration for him building, but he had to protect her at all costs. He had admitted everything to the sheriff and the bishop, but somehow, confessing all this to Abby was going to be worse.

He poured two cups of reheated coffee and plunked down a plate of glazed doughnuts he'd bought in town. "This is nothing like your delicious food," he said, trying to keep his voice light and his spirits strong. "And sorry, but not a mushroom in sight."

She took a sip of her coffee and stared at him over the edge of her cup. He wanted to vault over the table to hold and kiss her again. She seemed watchful, maybe distrustful of what was coming. Such a bright, beautiful woman, and here he was probably going to blow it all.

"Abby, I haven't told you everything about my life in the world, though Sheriff Freeman knows and I explained things to Bishop Esh. One reason I came back here was that I lost my job in Cincinnati. Someone robbed the store where I worked of a fortune in gems and jewelry, and the owners and police there decided it was an inside job, meaning someone on the staff—"

"I know what that means." Wide-eyed, she put her coffee cup down with a clink. "So they are blaming you?"

"I'm under suspicion, still under surveillance by the police and an insurance investigator."

"Then it's them!"

"I'm not sure. Abby, I vow to you, I had nothing to do with it. Unfortunately, I had been in the store earlier that night to drop off some boxes they needed the next morning. I had been given the security code, which I punched in. Although I left without touching a thing I shouldn't, I was the last one in there before the theft. My fingerprints were here and there, and some of my boxes were used by the thief or thieves to carry out their loot. And just a couple of days before, I'd watched one of the owners, Mrs. Tornelli, get into the safe, so they thought I could have seen the combination."

Abby looked both angry and sad. "I see. I guess they don't get it—that even though you left the Amish, you would tell the truth."

"Thanks for that, but I'm not done. I think Mrs. Tornelli—Triana—told the police detective and the insurance investigator to keep an eye on me, even here."

"So that has to be it! The arguing on the bridge, the lost diamond carefully taken back. Maybe the detective and investigator were watching you that night I heard the voices. They got angry I shone a light on them, and took off."

He thought it unlikely. But he might as well get everything out, and then let the chips fall where they may.

He took a swig of lukewarm coffee and interrupted whatever she was going to say next with, "There's more."

Abby sucked in a sharp breath, then just stared at him, her lush lower lip quivering.

"This is going to sound prideful," he told her, "but Triana Tornelli came on to me, and—"

"Came on to you? Came here, you mean?"

"No. She tried to seduce me—suggested we have an affair, a secret lovers' meeting without her husband knowing it, and I turned her down. We were not lovers. She held some power over me, and I needed her goodwill, but—"

"Ben," Abby said, reaching across the table to cover his clenched hands with one of hers, "I have a confession, too. I got on a computer in the library bookmobile and saw the Tornellis' picture."

She looked as if she'd just confessed to a mass murder. Despite his own grief, he had to bite his lower lip to keep from smiling. How genuine and generous his people were, and he'd had to jump the fence, then return, to realize it. Open, honest, Abigail was more precious than pearls to him.

"You did?" was all he could manage at first, since his voice had choked up. "But were you going to ask or say something more about her—her and me?"

"Ben, I believe you. You think I don't get it, after all the times I hung around, that she could want to do more than kiss you? But the thing is, if she did get those investigators after you, was it because you turned her down or because she's wanting you to take the blame for whoever took their expensive stuff? It has to be someone else who worked there that stole the jewelry!"

Abby leaned across the table as if there were others around to hear, and lowered her voice. "I also looked at the prices for jewelry on their website—sky-high, completely crazy costs. But we now have some other possibilities for who dropped the diamond and then stole it back. Can that female insurance person afford diamond earrings?"

"Never saw them on her, but—"

"But maybe she's been paid in some Tornelli goods instead of just money. Now, in the really pretty picture of her online, Mrs. Tornelli wore emeralds, but I'll just bet she has diamond earrings, right?"

He felt both relieved and elated. This Amish girl was on his side. She was thinking clearly. She had accepted what he'd told her at face value. Man, not that the Plain People's ways were perfect, but he'd lived in the big, bad outside world too long! Abigail Baughman would be called naive by the modern folk, yet what was wrong with trust—trust and love?

"Right," he said. "But however great a picture she takes, neither she nor any woman I have ever met could hold a candle to you."

Abby blinked back tears. They held hands, both hands, leaning toward each other across the table. "And here I'll never have a picture taken of my face to prove that," she said, her tone teasing, her fingers trembling despite the little smile she wore.

He could not believe how she was backing him up. Inner strength radiated from her, warming him—heating him. But if he pulled her over here into his lap, they'd never finish this conversation and decide what they must do, especially tonight. It was getting dark outside, and he'd hardly noticed.

"So," Abby went on, when he just stared at her, "my thief could be either of those women, or Mr. Tornelli, too. Are the insurance woman and the police detective thin? The Tornellis looked pretty slender."

Ben shook his head to clear it, then realized she would think he was saying no. "*Ja,* they're all in good shape, as *auslanders* put it. Are you saying your pursuer today was thin?"

She nodded. "But then so are all the others I can mention to the sheriff. Elam, Burt Commons. You know, I just assumed my thief and stalker was a man, but maybe not. I think someone must have been pretty slender to get through my basement window. But now the next question—why? If it's Elam or Burt Commons, I guess I know. Elam wants me to sell my house to the gun club in town, and he'd get a cut of the sale. Plus he's upset I turned down his proposal to wed him. Burt is furious I intervened when he was after you. But, land sakes, why would the outsiders be after me, if it's them?"

"Maybe whoever was on the bridge arguing thought you were watching them, then when you took the diamond... I don't know. I do know you either need to stay here all night, or I'm going to take my sleeping bag across the bridge again and camp out in your kitchen or front room."

"Ben, you know we can't," she protested, finally letting go of his hands.

"We've already stepped over the line big-time. I'll explain everything to the bishop tomorrow, and you can tell the sheriff—our two main confessors, right? Just one more night, and we'll get help tomorrow. I'm sure the bishop will get someone to come out and stay with you—maybe with me, too, until we can really be

together. And I want that. I want us to have a future
getting to know each other better. This whole thing has
been a blessing in dis—"

"Simply a blessing. I think so, too, but not in disguise. The one in disguise is the evil person who's been
sneaking around, and I just hope and pray the sheriff
will find out who and stop it."

"As they say in the big, bad world then, my place or
yours tonight? I promise I'll control myself better than
I did a while ago."

"Just for now, I hope," she said, standing and shaking out her soil-smudged skirts. Her *kapp* was still a
bit awry from when they'd kissed.

"Okay," he said. "I say we lock up tight here and
head across the bridge. With you and your house being
watched, it's more important to guard your mushrooms
than my boxes. But first, I want you to take a look at
something in the back room—the second bedroom, not
where I sleep."

"Not another surprise, after all you told me."

"One, I hope—I think—you'll like."

ABBY FOLLOWED BEN ACROSS his workshop/living area
and peeked in as he flicked on an electric light. Lined
up around the four walls of the mostly empty room
were what she would call hope chests. Among the Plain
People, *maidals* cherished them and filled them with
heirloom quilts, towels and linens. Liddy had kept her
big battery-run clock tucked in amid the sheets in hers,
a chest she might have started with Ben in mind, but
which had gone with her when she and Adam moved
to Pennsylvania.

"They're just perfect," Abby told him, standing in

the doorway. Her mind darted to one of the earlier circle letters she'd received from Sarah and Lena, in which they'd all talked about their hope chests, as well as their hopes and dreams for homes and families of their own someday.

"Which one do you like best?" Ben asked, eager as a boy. "Take a look. Even if you have one already, a second one can never hurt."

"I do have one that was my *grossmamm's*. It's special to me, so I won't say my favorite here right now." She longed to examine each chest, but still didn't go into the room.

"You're right," he said, coming back toward her. "The rules of the *bann*—take nothing from the hand of the one shunned."

"But someday, I would treasure a second one, if I had a come-calling friend. I suppose I'd be off my bean enough to want one carved with mushrooms."

He smiled at her, something she hadn't seen much. "Then," he said, "I'd better pay more attention to mushrooms, and not only their virgin spawn inoculator when I'm over there tonight. It will take me just a minute to get some things together and lock up." He turned out the light and headed for the other bedroom, still talking over his shoulder. "For once, let's go across the bridge together. I don't want you out there alone, especially not in the dark."

Sounds came from his room: a closet door banged, a drawer closed.

"Okay, *ja*," she called to him. "Only one more night, and we'll have others to help us...." Her voice trailed off wistfully. Despite the dangers, there was something wonderful about helping each other, just the two of them against bad things in the world. But there was the bright promise of a future, in the broad light of day or in the depths of night. Surely, nothing evil could hurt them now.

CHAPTER EIGHT

THEY LOCKED THEMSELVES inside Abby's house. While Ben looked around, checking the windows, she fixed them mushroom soup and sandwiches, and they ate by lantern light. Although they were both on edge, Abby nearly nodded off after dinner.

"I haven't slept well since that first night I heard voices out there," she told him as she washed the dishes. "Sorry," she added with a yawn. "It's not the company, really. I finally feel safe, now that you're here."

"We're both emotionally wrung out, plus you had that run through the woods." For the tenth time, he got up to glance out the windows toward the bridge. "It would shock me if this turns out to just be pranksters picking on a lone, isolated woman, but people are nuts these days. It will be good to turn things over to Bishop Esh and the sheriff in the morning. I'll put my sleeping bag on your rag rug, stretched across the doorway between the living room and kitchen."

"And," she said, stacking the dishes in the rack to dry, "I'd better take a bath and get to bed. I know I'm still a mess after hiding in that log."

"You look great to me. A little wild, but as natural and lovely as all of Eden County." He turned toward her and she to him, between the table and the sink. He gently tugged at a curl that had come loose from her *kapp,* and stroked the slant of her cheek with his thumb. "Abby, thanks to you, I'm finally really happy to be home. Despite everything we've been through here, I'm glad and grateful to have found you."

It was going to happen again—a kiss, a caress. But then he moved to the kitchen door, filling it completely, making the entire house seem to shrink. She wanted to be kissed good-night. She could tell he wanted that, too. But if they did, he'd have much more to confess to the bishop than he'd planned. She had already stepped over the line with a shunned man and could be put under the *meidung,* too.

"Good night, then," she said, and edged toward the door. "Turn out the lantern when you're ready, *ja?*"

"*Ja,* Abigail Baughman." He moved slowly out of the doorway to let her pass. "There's a worldly saying, 'Tomorrow is the first day of the rest of our lives.' Let's make that so."

Later, despite a warm bath, full stomach and utter exhaustion, Abby had trouble sleeping again. Mostly because Ben was just one closed door and one room—one shout—away.

AFTER BREAKFAST, Ben helped Abby harness Fern to the buggy. "I'll walk just ahead of you over the bridge, throw my stuff in the house, do a quick change of clothes, then be ready to go," he told her.

"I hope you don't mind driving that truck into town at about four miles an hour," she said as she climbed up and took the reins. "I could start ahead of you."

"No way. Until I see you walk safely through the sheriff's front door, I'm keeping you in sight. Maybe a long time after, too," he added, reaching up to squeeze her knee. "Wait for me by my truck."

She giddyapped to Fern and turned toward the bridge, though she felt she could have simply soared across the river. A future with Ben. A miracle that he could learn to love her, too. Wait until she wrote all that had happened in the next circle letter.

The steel buggy wheels bounced and rattled over the plank flooring of the bridge, scattering the pigeons roosting in the rafters above. They fluttered out the windows with their wings flapping.

She glanced at her locked-up house and gardens guarded by the fringe of forest. Harvesting her mushrooms would be delayed today. As for dealing with the sheriff, it wasn't the Plain People's way to trust law officers, ever since their Amish ancestors had been pursued and murdered in Europe years ago. But she and Ben had no choice, and surely Bishop Esh would understand.

Abby reined Fern in on the other side of the bridge as Ben went into his house. Again, she turned back to look across the river at her home and land, then at the old bridge itself—and screamed.

Ben blasted out of the house, banging the door into the wall.

"What! What?" he cried, when she pointed toward the bridge, close to this side.

When he leaped up into the buggy, he saw it, too: two bodies swinging underneath, an Amish woman and an *Englische* man, hanged, with nooses around their necks.

"WH-WHAT...WHO?" Ben stammered. "It looks like..."

"Like us."

He jumped down and ran the short way to the bridge,

with Abby scrambling after him. Why had they not seen this from the other side? Oh, she thought, a supporting truss hid the bodies from her windows. So, was this meant for only Ben to see? Surely, the bodies hadn't been there yesterday.

Her pulse pounded, matching their thudding steps on the bridge. The pigeons flapped and flew again. At the second window, Abby and Ben peered down in horror before they realized they were looking at store mannequins.

"Oh, thank the Lord!" she cried. "Not real—not people. But they look real, even this close, with hands and feet and faces. Maybe someone wanted you to see it at night and get spooked, thinking it was ghosts of the lovers who hanged themselves here years ago. Or you'd take it as a warning and make me leave—or leave yourself."

"It could be more than a sick prank—maybe a trap or diversion." He leaned way out the window to look toward his house, then hers. "I don't see anyone. Keep looking both ways," he ordered, as he pulled his cell phone out of his jeans pocket. "Since I've decided to return to the church, I've been trying not to use this, but I'm getting the sheriff here, even if I miss the meeting with the elders."

"Ben, you can't miss that!"

"They'll have to understand when we tell them everything. This way we'll protect the evidence and show it to the sheriff and the bishop—maybe the Cincinnati detective, too. I swear that insurance investigator could be behind this, trying to panic me into some kind of confession, or get me to move back to Cincinnati where she can watch me better. She's been desperate to nail me, even before I came back here."

He began to pace while he made the call. Abby kept looking both ways on the bridge, at her house, then Ben's, even up and down the river. The rapids rushing over the rocks below made her dizzy, as if the bridge— the whole world—were moving.

BEN WAS UPSET when the sheriff answered and said he wasn't back in town yet, but was on the road from Cleveland, "'bout an hour out." In a rush, Ben explained things.

"Okay," Sheriff Freeman said, "I'll use my siren and light bar and be there in half the time. Sit tight."

Abby looked upset when he told her.

"I think we should cut these figures down and take them into town, not wait here," she insisted.

"They're the best evidence we've had for all this, especially since the diamond and note telling you to get out disappeared. Fingerprints or DNA could be on those plastic bodies. I've been fingerprinted and all that, so I know. Abby, this is my chance to be cleared, to be myself again, be Amish, be with you."

"All right. I trust you."

"I'd even like to drape the mannequins with sheets, preserve whatever hair and fibers might be on them."

"Hair and fibers? You mean their wigs and their clothes need to be protected for fingerprints?"

"No, not like that. I read up on all the evidence the police got after the jewelry theft, things they said pointed to me. I was advised to hire a lawyer, but I didn't—still Amish to the core."

"In the online photos of you carving your boxes, you never let them show your face."

He nodded. "Now here's my plan. I'm going to run over to my house and grab two clean sheets. You'll be able to see me go in and out. Be right back!"

He was so excited about clearing his name, she thought, but she understood. To have something that terrible hanging over one's head...

As the pigeons fluttered back into the rafters above, she looked up. What was that stuck in one of the old swallow nests up there? It looked like a short string of pearls, maybe a bracelet.

Abby glanced at Ben again, saw him unlock his front door and rush inside. She took two steps back and squinted up into the dim rafters to see better. What if some other piece of jewelry had been dropped here and some bird or squirrel had found it?

Wait until she told Ben! If she just had a ladder to get up there to check that nest...

She could see he hadn't come back outside yet. She ran for her buggy, got in and made her way back onto the bridge, directly under the nest. Yes, for sure this was the spot where she'd found the diamond. "Whoa," she told Fern. From this higher vantage point, she could see the nest better. *Ja,* a pearl bracelet, like the one she'd seen spilling from Ben's boxes on the jewelry store website. But where was Ben? Wait until she told him and the sheriff this latest twist.

Trusting Fern to stand stock-still, she balanced a foot on the splashboard and the other on the seat. Steadying herself with one hand on the buggy's roof, she stretched, reaching for the dangling pearls. But she noticed something else. Wedged into the angled space where the bridge roof met the side beams was a polished wooden box—no, two of them, maybe with two more jammed behind. Ben's boxes?

She got down inside the vehicle and pulled out the buggy whip she never used. If she could just slide one of those boxes out of its niche, maybe she could catch it and—

Fern snorted. The buggy shifted. Abby bounced back in the seat as the box she'd loosened tipped and fell, showering jewelry over her, until it thudded onto the bridge floor in a final spray of shining gems.

Knocked back hard into the seat, she saw what had startled Fern. Her hemp-masked pursuer stood ten feet away, without gloves this time. Beautifully manicured hands with painted crimson nails and big, gold rings pointed a gun at Abby. Just beyond, someone was dragging an unconscious—or dead—Ben toward her on the bridge.

Abby gasped and let out a little scream.

"I see," the woman said as she came closer, "you found the jewels Benjamin stole from our store. Pity he's so full of remorse that he's going to hang himself here. And you, madly in love with him, will join him in a suicide pact, just like those sad lovers years ago. Hurry up, Cesar," she shouted over her shoulder. "Let's haul up the mannequins and get this over with! If all we've done hasn't made Miss Amish here leave so we only have to deal with Ben, nothing will. And we don't need that insurance harpy showing up before we're through! We can just reuse these nooses, so let's get going!"

"I had to hit him really hard to knock him out," Cesar Tornelli said. He was struggling, huffing and puffing as he dragged Ben.

"Ben would not have stolen this," Abby said, her voice shaking as she swept necklaces and bracelets off her lap. "You put Ben's boxes with your store's jewels here, didn't you? I'll bet you kept some back and hoped they wouldn't be found, so you could have the insurance money *and* the jewels. You thought if you hid some of them here, Ben would be blamed!"

Abby kept telling herself that in less than a half hour the sheriff would arrive.

"You're crazy," Triana—this woman had to be Mrs. Tornelli—said. "We suspected Ben, traced him here when he left town, and how nice you've found our stolen property for us."

"Quit wasting time," Cesar ordered. "Keep an eye on her, and I'll haul up the bodies. And, yes, Amish Abby," he said as he leaned out the window to tug up a mannequin, "we did have to steal our own jewels because we were facing bankruptcy. We had no other choice, just as we have no other choice now."

For sure, Abby thought, they intended to kill her and Ben. They'd clearly identified themselves, admitted their sins and made certain Ben was in no shape to fight them. At least she could tell he was still breathing.

"Now you shut up, Cesar," Triana said. "She probably doesn't even know what bankruptcy means."

"I know what bankruptcy of character, of morals, means," Abby told them. She felt terrified and panicked, but also defiant. Her dander was up, as *Grossmamm* used to say—and that wouldn't do her any good at all. But she'd do anything to keep them talking until Ben woke up or the sheriff arrived.

"I'm going to get out of my buggy and tend to Ben's head," she told Triana, making a move to get down.

Surely they didn't want her found with a bullet from their gun in her.

"Just stay put!" the woman ordered, both hands on the gun. "Enjoy those jewels, because... Look, I—we're really sorry you got tangled up in this. But we figured you saw us hiding the boxes when you shone your light in, and could ID us. When we came back, I saw you find an earring that could be linked to me. This whole mess has just gotten out of hand."

Cesar drew in the first mannequin—the Amish-dressed woman—and Abby's insides cartwheeled. The figure was clad in one of her dresses and aprons, which she hadn't missed at all. *Think!* she told herself. *Find a way to stall!*

She tore her gaze away from the mannequin sprawled amid the scattering of jewels. "So, Triana," she said, "did you tell Cesar that you came on to Ben, tried to seduce him to have a worldly affair? I assume that's another reason you want to get rid of Ben, besides pinning your theft on him. You wouldn't want him to tell your husband you're sick and tired of him."

"Just shut up!" Triana ordered as the gun wavered in her hand.

But Cesar had turned toward his wife before leaning out the window to haul up the male mannequin. "What?" he demanded, his voice dripping menace and reined-in fury. "Is that why you set up this whole thing—ordering me around, trying to scare her away and now getting rid of Benjamin, instead of just letting him take the fall for us?"

"She's lying—she's desperate," Triana insisted, stepping closer to the buggy and pointing the gun straight at Abby.

"The Amish try not to lie," Abby told Cesar, ignoring the woman and fighting to keep calm. "And however attractive your wife is, we also refuse to have marriage relations with a man or woman wed to someone else. I realize you don't know me, Mr. Tornelli, but Ben and I are telling the truth about your wife, so you better hope she doesn't double-cross you some other way."

"You lying little—" Triana began, just as Cesar came around the buggy, took her gun and slapped her right through her hemp mask.

Up this close, Abby got a glimpse of her lipstick through the mouth hole, and dark lashes through the eye slits. When Abby had flashed the light at them on the bridge, she had thought at first the woman was Amish, but it had been Triana's sleek, silver hair and not a prayer *kapp* she'd glimpsed. They must have feared she would describe them to Ben and he'd—

But Abby's hopes that she'd stalled their plans were crushed when Cesar shoved Triana toward the window and ordered, "Haul that other one up and let's get this over." Now *he* trained the gun at Abby. If only she could seize the reins and get Fern going. Would a fiberglass buggy stop a bullet? But she could not leave Ben behind. How much time had passed? *Dear Lord, please get the sheriff here fast.*

Each time Abby so much as moved, pieces of jewelry and gems slid off her onto the buggy seat and floor. Could she throw some in Cesar's face, or hit him with the buggy whip? She felt filled with fear and fury. Now she understood how Ben had beaten up Steve Commons when he'd attacked Ben's sister. Oh, *ja,* if given the chance here, she would not turn the other cheek.

The male figure—garbed in Ben's clothes, for all she

knew—scraped over the windowsill and hit the floor. Triana was breathing hard, and Cesar was cussing her out. If only they would start to fight each other with more than words...

"Get the ropes and nooses," Cesar said. "We can't leave marks by tying their hands behind their backs."

"There will be hair and fiber evidence, anyway," Abby told him, using another tactic. She tried to remember what else Ben had said about being investigated. "You obviously hit Ben inside his house. You think his blood and your hair and fibers won't be there?"

"What the heck is this, *NCIS Amish?*" Cesar asked. "Girl, I regret that you got caught up in this, and I half wish I was tossing Triana over the side instead. Now just climb down here slowly."

She did, but dared to kneel beside Ben. Sticky blood matted the hair on his left temple. She dabbed at it with her apron and then saw her chance.

Triana, who looked furious, was walking in front of Fern and the buggy to get the nooses. Again Abby assured herself that the Tornellis didn't want to have bodies with a bullet from their gun in them. They wanted it to look as though Ben was so ashamed of what he'd done that he'd hanged her and himself, or even that they'd made a *verboten* lovers' pact and jumped off the bridge together.

"Fern, giddyap!" she cried.

The horse jerked the traces; the buggy vaulted forward. Its corner slammed into Triana, throwing her down. Cesar jumped back to keep from being hit by the opposite wheel.

Ben's eyelids flickered open and he moved. He must

have been conscious even before she yelled. He rolled away from Abby into Cesar, taking him down.

On the floor of the bridge, the two men struggled for the gun. If Ben hadn't been wounded, Abby knew he would have won, but Cesar seemed to be stronger. *Use no violence, turn the other cheek.* The words came to her even as she ran over and kicked Cesar's arm to make him drop the gun. When she saw Ben pull one of the man's arms behind his back to control him, she grabbed the noose on the floor and ran over to Triana, who was gasping for breath and moaning in pain. It looked as if the steel buggy wheel had run over her foot. Fern must have just kept going, because Abby couldn't see any sign of horse or buggy.

She yanked the hood off the woman. Triana didn't look one bit beautiful now, tears making black streaks run down her cheeks from her dark-lined eyes. Abby tied her hands behind her back, tightening the noose around her wrists. Triana Tornelli sat sobbing in the strewn beauty of the stolen jewels, which crunched under Abby's feet when she ran back to Ben.

It seemed to her an eternity before the sheriff came, because Ben was bleeding and had a horrible headache. Sheriff Freeman approached on foot with his gun drawn. Abby said to Ben, "Now you'll really be late for your meeting with the elders. I hope they don't think you changed your mind."

"If you vouch for me, they'll understand. I think you can tell them how sometimes the rules need to be broken," he added, as the sheriff handcuffed and put both prisoners in the back of his cruiser.

"Well, I'll be," Sheriff Freeman said when he returned, this time leading Fern and the buggy. He stared again at the litter of jewels while they waited for the county emergency squad to check out Ben's head and Triana's broken foot. "Wait till I call the big city police and that pushy insurance adjustor and tell them us 'rural rubes' solved their case!"

Somehow, though the Amish had no telephones, word spread of the arrests of the *auslanders* and their stolen treasure. Buggy after buggy and a few cars drove up, so the sheriff put yellow police tape across both ends of the bridge to keep gawkers out, while the medics patched up Ben's head on his front porch.

"I'm not a bit worried one of your people will take any of those sparklers," the sheriff told them. "But we got some folks I don't trust far's I can throw them," he muttered, then hustled over to tell Burt Commons to get off Ben's property and stay off.

Bishop Esh drove up in a buggy with two of the elders and came over to talk to Ben. Abby had been sitting beside him on the swing, but moved to the lowest porch step while the medics packed up their things. Though she knew she should move even farther away from Ben, she didn't. Surely, when the Plain People heard what had happened here today, they would understand and forgive.

"How about we have our meeting right inside your place, so you won't have to drive in today," Bishop Esh said to Ben. "That is, if you're up to it. We're real glad to see you came through all right."

"I'd appreciate that," Ben told them. Bandaged head and all, he stood up. Abby could tell he was a bit woozy, but there was no stopping him, nor did she want to. Oh, no, she wanted everything settled right now, right here, because she never wanted to let Ben Kline out of her sight again. From now on, if he was willing, oh, *ja,* they were going to be hanging out together.

AFTERWORD

IT WAS A DAY Abby would always remember, and not just because the first snow fell, silvering the bare trees and etching the old boards of the bridge. Why, the Hanging Bridge looked like it wore a white linen prayer *kapp*. It was also the first day after the church service in which Ben was restored to his people and the Amish faith. And it was the Monday morning he had gone to sell his truck and buy a buggy. A courting buggy, he had promised her, and he was going to officially come calling.

She felt as nervous as she had while waiting for her *rumspringa* days of freedom to begin. But she recalled how strong Ben's voice had rung out in church six weeks ago when he had knelt among the brethren and asked to be returned to the Amish church and community. Bishop Esh had preached on the prodigal son who came home to his family and people. There had been tears in many eyes, including hers.

And then the six weeks of waiting, with everyone watching Ben's behavior, had begun. Those days had been hard for Abby, too, for he was still under the *bann*. Each week she had invited a different friend to come live with her to help her get through the days when she and Ben could not be alone, but yesterday he had been fully forgiven and reinstated during a worship service. On his knees, Ben had promised to "work with the church," and had been welcomed back with open arms—including hers. Ben's *bann* was over.

The final words of the bishop as he blessed Ben echoed in her heart: "The Lord has delivered your soul from death. Therefore, walk before the Lord in the land of the living...." Both she and Ben had escaped death, and he had promised her they *would* walk together in the land of the living.

As she paced back and forth in her kitchen, watching the road by his house for any sign of him, she read snatches of the latest circle letter, which lay on the table. She had it memorized, especially the parts about Sarah and Lena's best wishes and fervent prayers that everything would work out just fine for her and Ben. *Ja,* she thought, better than for Cesar and Triana, who were both going to prison. Better than for the insurance agent, who was losing her job for targeting Ben after being led astray by the Tornellis.

When she caught a glimpse of a buggy turning toward the bridge, Abby sucked in a deep breath and clasped her hands. She'd already seen Ben's fine new mare, a former harness racer he'd bought at the livestock auction in Kidron. But—oh, maybe it wasn't Ben, because it was hardly a small, two-seat courting buggy, but a big, six-seat family sedan. He'd gone over to Sugarcreek to buy a buggy, because he didn't want to get one from the place where Elam Garber worked, even though her former friend was going to wed Ruth Yutzy. But it had to be Ben. Her people were real good at telling who was coming on the road just by the size and gait of the horse.

Suddenly, Abby felt hit with the jitters. Go out to greet him? She'd waited years for this. Stay put and let him come up and knock on the door? What had Liddy used to do when Ben came calling and Abby would peek out her bedroom window and wish he was coming for her?

But she couldn't wait a moment more. Smoothing her best apron over her lilac-hued dress, she pulled a tan woolen shawl around her shoulders, made sure her *kapp* was on straight, and went out onto the porch into the brisk air. It sure made a pretty scene with the falling snow, the buggy and the bridge.

Oh, *ja,* it was Ben, smiling at her. But when he got down, he didn't come straight toward her. He leaned back into the big buggy and lifted down a large, carved, polished chest and carried it over to her.

"A hope chest full of hope, and I hope I don't get this or me turned down," he said as his eyes went thoroughly over her, immediately warming the bite of the wind. He held the big box toward her so she could see it better.

"Oh, Ben, you carved mushroom handles and corners!"

"Right. Mostly turkey tails and shaggy manes."

"It's just beautiful!"

"Like you, Abby. Strong, too. Well, do I have to stand here in this wind holding it, hoping you'll ask me in and accept it?"

"Of course I accept it!" she said, fighting tears of joy and sweeping wide the door for him. "And that is one great-looking horse and buggy, but a big one."

He put the chest down on her kitchen table and opened it for her to see inside. Within its smoothly sanded, polished interior lay an inch-thick stack of money, held together with a rubber band. As he pulled it out and flipped through it, she saw it was all one-hundred-dollar bills! For one wild second, it flew through her head that the Tornellis had accused Ben of theft and—and now here he was with...

"The insurance company did what they called 'settled' for 'undue harassment' by one of their agents," he explained. "They were impressed, I guess, that I didn't sue them. We made the right decision not to, but this comes my—our way, anyhow. I think we might want to use some of it to add a couple bedrooms on the back of this house, fix up my old place and rent it out, and live here—if you'll marry me. Abby? You all right? I'm trying not to touch you yet to sway your decision, but it's not like you to not have a word to say."

"A word to say," she repeated, feeling dazed and trying to catch her breath. "Here's a word then—*ja! Ja,* Ben Kline!" she cried, and took two running steps into his arms.

He picked her up and twirled her, until, laughing and breathless, he leaned back against the kitchen counter, still holding her. "I figured with that windfall of money," he said, "I'd just spring for a family sedan so we have room for our *kinder,* your mushrooms and my boxes and chests. As for children, we are getting a late start and are going to have to work real hard to catch up."

"I like your ideas—all of them." She barely got the words out before he kissed her hard. She threw her arms around his neck and gave him just as good back. When she came up for air, her head still spinning, she said, "We've kind of had a crazy courtship, so far. You think Bishop Esh would let us have a church and wedding service on the bridge this spring?"

"This spring? I've been thinking about six weeks away—the new year, a new life—but if you want a wedding on the bridge, we can try. Abby, my love, you're a gem!"

* * * * *

To my loving husband, as always.

FALLEN IN PLAIN SIGHT

Marta Perry

CHAPTER ONE

"IF YOU ARE NOT CAREFUL, Sarah Elizabeth Weaver, you will end up a *maidal,* as lonely and sad as that old man you work for." *Mamm* had what she obviously considered the last word as she drew the buggy to a halt by the Strickland house.

"Mamm..." Sarah hesitated, ready to jump down, but not wanting to leave her mother for the day with harsh words between them. "I know you want to see me married, with a home and family of my own. But I'm just not ready."

Her mother shook her head, a mix of sorrow and exasperation on her face. "When will you be ready? Independence is all very *gut,* but having someone of your own is better, that's certain sure. *Ach,* well, go on to work." She waved her hand toward the huge old Victorian house, its gingerbread trim and fancy touches a far cry from a simple Amish farmhouse. "But think on it. All of your friends are starting families already."

"I will, *Mamm.*" Sarah slid down. Easier to say that than to argue over a subject on which they'd never agree.

Anyway, not all her friends were married. She still had two dear ones, Abby and Lena, who weren't. But since they all lived far apart, their only connection was the round robin letters they sent from one to the other. They understood, even if *Mamm* didn't.

But she couldn't take comfort in Abby's unmarried state much longer. The long-awaited letter she'd received yesterday had contained surprising news. Her friend would soon wed Ben Kline. They'd been brought together at last after Ben's return from the *Englische* world. That news from Abby had probably been what started *Mamm* on her current train of thought about marriage.

Sarah waved as her mother clicked to Bell and the buggy moved onto Springville's main street. *Mamm* had stopped saying it, but they both knew who she had in mind for a son-in-law. She and Jacob's mother had been planning their children's marriage since the two of them were in their cradles.

But if they'd been serious about marrying Jacob and her off to each other, they'd have been better not bringing them up so close that they were like brother and sister. Jacob was her best friend and the brother she'd never had, but to think of falling in love with him was laughable. Why couldn't *Mamm* see that?

Sarah unlocked the door into the back hall off the kitchen, pausing there to hang up her black bonnet and sweater and straighten the apron that matched the deep green of her dress. Getting dressed for work was simplicity itself when you were Amish. She'd had a choice between green, blue and purple dresses, all cut exactly the same.

Exactly the same, just like all her working days. She'd been taking care of the house for elderly *Englischer* Richard Strickland for over three years, and nothing ever changed, because that was how he liked it. Probably that was partly due to his bad eyesight. He didn't want to trip on anything that had been moved.

She went on into the kitchen, reaching automatically to pick up the breakfast dishes on the table. And stopped. The table was bare, except for the napkin holder and salt and pepper shakers that always sat in the center.

Every day she let herself in the back door at eight-thirty, and every day she found Mr. Strickland's breakfast dishes on the table. Her employer would be in the sunroom on the side of the house, enjoying a second cup of coffee while he listened to the news. But the coffeemaker was cold, the sink was empty and shining, and no sound broke the stillness of the old house.

A chill spread through her. Sarah spun, moving quickly toward the front of the house. Mr. Strickland must be ill...nothing else would cause him to change the immutable habits of a lifetime. She hurried through the hallway, thoughts racing faster than her feet—*call Mr. Strickland's doctor, or the rescue squad if it looked very serious. They could be here faster and—*

She skidded to a stop a few feet from the bottom of the stairs. Neither the doctor nor the rescue squad would be of help. Richard Strickland lay tumbled on the polished stairs, one hand reaching the tiled floor of the hall. Sarah didn't need to touch him to know he was dead.

She had to, of course. She knelt next to him, silent prayers forming in her mind, and searched for a pulse. Nothing stirred under her fingers, and his skin was cold. Pity and grief seemed to have a stranglehold on her throat. Mr. Strickland hadn't been an especially likable man...eccentric, the charitable said. He was the last of the Strickland family, a name that had once meant something in Lancaster County, and folks just shrugged off his crankiness. But she was used to him, fond of him, even.

Standing slowly, Sarah went to the telephone in the small alcove off the hall and dialed 911. After she'd said what she must, she went back to kneel by the body, her lips moving in silent prayer.

Even so, she couldn't keep her eyes from seeing, or her mind from wondering. What had Mr. Strickland been doing on the stairs in the night? And it must have been night, because the upstairs hall light was on. He never came downstairs after he'd taken his pills in the evening, because he said they made him dizzy. And he also never came out of his bedroom until he was fully dressed, so why would he be wearing a robe and slippers?

The doorbell pealed, followed by insistent knocking, and in a few minutes the hall was filled with people. The retired doctor who lived just down the street conferred with the ambulance attendants. A young patrolman stood by the door, looking so pale Sarah wondered if he'd ever seen a dead person before. Adam Byler, the township police chief, was deep in conversation with Leo Frost, Mr. Strickland's attorney.

Sarah sat on a straight chair against the wall, hands folded in her lap, blinking against the tears that threatened to fall, wondering when she'd be able to go home. Wondering what, if anything, she should say.

Her gaze was caught by the leather slipper that lay on the tile floor, and she frowned.

Chief Byler picked up the slipper, holding it out to Mr. Frost. "This is probably the culprit," he said. "It looks as if Strickland was coming downstairs in the night, and he tripped on the slipper. Easy enough to happen, and these leather soles are slippery."

But Mr. Strickland wouldn't come down in the night, wouldn't wear those slippers.

Sarah pressed her lips together. She could practically hear *Daad's* voice in her mind.

Amish have a duty to obey the law of the land and respect its officials, but we don't become involved with them.

What would *Daad* say she should do now? Speak or be silent? She suspected she knew the answer to that. So she sat, silent, her gaze on her hands.

"Sarah?"

She looked up, startled, to find that Chief Byler stood in front of her, along with Mr. Frost.

"I know this is upsetting for you, but I have a few questions."

"Ja." She rose. For sure she should answer any questions the police asked.

He glanced at the paramedics, who were moving a stretcher into place. "Let's go into the kitchen to talk."

Nodding, she led the way back down the hall. He was being kind, but it didn't bother her so much as he might think, being near the body. Death was a part of life, and she'd been old enough to help lay out the body when her *grossmamm* passed. It was only the *Englische* who thought people should die in hospitals and be taken off to funeral homes.

Chief Byler put a notebook on the kitchen table. "Did Mr. Strickland seem well when you left yesterday? And what time was that?"

"Four o'clock," she said promptly. "That was my time. Mr. Strickland had dinner at one o'clock, like always. Roast chicken, it was, so there was plenty left for his supper."

"And did he seem all right then?" Byler asked.

"*Ja,* he seemed fine." Her voice thickened despite her efforts. "He was upstairs in his study, working at his desk. I asked if he needed anything, and he just said no and that he would see me tomorrow."

But he hadn't.

Chief Byler nodded. "And this morning?"

She hesitated, putting her thoughts in order. Surely, since he asked, she ought to tell him what she'd noticed.

"It's all right, Sarah," Mr. Frost said, his lined face kind. "Just tell it the way it happened."

"I unlocked the back door and came in. Hung up my things and went to the kitchen to do the breakfast dishes, but there weren't any." She felt the chill again. "I knew something was wrong. Mr. Strickland's routine was always exactly the same."

"True enough," Leo Frost said. "Richard insisted everything be done exactly the same way at the same time every day. He went through I don't know how many housekeepers because he couldn't find anyone to suit him, until I found Sarah for him." He patted her shoulder. "You always made him comfortable and as happy as he was likely to be, my dear. I know he wasn't easy to get along with."

That was true enough, but it might seem rude if she agreed, so she kept silent.

"So you found him and called 911," Chief Byler said. "Apparently he'd been dead for some hours, according to the doctor. If there's anything else…"

He paused, as if waiting for her to say something.

The words hovered on her tongue. But the odd things

she'd noticed— would they mean anything, or just sound like so much foolishness to an officer of the law?

A step sounded in the back hall, and then Jacob was standing there, looking solid and safe and familiar in his faded blue work shirt, suspenders crossing broad shoulders, his summer straw hat sitting squarely on his light brown hair. "Sarah? *Was ist letz?*"

What's wrong? At the question, the tears she'd held back overflowed, and she ran to him.

His arm encircled her shoulders firmly. *"Komm,"* he said. "I will take you home."

JACOB LOOKED OVER SARAH'S head at the two men. Both Leo Frost, the lawyer, and Chief Byler were usually thought of as friends of the *Leit,* the Amish people. If they objected to her leaving…

Well, it was his job to look after Sarah, like always.

Frost and Byler exchanged glances and the chief shrugged. "That's fine. You go along home. I know where to find you if I have any more questions." A smile tempered the words.

"I'm sorry you were the one to find him, Sarah. Try not to dwell on it." Leo Frost looked at her with concern. "I'll come by the house and check on you later."

Sarah managed to smile at Frost, but it was a wobbly effort that worried Jacob. The sooner he got her home, the better.

"Danki." With a word of thanks, he steered Sarah to the door, stopping while she grabbed her bonnet and sweater, and out into the warm spring air.

He helped her up to the buggy seat and climbed in himself. He didn't like that frozen look on Sarah's face. Whether she'd admit it or not, it had been a shock to find her employer dead. She'd been fond of the old man, despite his crankiness, and she was grieving.

Sarah didn't speak until the buggy had passed the outskirts of Springville and started along the narrow country road. She stirred, fiddling with her bonnet strings as if she didn't remember putting it on.

"*Danki,* Jacob." Her voice was husky. "How did you know?"

"*Ach,* you know how fast news travels around the township. Bishop Amos stopped by the machine shop to tell your *daad.* The bishop always knows everything."

She nodded, finally smiling a little. "*Ja,* the Amish grapevine works well, for sure."

"I'm sorry, Sarah. I know you cared about Mr. Strickland." She'd spent nearly as much time with him as with her family in the past three years since she'd been taking care of the house for him. Of course she'd miss him.

"It's not just that." The words burst out of her as if she couldn't hold them back. "Can I tell you something, Jacob?"

He studied her face, the warm, creamy skin dotted with freckles already, a strand of brown hair escaping from under her *kapp* to curl against her cheek, her blue eyes serious.

"*Ja,* for sure. Always." She ought to know that.

Sarah took a deep breath and blew it out. "I went in the hallway and saw Mr. Strickland." Her voice shook a little, and he reached across to take her hand in a comforting grip. "He was lying on the stairs, head down. He had on a robe and slippers, and the light was on in the upstairs hall, which must mean he'd fallen during the night."

Jacob nodded, not sure what she was driving at.

"Chances are he died right away, pitching down those stairs. If you're worrying that he lay there—"

"No, it's not that." She shook her head in that decisive way of hers, impatient as always. "Don't you see? It was all wrong. Mr. Strickland never came downstairs in the night. He said the medicine he took before bed made him a little dizzy, and he wouldn't risk it. He was very particular about that...made sure he had a pitcher of water and a little tin of crackers in his bedroom in case he wanted them."

Jacob considered for a moment. "Maybe he felt sick."

"Then he'd have called for help. He always had the phone right next to him." She shook her head, her bonnet strings fluttering in the breeze. "He never came out of the bedroom without being dressed. Nobody saw him in his robe and slippers. And those slippers—he showed them to me once. Said they were so slippery it was like the person who gave them to him wanted him to have an accident. It's just all wrong."

It would be easy to dismiss her worries, Jacob decided. Whether Sarah wanted to hear it or not, just because a man always did things a certain way didn't mean he wouldn't change if he had to. If he heard someone in the house, for instance. But surely the police would be able to tell if someone had broken in.

"Well?" Her voice crackled with impatience. "It shouldn't take that long to tell me what you think."

"Always in such a rush, Sarah." He kept his voice light and teasing. "Always jumping to conclusions and landing yourself in trouble, *ja?*"

That distracted her, as he'd known it would. "I'm not in trouble. And if I were, I'd find my own way out." Her forehead wrinkled slightly. "But should I tell Chief

Byler what I noticed? I know I shouldn't get involved with the police, but isn't it wrong to hold back?"

He pondered that. Sarah wouldn't be able to let go of the questions in her mind. Knowing her as he did, he could feel sure of that.

"Mr. Frost isn't the police," he observed.

She nodded, the sparkle coming back into her eyes. "*Ja,* that's true. If I tell him, he can decide if the police need to know. *Danki,* Jacob." She squeezed his arm, and it seemed to him he felt that touch in his very bones. "You are a *gut* big brother."

Her words were easy, and he was glad he'd been able to put the light back in her face, chasing away the sorrow and worry. But he wished she'd called him anything else.

"*Ach,* I have forgotten." Sarah's hands flexed as if she'd grab whatever it was that had gotten away. "I didn't say anything to the chief about telling Hank Mitchell. Poor Hank. He must have been at his college classes, and he'll come home, not knowing. Someone should tell him."

"Not you," Jacob said, before he could think how sharp that sounded. "It's not your job to take care of Mr. Strickland's cousin." Truthfully, he was getting tired of hearing the man's name since he'd come to live in the garage apartment at Mr. Strickland's place.

"Distant cousin, I think," she corrected. "That's the only reason Mr. Strickland let him live in the garage apartment. He doesn't—didn't—like strangers around, but he said you couldn't turn away kin."

"Well, whatever he is, he's not your responsibility." Leo Frost would deal with the man, as well as the apartment and the house. That was his job.

And Sarah's job, it seemed, had ended.

She was glaring at him, he realized.

"You sound like my *daad*," she said, her tone frosty.

He'd made a mistake, for sure. But what with her calling him her big brother and comparing him to her *daad*, he could hardly admit that he was jealous.

The horse turned automatically into the lane between their homes and headed for the barn. Jacob didn't speak, because he couldn't find anything to say.

He was always the logical one, but he didn't feel that way at the moment. He didn't want to go on being Sarah's brother, because the feelings he had were not at all brotherly. But he couldn't say anything, because once he did, there was no going back, and he might lose her friendship and be left with nothing.

CHAPTER TWO

SUPPER WAS NEARLY OVER, and Sarah was grateful. Her younger sisters had been agog over the fact that she had found a body, and their questions had gone on until her throat was tight with pressure.

If anyone had asked her a few days ago, she would have had to admit that Richard Strickland was crotchety, irritable and intent on having his own way. Despite that, Sarah had grown to love him, as she'd love any creature she took care of, whether it was an ailing foal or an elderly *Englischer*. It seemed impossible that he was gone.

He was gone, and she was the only one who suspected his passing was more than a tragic accident.

"But how did he look?" Ten-year-old Emma's eyes shone with excitement. "Was he all bloody?"

"I don't think Sarah wants to talk about it anymore." Jacob, who was taking meals with them while his mother was off visiting his married sister, intervened.

"*Ja,* for sure." *Daad* frowned at Emma and Rachel. "That is enough from the both of you. Go outside and do your chores now."

Rachel, twelve, shot a resentful look at Emma, obviously thinking she had reminded him that they were still at the table. But they both went out quietly, saving any argument until they were out of earshot of their father.

"*Ach,* it's a sad thing for sure, the poor old man dying alone that way," *Mamm* said. "But there was nothing you could have done to make things any different, Sarah, so you must not fret. It was God's will."

God's will—the answer Sarah had been trained to accept since birth. But in this case, maybe it was also someone else's will. A cold hand seemed to grip her neck. If what she'd noticed meant anything, it might be that someone else was responsible for Mr. Strickland's fall.

She backed away from that thought quickly. It couldn't be. She was imagining things for sure. She'd tell her worries to Leo Frost, as Jacob had suggested, and then she could forget about them.

"Now that you will not be working for Mr. Strickland any longer, I am thinking you could help us keep the books in the shop. And help your *mamm,* too."

Sarah eyed her father's weathered face, creased with lines of sun and toil and smiling, his brown beard streaked now with gray. She knew exactly what he was thinking—that it was time his eldest daughter stopped working in town and started working on getting married. On that subject, as on so many others, he and *Mamm* thought as one.

"You know I am always glad to help, *Daad.*" She meant the words, but perhaps not in the way he wished. She could see a battle ahead.

Jacob moved slightly, craning to look out the window. "A car is coming up the lane. Mr. Frost, I think."

Jacob was right, and in a few minutes the lawyer was seated at the kitchen table, a slice of *Mamm's* apple crumble pie and a steaming mug of coffee in front of him.

Leo Frost, white-haired and bright-eyed, was officially semiretired, but he still dealt with some of his old clients, like Richard Strickland. He was a favorite among the Plain People of the township, always ready to give advice and help on the rare occasions when they had to deal with the *Englische* law.

"Wonderful pie, Elizabeth. This was just what I needed after such a trying day." His smile included all of them, but he studied Sarah especially, as if judging how much she had been affected by what had happened.

"We are sorry for the loss you have suffered." *Daad,* naturally, spoke for the family. With Leo present, the conversation had switched from Pennsylvania Dutch to English, something they did so naturally it was almost automatic.

"Yes, well, there are only a few of us close enough to Richard to feel a sense of loss—primarily Sarah and me, I suppose. Richard had outlived most of his family and friends." The lawyer shook his head. "Truthfully, he was such a difficult personality that he didn't have many friends. He was fortunate to have Sarah to look after him." He smiled at her, and she discovered that her answering smile was a bit wobbly.

"I was wondering what will happen next," Jacob said, asking the question she wanted answered. "With the police involved and all."

"That shouldn't cause too much delay in settling the estate, I hope," Leo said, frowning a little, as if not used to having clients die in a way that involved the police. "However, everything in the house will have to be inventoried before I can get on with disposing of the property according to his will."

Daad nodded, but Sarah suspected he felt the prospect foreign. Elderly Amish people often made disposition of their belongings before they passed, and they seldom had enough to warrant an inventory.

"Actually, that's one reason I wanted to come and see Sarah." He smiled at her. "I was hoping she would agree to continue working for a time—long enough to help me inventory the items in the house and get it ready for transfer. According to Richard's wishes, it's going to the historical society. But sorting and packing is a big job, and she's the person who knows the most about the place."

Mamm glanced at *Daad,* looking dismayed. Clearly, she had expected Sarah's job to end promptly with Mr. Strickland's death.

"I don't know...." For once, *Daad* seemed at a loss. "We had hoped...had thought that her job was over now. How long would it take, this inventory?"

"It's hard to say," Leo replied. "Goodness knows, that house is filled with stuff, some of it outright junk, some of it quite valuable. I would think at least a couple of weeks. Naturally, Sarah will be paid for as long as it takes."

Daad was frowning again, and Sarah gripped her skirt with both hands to keep from bursting into speech. She wasn't ready to give up her independence yet, and Mr. Frost's offer would provide her with an opportunity to look around for another place. More importantly, it would give her a chance to talk to him about what she'd noticed, something she could hardly do in front of her parents.

"I don't know that I like our Sarah being alone in that house all day." *Daad* seemed on the verge of refusal.

"I would be in and out several times a day," Leo said quickly.

"I could drive Sarah to work and check the house every morning, if you want," Jacob offered. "Then go back and bring her home."

Daad wavered, obviously trusting Jacob's good common sense.

"I'd be most grateful," Leo said. "I don't know how I'd do it without Sarah's help."

Putting it on to the basis of a need for help pushed *Daad* the rest of the way. He nodded. "*Ja,* I suppose it is all right. If Sarah wants."

She could feel their gazes on her, and tried not to let any trace of her thoughts show in her face.

"*Ja,* for sure I will be glad to help."

Although she had to admit that a little shiver of apprehension snaked down her back at the thought of being alone in the house where Mr. Strickland had died.

BY THE TIME SARAH REACHED the Strickland house the next morning, she was embarrassed to remember her fears. The place looked the same as always, a fine old Victorian that was said to have once been the grandest residence in town. And while Mr. Strickland's death was sad, it was in the nature of things. She'd almost managed to reason away the inconsistencies that had bothered her the previous day. Almost, but not quite.

Jacob, who had kept his promise to drive her to the house, jumped down easily from his seat beside her, tying the horse to the fence.

"You don't have to come in with me." She got down and unlatched the gate, holding it. "I know you were just trying to reassure *Daad* so he wouldn't be upset about my coming."

Jacob pushed the gate the rest of the way open and walked through. "You might fool your *daad,* but you can't fool me, so don't bother to try." He held the gate for her. "When you were talking so calm about coming back here, you felt scared."

"Did not," she said instantly, an echo of their childhood.

Jacob grinned. "Did, too."

Giving in, she went up the walk. "Well, maybe I felt a little funny, is all. Especially since…" She stopped, not wanting to finish the thought.

"Especially since you saw things you thought were wrong about Mr. Strickland's death." Jacob waited while she opened the door.

"I've decided I was being foolish," she said firmly. She took her bonnet off and put it on the usual hook, followed by her sweater, and smoothed her apron down and her hair back under her *kapp.* Then, satisfied she looked as she should, Sarah turned to Jacob. "It's like you said. There could be explanations for all the things I saw that were out of the ordinary. And if I told the police, they'd laugh."

"Chief Byler would never laugh at you. He's not that kind of man." Jacob followed her into the kitchen. "But maybe it's best if you forget the whole thing, anyway. No sense stirring up trouble."

Sarah flared up at that. "You're the one who suggested I talk to Leo Frost. Remember?"

"Ja." Jacob grasped the back of a kitchen chair. "But I don't want you to get into trouble."

His strong hands nearly covered the top slat. Funny

how she so easily forgot that they were both grown up already. But that was all the more reason why Jacob should stop treating her like a little child. Just because he was partners with *Daad* now in the machine shop, that didn't mean he was the boss.

"I won't get into trouble," she said firmly. "And you don't need to go looking around the house, either. Mr. Strickland wouldn't have liked it, and you can see everything is okay."

Jacob studied her face for a moment, as if trying to read any fear there. Then he shrugged. "I will just walk through the downstairs, *ja?* Then I can tell your *daad* all was quiet."

Not waiting for permission, he walked toward the front of the house. She could hear his footsteps on the hall floor, and that made her picture the hall the way she'd seen it when she'd walked in yesterday.

She wrenched her mind away from that image. She would go in later, when she was by herself, without Jacob watching her to see any betraying signs of fear.

He was back in a moment. "Everything is okay. I'd best get to the shop. See you at the usual time?"

"*Ja. Danki,* Jacob."

He went out, taking his solid, reassuring presence away, and the house felt empty and unwelcoming when the door shut behind him.

Sarah busied herself washing up the coffee cups the officers had used the previous day. Leo Frost would probably come soon, and she didn't want him finding dirty dishes in the sink.

Should she tell him the things that worried her? He hadn't seemed to notice anything, any more than the police did.

Her mind seesawed back and forth. If she told him...

She stopped, a cup poised above the dish drainer. Had she heard something...some sound that shouldn't be there? Old houses made noises, but after all this time, she was used to the sounds this house made. That had sounded like a step.

It came again, clearer this time. From the front hallway. Sarah put the cup down very carefully. She could tiptoe to the door and be out before anyone realized she was here. Couldn't she?

Ach, she was letting this business make her *ferhoodled.* It would be Leo Frost, for sure. He'd said he'd be here this morning, and he had a key. What would he think if he found her huddled in the kitchen, afraid to move?

She tossed the dish towel onto the drainer and hurried through to the front hall. Someone grabbed her arm in a hard grasp. She gasped in shock and drew in breath to scream before she realized who it was.

"Hey, hang on, Sarah. Where are you going in such a hurry?" Hank Mitchell, Mr. Strickland's distant cousin, grinned down at her, his easygoing face relaxed.

"Hank. What are you doing here? I thought it was Mr. Frost." She took a step back, putting some space between them, and his hands dropped to his sides at once.

"I was upstairs, looking for you. I didn't have a chance to talk to you yesterday." The smile slid from his face. "Just wanted to say how sorry I am. I wish I'd come to the house before I left for class yesterday. Then I'd have found him instead of you."

Hank must have left earlier than usual for the classes he took at the school in Lancaster. "It couldn't be helped," she said. "No matter who found him."

"Still, it must have been a shock. Are you okay?"

"Fine." She forced a smile, wishing they weren't having this conversation at the bottom of the staircase. "You must have heard Jacob and me when we came in the house just now. Why didn't you speak to us then?"

Hank shrugged. "I get the impression your friend Jacob doesn't exactly approve of me."

"I'm sure he doesn't...well, he doesn't know you." It was hard to reply to that comment without lying, because she had the distinct impression Hank was right about Jacob's attitude.

"Yeah." He grinned. "Hey, did you say Mr. Frost was coming over?"

She nodded. "I expect him soon, if you'd like to speak to him."

"No need. I'll catch him later." Hank was already headed for the door. "I'm just glad Frost is going to be with you. If Jacob isn't here on time, maybe you'll let me drive you home."

He was gone before she could say that Jacob was always on time. She paused, frowning at the stairs and barely seeing them. Hank had known that Jacob was coming back for her. They'd been speaking *Englische* when they came in the house—she because that was what she always spoke here, and Jacob because he'd naturally answer her in the same tongue.

So Hank had heard them. Had he also heard her saying that she thought something was wrong about Mr. Strickland's death?

CHAPTER THREE

JACOB ARRIVED EARLY to pick Sarah up for her ride home. Even knowing she wouldn't be ready yet, he'd been restless, having trouble concentrating on the work at the machine shop. His thoughts returned again and again to her list of oddities about Mr. Strickland's death.

All of them were things that could be easily dismissed, for sure. But Sarah was bothered, and so he was.

He slid down from the high buggy seat. Since Mr. Strickland's house had no place to stable a horse for the day, someone always had to bring Sarah back and forth. This time, he was especially glad he was the one to do so.

Hank Mitchell was clipping a hedge behind the house, a ball cap pushed back on his curly brown hair, his tight jeans riding low on his hips. The *Englischer* was friendly enough, Jacob supposed. Not his fault that Jacob was tired of hearing his name on Sarah's lips.

When no one came in answer to his tapping, Jacob opened the side door. "Sarah? *Wo bist du?*" *Where are you?*

Steps sounded on the narrow back stairway that led from the kitchen to the second floor, and she appeared, frowning a little.

"You are early, ain't so?" She glanced at the clock.

"We finished up that reaper we were rebuilding, so your *daad* said I should leave. Maybe see if you needed any help."

Sarah's shoulders lifted, her nose wrinkling. "I don't even have enough to do myself. Leo Frost was supposed to come this morning, but then he called to say he was busy and would stop by later. He still hasn't, so I was *chust* tidying up."

The frown was still there, and Jacob sensed it didn't have anything to do with either his early arrival or Frost's late one. "Something is wrong, *ja?*" He hung his straw hat on the knob of the ladder-back chair, prepared to wait as long as needed.

Sarah's lips pressed together, and for a moment he thought she wouldn't answer. Then she nodded. "Things are not where they should be."

"Things? What things?" She should know he would keep asking until he had a better answer than that one.

"Things," she said, waving her hands as if to take in the whole house. "You know how Mr. Strickland had all these little decorations around, like his seashells from when he went to the ocean as a boy, and the teapots his *mamm* collected."

Jacob nodded. The *Englischer's* house had always seemed cluttered to him, with gimcracks on every table, but Sarah said they gave the man pleasure. "Are they gone?"

His thoughts went immediately to theft. If a thief had gotten into the house, that would explain why Mr. Strickland had tried to come down the stairs that night.

"Not missing, no." Sarah's frown deepened. "Just moved. Rearranged, some of them, like someone had looked at them and put them back in the wrong place."

"*Ach,* Sarah, Mr. Strickland probably did it himself. Or you did, when you were cleaning." Relief washed through him. Not a thief lurking around the house, then.

"Jacob Mast, you know perfectly well I would put everything back where it belonged. That's the first thing I learned, working for Mr. Strickland. Everything must be in place."

"Maybe he did—" He tried to go on, but Sarah spoke over him.

"It was because of his bad eyes, you see. He might pick a piece up, hold it in his hands as if it comforted him. Even lift it a few inches from his eyes to see it better. But always each piece went back exactly where it belonged, so he could find it the next time."

That made sense, Jacob supposed, but it still didn't mean Mr. Strickland couldn't have changed his habits for some reason. But since Sarah was already annoyed with him, maybe it wasn't best to point that out.

"I see Mr. Frost coming up the walk now," he said instead, grateful for the interruption. "You should tell him."

But Leo Frost, once he was settled at the kitchen table with a cup of coffee, didn't seem to take Sarah's revelations that seriously. She told him everything, including what she'd noticed the day before. He nodded, patted her hand and promised to discuss it with Chief Byler.

Surprisingly, he paid more heed when Sarah mentioned that Hank Mitchell had been in the house that morning. But no more than Jacob himself did. He'd known he should have checked the entire place, and he'd let Sarah persuade him not to. He wouldn't make that mistake again.

Leo Frost's blue eyes turned cold. "I suppose Richard gave him a key, but I'll have to get it back from him. I don't like the idea of just anyone being able to get in. Richard Strickland had a lot of worthless junk, but he also owned some very valuable antiques."

"I did not mean to get Hank in trouble," Sarah said. "I'm sure he was just looking for me, as he said."

"I'm not blaming you, or Mitchell either, for that matter." Leo patted her hand again. "But I know very little about that young man, and I'd prefer that you not let anyone in unless I tell you to."

Sarah nodded, her gaze on the tabletop, and Jacob knew she was feeling at fault.

"I'll take care of collecting his key," Leo said. "Now, as to the work. Tomorrow you can start sorting through the clothes and packing them in boxes to go to the thrift store." He glanced around the kitchen, shaking his head. "I'd like to auction off the whole lot, but that wouldn't be right, so we'll have to take our time and go through everything. Any papers you might find should be put aside for me to see." He rubbed at the line that had deepened between his snowy eyebrows, as if finding all of this too much.

Sarah, obviously seeing the signs of stress as well, reached out to pat his sleeve. "If you are upset about sorting Mr. Strickland's things—"

"No, no, it's not that." Leo's face warmed as he smiled at her. "At my age, you expect your friends and clients to start dying off. The reason I'm upset came in today's mail. I received a note from Richard, saying he wanted to change his will."

That must have given him a start, knowing his friend

was dead and then getting a letter from him. No wonder he seemed upset.

"But...I thought he was leaving everything to the historical society. He often talked about that." Sarah's bright eyes had clouded.

Leo sighed, shaking his head. "That was the way the last will read, and of course it's valid, since we didn't draft a new one."

"But if he wanted to make changes..." Sarah fell silent, obviously turning the possibility over in her mind.

"Even if he left a list of proposed alterations, it doesn't change anything. I just wish I knew what he was thinking." He smiled, but it seemed to take an effort. "He didn't mention anything about it to you, then?"

Sarah shook her head. "I suppose he might have wanted to leave something to Hank. He wouldn't have known about him when he made up his last will. But that's the only thing I can imagine."

"Like you, I'm troubled by any changes in Richard's regular behavior, but I expect we'll find there was some reason for everything." Leo waved his hands in a shooing motion. "I've kept you long enough. Go on home now. I'll see you tomorrow."

Jacob followed Sarah out to the buggy. He'd been worried about her when he'd arrived, and he was more worried now that he'd heard about Hank being in the house. Leo Frost hadn't liked it, either.

Jacob helped Sarah into the high seat and stood for a moment staring up at her. The black bonnet framed her face, seeming to dampen all her brightness.

"Why didn't you tell Mitchell to get out when you found him in the house?" The words escaped before he thought them through.

Sarah gaped at him. Little wonder. He was acting *ferhoodled,* for sure, out of worry about her.

"How could I do that?" Her quick temper flared. "It is not my house. And Hank was a relative of Mr. Strickland. You are being foolish."

"*Ach,* well, maybe you are being foolish, too, staying on here," he snapped back. "I wish I'd never encouraged it."

Sarah's chin tilted up. "It's none of your business what I do, Jacob. Now take me home, please."

He swung himself up to the seat next to her. Fuming and being foolish both at the same time. What was he going to do about his sweet, stubborn Sarah?

AT LEAST, SARAH DECIDED the next day, she had something positive to do. Sorting through Mr. Strickland's clothing was depressing, but it was better than wandering around the house looking for something out of order. She'd done that so much that she'd begun to see problems everywhere, say nothing of hearing every creak the old house made.

She glanced at the large stacks on the four-poster bed—shirts, pants, suits, ties, all neatly folded. Bearing Leo Frost's words in mind, she had kept her eyes open for any papers, but the dresser and closet had contained only clothes. Mr. Strickland had been meticulous, despite the fact that he'd seldom thrown anything away.

Sarah got up from sitting on the floor, and stretched her back. All the clothing was ready to be packed, but she had no boxes.

The grocery store kept a stack that anyone who needed them could have. She'd best take a walk and pick up a few boxes. Too bad she hadn't thought of that when Jacob had dropped her off. He could have loaded some in the buggy.

She headed for the stairs, detouring first to open the door to the study. It tended to swing shut, and she pushed the heavy doorstop into place and then trotted down the stairs and out to the kitchen to get her bonnet.

Springville was small enough that it didn't take much more than ten minutes to walk from one end to the other. She strolled past the drugstore and the fabric shop, an old-fashioned one that catered to the many Amish quilters in the area. The spring sunshine was warm on her shoulders, relaxing her.

She hadn't realized how depressing it would be cooped up in that house alone all day. Mr. Strickland might have been cranky, but he'd loved to talk, sometimes following her around as she worked, telling her his views on the latest political scandal or expounding on the mistakes of the township supervisors. She'd liked it best when he talked about Springville's early days, or when he'd relived the memories brought on by each of the curios he'd saved.

The stack of boxes was at the side of the market, as usual, and she took as many as she could carry, waving her thanks through the window to the clerk at the front register.

She'd reached McKay's Antiques when she heard someone behind her.

"Sarah…Sarah Weaver. Wait a minute."

Sarah didn't need to turn to know who it was. Maude Stevens, president of the Spring Township Historical Society, had been related to Richard Strickland through her late husband, and she was one of the few people whose visits he'd tolerated.

But *tolerated* was the right word. Mr. Strickland had always complained that he could see her beady eyes assessing the property she coveted for the historical society.

Sarah turned, juggling the boxes, and waited while the woman chugged up to her. In her middle sixties, Maude Stevens was built somewhat like the church wagon that carried benches from one Amish home to another for worship—square and squat. Today she wore a hat, a concoction of feathers and net that Sarah stared at in awe. Maude must have been at the Women's Club luncheon at the inn—that was the only thing *Englische* women wore hats to anymore.

"Glad I caught you." Maude put a possessive hand on her arm, nearly causing Sarah to lose her grip on the boxes. "Wait till I catch my breath."

Sarah nodded. She could hardly refuse. To do Maude justice, her eyes weren't really beady. They were as shiny as two black pebbles one of the *kinder* might bring in from the creek.

"What are all the boxes for? You're not giving away anything from Richard's house, I hope." The woman seemed to have recovered from her race down the street.

"Mr. Frost asked me to pack up the clothing." Best to make it clear that the lawyer was in charge, Sarah thought. "I've been doing that today."

"Clothes." Maude dismissed Sarah's reply with a wave of her hand. "That doesn't matter, but nothing else must be disposed of unless I see it first."

Sarah blinked, unsure how to respond. "I thought Mr. Frost was responsible for that."

"Leo Frost was just Richard's attorney," Maude said, dismissing him with the same gesture she'd used for the clothing. "According to Richard's will, the bulk of his property will go to me...I mean the historical society, which I represent. As such, I should be the one to supervise any disposition of the house contents. You can't be expected to know what's of value, Sarah. And I, after all, am a relative."

"Not quite correct, is it, Maude, dear?" The question came silkily. Donald McKay had stepped out of his antiques shop, apparently listening in on their conversation without embarrassment. "It was your husband who was distantly related to Richard. Your late husband. I'm sure I remember Richard making it clear that you had no claim on his estate at all."

"That's not true." Maude's face seemed to swell, its ruddy color darkening. "Well, it's true enough that it was my husband who was Richard's blood kin, but he always treated me like a...like a dear niece."

That was so false that Sarah could only stare at her. Mr. Strickland had put up with her visits with ill-concealed impatience.

"Really?" Donald McKay's pale eyebrows lifted above his gold-rimmed glasses. "I find that so surprising." His voice was almost a purr, as if he'd borrowed it from the tortoiseshell cat that slept in his front window. "I seem to recall hearing Richard say—"

"I must be off." Maude interrupted him hastily, not wanting to hear what he remembered. "I'll stop by the house later, Sarah. Remember, don't get rid of anything without my approval."

She was gone before Sarah could find a reply. The only consolation was that it would be up to Leo Frost to deal with her.

Sarah glanced at Donald and found his blue eyes

twinkling at her from behind his glasses. He smoothed his sparse blond hair with one hand.

"I hope you appreciate the favor I just did for you, getting rid of our dear Maude that way."

Once again, she didn't know how to respond. She should not admit to being glad to see Maude steam off down the street. "I'm sure she means well," Sarah said finally.

McKay chuckled. "That's what's called damning with faint praise," he said. "Maude makes it sound as if she, not the historical society, is the beneficiary. I'm sure that's how she thinks it should be."

"It was up to Mr. Strickland to leave his property as he wished," Sarah said, reminded again of the fact that he'd wanted to change his will before he died.

"True enough," McKay said. "At the risk of sounding too much like Maude, I'd be willing to come and help you sort out the valuables from the trash in Richard's collections. There are some antiques that should be safeguarded when the house is empty."

That at least she knew how to answer. "I'm sure the house will be safe. I'm there during the day, you know. And at night, Mr. Frost has asked the police to drive by and check on it, in addition to Hank Mitchell being in the garage apartment."

"That relieves my mind," McKay said. "I'm glad Leo is being cautious. But about valuing the antiques…"

"That would be up to Mr. Frost," she said quickly. "He told me not to let anyone in the house without his approval."

"How farsighted of him," McKay murmured. "I'll speak to him about it, then."

"Thank you for the offer." The boxes were becoming unwieldy, and the house had begun to look like a sanctuary. "I must go now."

McKay nodded, stepping back inside the shop. The sleeping cat opened one eye, looked at him and closed it again.

Readjusting the boxes, Sarah scurried down the street. It was normal, surely, for people to offer their help. In the case of a death in the Amish community, the family would immediately be surrounded by other Amish, ready to take over care of the farm, the children, or anything else that must be done.

It was natural, she assured herself. So why did it make her feel so uncomfortable?

CHAPTER FOUR

BY THE TIME SARAH reached the house, the boxes were slipping out of her arms. Seeing her struggle with them, Hank dropped his hedge clippers and loped over to rescue them.

"You should have told me you needed these. I could've been your pack mule." He balanced the boxes easily, giving her a smile that made him look like a mischievous ten-year-old.

"*Danki*—thank you," she corrected, switching to English. "They're not heavy, just unwieldy."

"As long as I'm living in the garage apartment, I'm supposed to be doing the chores around here." He shrugged. "I don't suppose that lawyer mentioned anything to you about when I have to leave."

"No. No, he hasn't." It hadn't occurred to her that Hank would be losing his apartment with Mr. Strickland's death. "I'm sorry."

"No problem," he said easily, waiting while she unlocked the door. "I guess I'll just be moving on." He leaned against the door frame. "Will you miss me, Sarah?"

She kept her gaze on the key. "I will be sorry to lose my job," she said. The door opened, and she held out her hands for the boxes. "But I wish you well in whatever you do next."

"I'll carry these in for you." Hank started to move past her.

"I'm sorry." She stepped in front of him, mindful of Leo Frost's orders. "I'm not supposed to let anyone in the house unless Mr. Frost tells me to."

Hank's expression of surprise was almost comical. "But…I'm always in and out. How am I supposed to get the plant food and the watering cans from the mud-room if I can't come in?"

"I'm sorry," she said again. "You should talk to Mr. Frost about it. I'm sure he'll understand." Or would he? Leo hadn't seemed especially pleased with Mr. Strickland's decision to let his young relative stay here.

"Guess I'll have to talk to him. Frost doesn't expect you to do the heavy work of sorting and clearing, does he? That's not right, especially when I'm here."

"That is *sehr* kind of you, Hank. I'm glad you understand that I must do as he says."

At least, she supposed she did. Maude Stevens seemed to think *she* should be giving the orders.

Nodding at Hank, Sarah closed the door and gathered up the boxes. If Mrs. Stevens was right… She stopped, shook her head and headed for the front stairs. That was for the *Englische* to sort out, not her.

By the time she'd reached the stairs, she realized she'd need the packaging tape, which was kept in the utility drawer in the kitchen. Dropping the boxes, she started back there, glancing at the telephone stand as she passed. And stopped, staring. When she'd left the house, she'd noticed that there were several messages on the machine, and had made a mental note to ask Leo what to do about them. Now the message indicator said zero. Someone had been in the house while she was gone.

SARAH WAS BEING QUIETER than usual this evening. Jacob glanced at her as she sat at the kitchen table across from him, her head bent over the record books from the shop. It had been her *daad*'s idea that Jacob should show Sarah how he'd been keeping the books, so that she could take over once her job had ended.

That, too, was her father's idea. Jacob wasn't so sure it was what Sarah herself intended.

She'd enjoyed the freedom working in town gave her. He knew his Sarah. She'd be looking for some way of continuing that freedom.

She smoothed a strand of hair back under her *kapp*, and his gaze followed the movement, imagining that silky strand flowing through his fingers.

She made a penciled check mark against one item in a column, and he leaned a little closer to see what she questioned. The repair to Simon Esch's mower, it looked like.

There was a fine line between her eyebrows, and he didn't think it had anything to do with the fact that Simon hadn't yet paid for his mower repair.

"*Was ist letz,* Sarah? You are troubled," he said quietly, not wanting her parents, in the next room, to hear.

She glanced around the lamplit kitchen, as if assuring herself that her younger sisters were safely engaged in a board game in the living room, where her mother sat with her mending and her father read the latest issue of *The Budget* for news of the Amish community. Darkness pressed against the kitchen windows, and the overhead gas lamp cast a golden glow on Sarah's face.

"I had three different people offering to help sort things in the house today, and it's hard to find a way to say no to them. But Leo was very clear about it—no one is to come in unless he gives the okay."

"Who were they?" Jacob could guess that one of them would have been Hank, who always seemed to be hanging around Sarah.

"Maude Stevens," she said. "Reminding me that her late husband was a relative of Mr. Strickland's. And Mr. McKay from the antiques shop, who seemed to feel he was the only one who could properly value the old pieces in Mr. Strickland's house. And Hank, of course."

Of course. "I hope you told them all to talk to Leo Frost," he said. "It is his responsibility to deal with them, not yours."

"I know, but what can I do when—"

She broke off, her head lifting, and in an instant he heard the sound, as well. A horse whinnying somewhere outside.

"That's Dick," she said, referring to one of the big Belgian draft horses her father used for plowing. "He seems too close. He must be out." She turned toward the living room. "*Daad,* Dick is out. Somebody must not have latched the stall door."

A squabble broke out immediately between Sarah's younger sisters, each blaming the other.

"I will *komm,*" her father said.

But Sarah was already snatching a shawl from the hooks in the back hall. "Don't bother. I'll get him."

"Let me," Jacob began, but she shook her head.

"Too many people coming at him will spook him for sure." Everyone in the township knew that Dick didn't have the placid disposition of most Belgians. "I can do it."

Jacob hid a smile. Sometimes he thought "I can do it" must have been Sarah's first sentence.

"I will just step out on the porch in case you need me," he said, intending to pacify her.

Sarah was already out the back door, and he followed her, pausing for a moment to let his eyes get accustomed to the dark. Stars clustered thick in the sky, but it was the dark of the moon, so there was little illumination. Sarah had gone without a flashlight, and he reached back inside the door to grasp one from the hook in case they needed it.

He stepped off the porch, hoping she didn't take it into her head to turn around and see him disobeying her instructions. She'd have a word or two to say about that, for sure.

His gaze picked out the white of Sarah's *kapp* as his night vision cleared. Her dark dress and black shawl made the rest of her invisible.

There was another whinny, this time closer still. He frowned. Dick didn't sound like he was waiting for someone to return him to the safety of his stall. He sounded spooked.

"There, now, Dick, silly boy." Sarah's voice was calm and full of affection. "*Komm* here now. I will take you back to your stall."

Jacob spotted the draft horse, a large, pale shadow. The animal drifted slowly toward Sarah, as if uncertain what to do.

"That's my boy," she crooned. "You don't want to be out in the dark." She held up her hand, taking a step closer.

Uneasiness was a chill breath on Jacob's neck, and he tried to shrug it off. Sarah had been dealing with the horses since she was four, and even her father admitted that few could handle them better. It was probably the uncertainty of the past few days that made him jittery.

"That's my boy," she repeated, then reached for the halter, the movement slow and gentle. "You got out and didn't know what to do, did you?" Her hand touched the halter.

The night seemed to explode with noise—thudding hooves, frightened whinnies, a rush of movement from the barn, so fast he could hardly sort it out. Not just Dick—all the horses were out, frightened, bolting mindlessly.

Jacob raced toward the spot where Sarah had been, heart pounding, his breath catching. *Sarah.* None of the horses would step on her if they saw her, but frightened, in the dark—who knew what might happen?

He reached the animals, lunging between them, not caring for the moment what happened to them as long as he could find Sarah. Then he saw her, a dark shape on the ground, and his heart wanted to burst with fear.

"Sarah!"

But she was already scrambling to her feet. "I'm all right. Get after the horses before they run onto the road."

Relief flooded through him. Sarah wouldn't sound that tart if anything was wrong with her.

"*Ja,* I'm trying." He grabbed the nearest halter, realizing that he had hold of Sarah's mother's buggy horse. A skittish mare at the best of times, she shied away, but he hung on, grimly determined, until she settled.

"I've got Bell, but if I let go to get the others, she'll run."

Sarah came toward him, dwarfed by the two immense draft horses she led. "Take Dick and Bill. As long as you have a hand on them, they won't move. Maybe they'll settle Bell."

"Watch out for that colt," he warned. Sarah's *daad* had a half-broken colt he seemed to think would make a good buggy horse, but Jacob had his doubts. The sound of a car out on the road somewhere alarmed him. If that colt made a break for the road, it could cause an accident.

Maybe he should try to get these three into the barn and help Sarah— The back door flew open. Alerted by the noise, Josiah, Sarah's father, came hurrying out.

In a few minutes' time, they were putting all the horses safely back into their stalls. Josiah, frowning, checked each of the latches. He shook his head.

"The girls can be careless sometimes, but not this careless."

"Someone has done this deliberately." Sarah stated the obvious conclusion.

"*Ach,* it's spring," Josiah said, as if that explained it all. "Some young person thought it would be a *gut* joke to let all the horses out."

True, the amount of mischief increased with the warmer weather, but Jacob wasn't satisfied. "Not an Amish kid, ain't so?"

Josiah shook his head. "I would hope that none of ours would be so heedless of the animals. They could have run onto the road and been hit."

"I heard a car," Jacob said. "When we were rounding up the horses, I heard a car on the road. I didn't think of it at the time, but what I heard was the engine starting."

Sarah stared at him, her eyes wide in the glow of the

battery lanterns. "You mean someone parked along the road," she said. "Someone *Englische.*"

"*Englische.* We will never know who." Josiah led the way out of the barn. "And we forgive them, whoever they are."

Jacob nodded agreement. What else could he do? But he didn't like this.

He caught up with Sarah as her father went in the house. "Wait a minute." He touched her arm to stop her. "What if this had something to do with what's been happening at the Strickland place? Sarah, I don't think you should go there anymore."

"Don't be so foolish. How could the horses getting out have anything to do with Mr. Strickland?" She pulled away from him and marched into the house.

But he had heard the worry under her curt tone, and he knew Sarah had been thinking just what he had.

CHAPTER FIVE

LEO FROST WAS WAITING when Sarah and Jacob arrived at the Strickland place the next day. Hank was nowhere to be seen. Either he had an early class or he'd sensed Leo's reservations where he was concerned; Sarah wasn't sure which.

The lawyer met them in the kitchen. "Sarah, Jacob, good morning. I wanted to go over a few things with you, Sarah."

Jacob made a movement toward the door. "I will go now, since Mr. Frost is here."

"Stay, please, Jacob." He stopped him with a gesture. "I'm sure Sarah has told you about her concerns over the way Richard Strickland died."

Jacob nodded, his strong-featured face giving no hint as to his opinion.

"I wanted you both to know that I discussed with Chief Byler the things you noticed. I don't want you to think I ignored your concerns."

"I know you wouldn't," Sarah said, but she could tell by his face what Chief Byler's opinion had been.

"We talked about it at length," Leo went on. "But you must understand that each of those things could have an innocent explanation."

"*Ja,* I see." That was it, then. No one would take her worries seriously.

Leo shrugged, spreading his hands. "There was no indication that the house had been broken into, and as far as I can tell, nothing is missing. As for Richard's will, I can't see that anyone benefits from his death, other than the Heart Association and the historical society." He smiled, creases deepening around his eyes. "Maude Stevens may be annoying, but I hardly think she'd hurry his death for the sake of acquiring this house for her group." Leo eyed Sarah closely. "You're still worried, aren't you? Why?"

She shrugged, finding it difficult to put her observations into words that wouldn't sound foolish.

"Has anything else happened?" he pressed.

She hesitated. "There was the answering machine on the telephone."

"What about it?" Leo seemed puzzled, and Jacob gave her a look that questioned why she hadn't told him.

"After Mr. Strickland passed, I noticed that there were three messages on the machine. I kept meaning to ask you what to do about them, but I didn't think of it when you were here. Yesterday, when I came back from town, there were no messages."

Frowning, Leo led the way to the little alcove off the hall where the phone was. The two of them trouped after him.

"You did not tell me about this." Jacob sounded accusing.

"I wasn't sure it was important." And she hadn't wanted Jacob to fret still more about her.

Leo stared at the answering machine, its unwinking red light staring back at him. He pressed the play button. The machine whirred and shut off. No messages.

He looked at her. "You're sure of this?"

"*Ja.* I noticed it. I am sure. It's the same brand as the one *Daad* has in the phone shanty." Leo would understand that while Amish didn't have phones in their homes, most had access to one in a special shed somewhere on the property—necessary for business and for emergencies.

Leo ran a hand over his thick white hair. "I have to confess that electronic gadgets baffle me. I can't even set my new alarm clock. Could a power surge have wiped the messages away?"

"I don't know." The Amish didn't rely on electric lines, just batteries, and she had no idea.

"Are you sure you locked everything when you went out?" Leo sounded frustrated, and she was sorry to have given him something else to worry about.

"I…I think so." She frowned. "I know I locked the front door."

"I suppose there are some extra keys floating around town," Leo admitted, "even though I collected the one Hank Mitchell had for emergencies. Richard was careful, but he never imagined anything bad could happen here."

Jacob stirred, as if the words had made him think of something. "Sarah, I think you should tell Mr. Frost about what happened last night."

"That couldn't have anything to do with Mr. Strickland." She tried to sound as if she were sure.

"I think you should tell me anything that's out of the ordinary." Leo's normally clear blue eyes were clouded with doubt.

"The horses got out last night," Jacob said, apparently determined to take over. "Sarah was trying to catch the draft horse when all the others came racing out, like something had scared them. They ran right toward her."

"You weren't hurt?" Leo reached toward Sarah.

"No, no, I am fine." She hurried to reassure him. "The animals would not hurt me."

"Not if they saw you," Jacob corrected. "But they might if they were spooked."

"*Daad* says it was probably just *Englische* teenagers looking for mischief." She glared at Jacob. "What could anyone gain by injuring me?"

"Someone might feel he or she would have easier access to the house if you weren't here." Leo's frown deepened. "I don't like this at all, Sarah. Maybe I should get someone else to handle clearing up."

"No one else knew Mr. Strickland and the house the way I do. If anything is missing, I would notice it. Would anyone else?"

"Probably not," he said slowly, as if he didn't want to admit it.

"Sarah..." Jacob began.

"I am fine, Jacob. Don't fuss."

"Well, one thing we can do is make the house more secure," Leo said. "I'll have dead bolts installed on all the entrances immediately."

"I can do that," Jacob said. "I'll go to the hardware store right now." He was determined to do something.

"Fine. I'll go with you." Leo clapped him on the shoulder. "Sarah, lock the door behind us, please."

She stood at the doorway, watching them leave together: the formally dressed *Englischer* lawyer and the straw-hatted Amishman. Despite the many differences between them, Jacob and Leo had one thing in common—this ridiculous need to take care of her.

JACOB HAD INTENDED to look after the new locks right away, but things didn't work out that way. He'd had to go back home to fetch his tools and got tied up helping Sarah's father. Finally, by midafternoon, he'd begun installing them.

They were all done now, except for the front door. He worked carefully, not wanting to leave a scratch on the polished wood surface. Sarah would have something to say about that if he did.

Of course, she'd have to be talking to him for that. Since he'd returned, her responses to him were of the yes and no variety.

Well, he understood his Sarah. She'd been annoyed that he'd pushed her into telling Leo Frost about the incident with the horses, further annoyed that he'd tried to take care of her. Interfering, she'd call it. She ought to know by now that he couldn't do anything else.

She'd been in the dining room for the past hour, wrapping dishes in newspaper and packing them into boxes. He'd heard the occasional clink of a plate and the rustle of paper. Now, it seemed, she'd gone into the kitchen, and he could hear her moving around in there.

What was he going to do about Sarah? He couldn't go on this way, hoping she'd look at him and see someone other than the friend of her childhood. He loved her. He wanted her to be his wife. But those thoughts always brought him back to the same place. If he spoke up, he'd risk losing what they had.

"Jacob, what is it? You're looking grim."

It was a measure of the intensity of his thoughts that he hadn't heard her approach.

She smiled at him, eyes questioning, and held out

a glass of tea, ice clinking. "I thought you could use a break."

He took the glass, recognizing it as a truce. "Are you done being mad at me now?"

"I'm getting there," she said. "I know you mean to be helpful."

"This isn't like getting you out of the apple tree or telling your *mamm* that I was the one who ate the cherry pie. If you are right about Mr. Strickland's death…" He stopped, not sure he wanted to put his fears into words.

She paled. "I know. I haven't been able to think of anything else since it happened. If someone was in the house that night…" She bit her lip. "Surely no one would want to hurt Mr. Strickland."

Her lost expression hit Jacob in the heart. He set the glass down and touched her arm. "Maybe the police are right. If he heard something, it is possible he would come down to check, ain't so? And even if someone did try to get in, that doesn't mean that person caused him to fall. It could have been an accident."

Jacob wasn't sure what he believed about Richard Strickland's death. He just knew he had to take that lost look from Sarah's eyes.

It didn't seem to be working. She rubbed her arms as if she was cold.

"I can't forget it, Jacob. I can't. I have to know what happened. I can't just keep wondering."

He longed to comfort her, but that wasn't what she needed now. She needed answers, and he didn't have any.

"If someone was in the house that night," he said, feeling his way, "why were they here? To steal?"

It happened sometimes, even in a place like Spring-

ville. Even the Amish weren't immune. People sometimes tried to rob or cheat them, knowing they were
unlikely to go to the police.

"Maybe a thief," she said. "But that wouldn't explain
the answering machine. Why would a thief come back
and wipe the messages off?"

"I don't know." He almost said that deleting the messages could be accidental, but concentrating on the possibilities was chasing the hurt from her eyes. "What
about what Leo told us...that Mr. Strickland was going
to change his will?"

She considered for a moment, and then shook her
head. "Leo was right—you can't think the people from
the historical society would do violence to stop him
from changing his will."

"I guess not." He smiled. "But I wouldn't want to
cross Mrs. Stevens."

She managed to return the smile, encouraging him.

"If someone is trying to get into the house, there
must be something here that he or she wants," he went
on. "It's like you told Leo—you're the best one to find
it."

Sarah looked at him, blue eyes shining again. "*Ja,*
I am."

It cost him a pang of worry for her, but he said it because he knew this was what she needed. "Then why
are you wasting time making iced tea?"

Her arms went around him in a quick, warm hug.
"*Danki,* Jacob." She ran lightly up the steps.

CHAPTER SIX

MR. STRICKLAND HAD HAD two favorite rooms in this house: the downstairs sunroom next to the kitchen, where he sat in the daytime, and the upstairs study—his office, he'd called it. Sarah had spent the past hour working her way through the massive mahogany desk in the study, methodically sorting papers for Leo to go over. She'd found nothing remotely suspicious, but since she didn't know what she was looking for, that was hardly surprising.

Now she sat on the rug by the floor-to-ceiling bookshelves next to the desk. The rows of books made an imposing array, looming over her when she glanced up at them.

There was something alluring in all those books waiting to be read. They should go someplace where they'd be used, but she'd have to have Leo's instructions before she could sort them.

The bottom shelves by the desk were different. Mr. Strickland had used those to store items he planned to deal with soon: stacks of magazines he hadn't finished reading, a wire basket filled with Christmas cards and another basket that held appeals from charities. She'd seen him working his way through those, consulting his ledger to find out what he had donated when. He'd been a generous man in his way, quietly supporting a number of good causes. But he'd been careful with his money as well, making sure he wasn't taken in by repeated requests to an organization that had already received its yearly stipend.

Sarah pushed the charity requests aside. Leo would have to take care of them. Would Mr. Strickland have made provision in his will for the charities he'd supported in his life? If not, some of the local ones would feel the pinch.

Next to the baskets sat a pile of leather-bound books she didn't recall seeing the last time she'd dusted in here. She lifted one from the stack and wiped it gingerly with her hand. Definitely not here when she'd cleaned, or it wouldn't have been so dirty.

She opened the book, curious, and found a much younger Richard Strickland staring at her from the page. They weren't books; they were photo albums.

She bent over, entranced by the black-and-white image of a man she could hardly imagine. Wearing a straw hat at a jaunty angle, a teenaged Richard leaned against a tree. Behind him, she could make out blankets spread on the ground, anchored by picnic baskets. Girls in white dresses and young men in sweater vests and straw hats lounged on the blankets. One girl walked toward Richard, holding a plate in her hands. Her head was tilted back, showing a sweet, heart-shaped face and a mass of dark hair.

Sarah carried the album to the window for a little more light and realized she'd have to turn a lamp on for that. While she'd been engrossed in what she was doing, the sunny day had turned dark.

She glanced to the west. Black clouds massed over

the distant hills. Spring, always changeable, had a storm in store for them.

Leaving the album for another time, she hurried to the upstairs hall, automatically putting the doorstop back in place again. She looked down over the railing. The tile floor seemed far away, and Jacob wasn't at the front door any longer. She went quickly down the stairs, running her hand along the smooth railing, trying not to think of Mr. Strickland grasping at it as he fell.

The hallway was deserted, the house quiet around her except for the creaking of a shutter someplace as the wind started to pick up. They'd have to hurry if they were going to beat the storm home.

"Jacob?" She walked back down the hallway, glancing into the living room and dining room as she passed. Where was he? Surely he wouldn't have left the house without telling her.

Another creak was followed by what might have been a distant footstep. Her pulse thudded in her throat, and a chill snaked down her spine.

Ach, she was acting *ferhoodled,* that was for sure. There was nothing in this house to be afraid of. She'd heard all its creaks and moans before. There was nothing different this time.

The sunroom was empty—forlorn, it seemed, without Mr. Strickland's familiar presence in his favorite chair. The boxes of clothes she'd packed earlier were stacked there, ready for pickup by the Goodwill truck.

She hurried into the kitchen, her worry about Jacob building. Where was he? "Jacob? This is no time for hide-and-seek."

No answer, but a sound came from behind her. She whirled, and saw that the basement door stood open.

"Jacob?" Foolish, to let her voice quaver that way.

"*Ja,* I am here." Footsteps sounded on the wooden cellar steps, and he appeared, looking as dusty as the album had been.

"What have you been doing to get so dirty?" Relief made her voice tart. "Don't you see there's a storm coming?"

He smiled, wiping his face on his sleeve. "Can't see much of anything down there. I was trying to be sure that the windows were secure. There's so much junk it's hard to get to them." He glanced at the kitchen window and his expression sobered. "Rain is coming for sure. We'd best get on the road or we'll be stuck in town. Where's your bonnet?"

"Here in the hall." She'd already gone to grab it, tying it quickly on her head. "What about the new keys?"

"They're on the table—no, here they are on the counter." Jacob hurried after her, holding out a ring of shiny keys. "You'd best take charge of them until you can give them to Leo."

They went out, Jacob heading for the spot under the walnut tree where he'd left the buggy, while she wrestled with the stiff new lock, finally getting it to turn.

By the time she reached Jacob, he was backing the mare between the buggy shafts. Sarah went automatically to the opposite side, grasping the harness when he tossed it over. "Poor Bess," she murmured. "You had a boring day, ain't so? Never mind. You'll soon be home."

"If she's not, we're all going to get a soaking," Jacob commented. He started around to help Sarah up, but she clambered into the seat on her own.

"Komm, schnell." She grinned at him. "I am already up."

Making no comment, he went back around and swung himself easily into the seat. Bess didn't need any urging to start moving. She had probably sensed the storm coming long before Sarah had noticed it.

Sarah waited until they'd cleared town traffic and were driving on the narrow, two-lane country road before she spoke. "I'm sorry I didn't see the sky darkening earlier. I should have noticed."

"What were you doing that had you so occupied?" He glanced at her, his blue eyes reflecting the blue shirt he wore. Funny, that she noticed that. She knew Jacob so well that she usually didn't even see him.

"Sorting upstairs in the study. I found some old photo albums that Mr. Strickland must have been looking at. You should have seen the picture I found of him as a young man."

"A ladies' man, was he?" Jacob's gaze was fixed on the road ahead as the mare trotted along.

"I'll bet he was. He looked so pleased with himself, out on a picnic with a group of his friends." It struck her as sad, suddenly—all those youthful faces, most of them just a memory now.

Jacob clasped her hand for a moment, seeming to read her thoughts. "He was a *gut* man, and he had a *gut* life."

She nodded, comforted. That was all any of them, Amish or *Englische,* could hope to have said about them.

A fat raindrop landed on her skirt, followed by another. "Here comes the rain." She pulled her lightweight sweater more snugly around her. Too bad she hadn't worn a jacket today.

"Like I said, we'll get soaked." Jacob reached under the seat to pull out a lap robe. He let Bess trot on by herself while he smoothed it around Sarah's shoulders. "There. That should keep the worst of it off." He smiled, his face very close to hers for a moment, and her heart seemed to give an extra beat. Then he was turning away to pick up the lines again. "Step up, Bess."

The mare, as steady and solid as her master, moved on, hooves clopping on the wet pavement.

Sarah snuggled into the robe, clutching it around her, still seeming to feel the weight of Jacob's palms on her shoulders.

"Car coming," Jacob said briefly, his hands steady on the lines.

A car swished by, too fast, she thought, for the road conditions. Hadn't the driver seen Jacob's battery-operated blinkers? Or did he just not care? His passing sent up a spray of water, and she pressed closer to Jacob, feeling his warmth.

"Foolish, driving so swiftly in the rain," he said. "Keep an eye out behind us and let me know if anyone else is coming up that fast."

"Ja." She slid her hand into the crook of his arm to keep her balance, and swiveled her head to watch. She couldn't see very far, not with the wind blowing the rain in sheets. A shiver ran through her. She should have been watching the weather. Should have suggested they wait out the storm.

Still, they were nearly home now. Another hundred yards and they'd be turning into the lane.

A white vehicle appeared out of the rainy mist behind them, so pale it seemed insubstantial. "Another one," she warned.

Jacob nodded, steering Bess to the right until the right-side wheels bit into the gravel of the berm. That should give the driver plenty of room to pass.

But the vehicle wasn't passing. Sarah gasped, hands digging into Jacob's arm. "He's coming right at us." She could hear the fear in he voice.

Jacob muttered something, steering Bess still farther over, practically to the edge of the ditch.

But it wasn't enough. Sarah barely heard the crash before she was ripped away from Jacob and sent flying from the buggy.

JACOB LAY FACEDOWN in mud. Shaking his head free, he pushed back with his hands, trying to make his mind work. The buggy, the rain, the blur of white...Sarah!

He scrambled to his feet, slipping and sloshing in the muddy ditch. Where was Sarah? His heart thudded so loudly he could hear it. Where was she? He tried to look around, but his vision was blurring. The rain, driving down now in torrents, made it worse. He couldn't see her....

"Sarah!" Her name came out as a croak, and he tried again. "Sarah, where are you?" He stumbled out of the ditch, peering around, trying to force his eyes to focus.

The buggy was tilted end up in the ditch, the shafts shattered. Bess stood trembling, tangled in her lines. He had to help the mare, but had to find Sarah first.

"Sarah!" he cried out, his voice breaking.

"Here." The sound was faint, but he heard it.

He spun, half running, half staggering toward the rear of the buggy.

Sarah was getting up—from the soft ground, thank the *gut* Lord, not from the macadam. He reached her, grabbed her wrists and pulled her against him. He wrapped his arms around her and held on tightly.

"Sarah." *Danki, Father.* "Are you all right? Do you hurt anywhere?"

He felt her shake her head against his chest. She'd lost her bonnet somehow, and her cheek pressed against him.

"You're certain sure?" He ran his palms up and down her back, needing to know for himself that she was in one piece.

"I'm all right." Her voice was muffled by his damp shirt. "Just…just shaky. And scared." She pressed closer to him. "I couldn't see you. I thought…"

She let the words drift off, but he knew. She'd felt the same thing he did—sheer terror at the thought of losing each other.

A car shrieked to a stop at the side of the road. The sound galvanized Jacob, and he drew back. He looked searchingly into her face. She was mud-streaked, her hair wet and plastered to her head. She was beautiful.

He touched her face, smoothing back a strand of wet hair. "Sarah, I—"

"Are you all right?" The car's occupant had reached them.

He released Sarah reluctantly and turned, to find Sam Robertson, who ran the local hardware store, staring at them. "I already called the police. Do you need the EMTs, Jacob? Sarah?"

Relieved that it was someone he knew, Jacob shook his head. "We are shaken, that's all." He suspected they'd both be sore tomorrow. "Bess… I must get Bess out of the harness."

Sam nodded. "I'll put some flares out so no other darn fool comes barreling down on us. Stupid people don't have sense the good Lord gave a gnat."

"I'll help with the horse." Sarah was already moving toward Bess, not giving Jacob a chance to suggest she sit down instead.

Still, he was glad of her help. Bess was a fine, steady animal, but this would try any horse's nerves. At least she wasn't attempting to kick the buggy into more pieces than it already was.

"Easy, Bess, easy." Sarah held the mare's head, her voice soothing. "We will have you out of this soon, you'll see."

Jacob took a moment to survey the tangle, tracing the lines of the harness and the possible dangers. One of the broken shafts was perilously near the mare's side; he'd have to get that away first.

It was hard to get a decent grip when his feet kept slipping in the mud and water, but finally he'd wedged the shaft out enough that he could pull on it. "Hold her head steady," he said, more for the sake of saying something to Sarah than because she needed directions.

"I am," she said, her voice calm. "She is being as *gut* as gold, aren't you, Bess?"

She stroked the mare's nose, crooning to her, as Jacob eased the broken shaft away from her flank and tossed it to the side.

He could breathe again. Now it was just a matter of getting the harness off her. Already he could hear the hiss of the flares on the road, and he spotted Josiah running down the lane from the house as one of Sarah's sisters hitched up the wagon. In the distance a police siren wailed, and a shudder went over Bess at the sound.

Jacob nodded to Sarah that the harness was unbuckled, and she led the mare away from the wreckage, letting the animal scramble out of the ditch.

He smiled at Sarah. They were both drenched and aching, and Bess was okay even though his buggy was probably a total loss. But it could have been so much worse.

"*Gut* job."

She nodded, smiling back in spite of the rain and mud. "You, too."

An hour later she and Jacob had changed into dry clothes and were warm again, sitting at the table with Sarah's *daad* and Chief Byler, mugs of coffee in front of them. Sarah's *mamm* bustled about the kitchen, slicing into the dried-apple pie she'd made that morning. Sarah stole a quick glance at Jacob's face, needing to assure herself that he was all right. She wouldn't soon forget the panic she'd felt when she feared he'd been injured, maybe killed, out there on the road. Her fingers trembled, and she pressed them around the mug, absorbing the warmth.

"Sam Robertson wasn't able to get a license number, unfortunately," Chief Byler said. "He was too far away and the conditions were too bad. He said the vehicle had passed him a couple of miles back, but of course there was no reason then for him to notice. Did you see anything?"

He seemed to address the question to both of them, glancing from her to Jacob.

Sarah shook her head. "I looked back and saw the

lights, so I warned Jacob." She frowned a little, teasing the memory out. "Something about the lights... It wasn't a car, I don't think."

"A van," Jacob said. "A white van. That's all I saw. Just a flash."

Just a flash, because he'd been too busy trying to save them.

"When I told Jacob, he got the buggy over as far as he could. The driver had plenty of room to pass."

"I don't doubt that," Chief Byler said. "Reckless driving, leaving the scene of an accident, driving too fast for conditions... He's piled up a list of charges to answer for, assuming we can find him."

Josiah Weaver cleared his throat. "It is kind of you, Chief Byler," he said. "But we will not press charges."

That was the Amish way. Forgiveness. Sarah discovered she didn't feel much forgiveness toward the driver. She would have to work on that.

"You won't need to," Chief Byler said, and there was satisfaction in his voice. He'd dealt with the Amish often enough to know their beliefs. "This isn't a matter of vandalism against private property. Hit-and-run is a criminal act and doesn't depend upon your pressing charges. Jacob and Sarah will just have to say what they saw if it comes to a trial."

Sarah could almost sense her *daad*'s struggle. He didn't want to be involved with the law, but he would never knowingly disobey it, either. Finally, he nodded.

Chief Byler turned back to them, his strong face serious, eyes intent. "You understand, I hope. If not for Jacob's good driving, someone could have been killed today. We can't let that person go free to hit someone else, who might not be so lucky."

Jacob nodded. "I wish I could help, but I was too busy trying to control the horse to see more."

"It happened so fast," Sarah added. "Just a blur of white, and then I was flying through the air."

Mamm made a small sound and touched her daughter's shoulder. Sarah looked up at her, managing a smile.

"Well, I'm just glad you two are all right." Chief Byler rose. "If you think of anything else, no matter how small—" He stopped when his cell phone rang. "Excuse me." He turned away, putting the tiny phone to his ear, his answers too low to be intelligible.

He snapped the phone closed, a new energy seeming to charge his body. "That list of charges just got longer. The van was stolen this afternoon from over in New Holland. They found it abandoned about two miles down the road. No sign of the driver." He was out of the house almost before they could say goodbye.

"*Ach,* he's gone without his pie," *Mamm* noted mournfully, not liking it when any visitor to her house left without being fed.

"Teenagers," *Daad* said, with an air of finality. "That's what he'll find. Some *Englische* teenagers stealing a car for a joyride."

"Maybe so," Jacob murmured, but he sent a worried look in Sarah's direction.

She understood what he was thinking. The incident with the horses last night, now the buggy crash today. Either one of those things might have injured her enough to keep her away from work.

Well, if that was the case, the guilty person would be disappointed. Thanks to the new locks Jacob had installed, no one would get into the Strickland house unless she let them in.

CHAPTER SEVEN

MAMM HAD BEEN URGING HER to go to bed since the police chief left, but Sarah managed to evade her.

"I'm all right, *Mamm*." She bent to press her cheek against her mother's. *Mamm* was sitting with her mending in her lap, but hadn't yet taken a stitch. "Really. I'd rather do something."

"Play Chinese checkers with us?" Emma asked, her tone hopeful. She was poised by the stack of games on the bookshelf, ready to pull the game out.

"*Ja,* that's a *gut* idea." Sarah smiled at her little sister. "That will get my mind on beating you." She knew she'd said the right thing when the lines in *Mamm*'s face relaxed.

"Set it up," Sarah instructed. "I'll be back in a minute, soon as I tell Jacob something."

She hurried toward the kitchen, listening to her sisters squabbling good-naturedly about who would go first. The door was closing behind Jacob, but he must have heard what she'd said, because he was waiting on the porch when she got there.

The evening had turned chilly, and she drew her shawl around her. Jacob leaned against the porch railing, his face a pale oval in the dim light. She didn't need to see him to know that he was waiting for her to speak.

Now that she was here, she didn't know what to say.

That moment after the accident, when she'd clung to him, pressing her body against his... Her face flooded with heat at the thought of it. She had to say something to put that in its proper perspective and return things to normal between them. She just didn't know what.

"*Mamm* is determined to send me to bed," she said finally. "You'd think I had a cold instead of a few bumps and bruises."

"She loves you." His voice sounded deep, coming at her out of the dark. "She was scared, that's all."

"*Daad*'s got a bee in his bonnet about *Englische* teenagers," she said, not wanting to think about being scared. "He's sure that's who is responsible."

"He hasn't forgotten about the kids who splashed the red paint on the barn last year, ain't so?"

She could hear the smile in his voice, and she found it soothing. *Daad* had forgiven those kids, of course, and his solution had been to paint the whole barn red.

"Well, I guess he could be right in this case," she stated. "Taking a car, going for a joyride—that's the sort of thing teenagers would do."

"Do you think that, Sarah, or are you trying to convince yourself?"

She shook her head, moving to the railing to stand next to him. "If it was deliberate, I'd think the driver would have done worse than sideswipe us."

"Not if he just wanted to convince you to stay at home instead of going to the Strickland house."

She tilted her head to look up at him, remembering the summer he'd suddenly shot up to become taller than she was. "Is that what you want me to do?"

He didn't answer for a moment, and then he shrugged. "Maybe so, but you won't, ain't so?"

She thought there was a note of frustration in his voice, and knew that was exactly what he wanted.

"You are the one who suggested I go, Jacob." She couldn't help sounding defensive. "If there is a clue to why Mr. Strickland died in that house, I am the most likely person to find it."

"*Ja,* I said that." His words were heavy, as if weighted down with his worry. "But that doesn't mean I can stop fretting."

"You should. After all, you're the one who put new locks on all the doors. No one can get in now, and I will be careful."

Jacob's hands clenched the railing, and she could feel tension coming off him in waves. "That's not enough. I should see about taking time off work to help you. You'd get it done faster, and I'd be there with you."

Annoyance flared up in her, a welcome relief from the remnants of fear. "I am not in need of a babysitter, Jacob. You seem to forget that I am all grown up."

"Grown up? Then why do you sound like a stubborn little girl?" He seemed as annoyed as she was.

"I do not." As soon as she said it, Sarah knew this kind of argument was the last thing she wanted. She wanted…

Jacob grasped her shoulders. For an instant she thought he was going to shake her.

And then he drew her toward him and kissed her. His lips were firm and warm, and after the initial shock she felt herself lean into the kiss, wanting to put her arms around him, to hold him close—

But almost before she could think, he'd pulled away, turning to take the porch steps in one long stride, and vanishing into the dark.

SARAH'S MOTHER HAD already planned to drive her to work the next day, to Sarah's great relief. After a sleepless night, she was still too uncertain of her own mind to want to face Jacob again so soon.

Fortunately, *Mamm* was too busy with her own plans to notice Sarah's preoccupation. A basket filled with sticky buns fresh from the oven sent a tantalizing aroma wafting around the two of them as they rode. Sarah hadn't felt much like eating breakfast, but the smell of those sticky buns would tempt a marble statue.

"I hope your aunt remembered to make arrangements for the taxi," *Mamm* said, always fretting over any plans she hadn't carried out herself.

"I'm sure she did. If not, Cousin Barbara will have reminded her."

The taxi wasn't really a taxi, of course, just a car driven by an elderly *Englischer* who was willing to take the Amish places they couldn't get by horse and buggy. The church had no rules against riding in a car, only against owning one yourself, because that made it too easy to be running around away from your family.

This trip to the big fabric store in a nearby town had been in the planning stages for a month, it seemed. Sarah's mother and three friends would shop and then have lunch at a restaurant to celebrate Cousin Barbara's birthday. Afterward, *Mamm* intended to wait at Aunt Mary's until Sarah was ready to go home.

Her sister, Mary, their cousin Barbara and Jacob's *mamm* had been *Mamm*'s dearest friends since the four of them had been born, practically. The same age, they'd finished school the same time, of course, and had even married the same year.

That was how things were in the Amish community.

Friendships didn't change from moment to moment, as Sarah sometimes thought they did in the *Englische* world. Your closest friends were there for life.

Which made that kiss from Jacob all the more inexplicable. And made her reaction to it even less understandable. She'd thought about it half the night, and dreamed about it when she finally fell asleep.

She and Jacob were like brother and sister. They always had been since they were born within a month of each other and lived next door to each other, that was only natural. Especially after his *daad* had passed and Jacob began working in the machine shop.

Sarah saw him every day of her life. How could she start thinking of him as anything other than a brother?

But there'd been nothing brotherly about that kiss last night. She touched her fingertips to her mouth, seeming to still feel the imprint of Jacob's lips.

At least she had a quiet day of work ahead of her. Maybe somehow her feelings would become clear.

Mamm pressed a couple of wax-paper-wrapped sticky buns in her hand once she'd climbed down at the house. "Have those for a snack. And *chust* walk over to Mary's when you're done, *ja?*"

"I will, *Mamm. Danki.*" Clutching the warm rolls, she waved to her mother and hurried up the walk.

Hank came around the back of the house toward her as she approached the door, almost as if he'd been watching for her. "Hi, Sarah. Wow, something sure does smell good." He eyed the rolls.

"My *mamm*'s sticky buns." The new key stuck at first, but then turned and the door swung open. "Would you like to have one?" She could hardly not make the offer, since he was standing right there.

"That'd be great." He hesitated, glancing at the open door. "Maybe I'd better eat it out here."

True, she wasn't supposed to let people in unless Leo approved of them. But what harm could it do for Hank to come into the kitchen? It wasn't as if he hadn't been there a hundred times before. Besides, she'd be right there to make sure he didn't take anything out of the house.

"You'll have sticky syrup all over you if you do. *Komm,* please." She went in, setting the package and her keys on the shelf while she took off the jacket she'd worn against the early morning chill.

"That's nice of you." Hank followed her to the kitchen. "I'm not much of a cook, so mostly I eat macaroni and cheese from a package. Or peanut butter sandwiches."

"This is better." She put one of the buns on a plate and handed it to him, then filled a glass with cold water, sticky buns not being something you'd want to eat without a drink. "My mother baked these fresh this morning."

Hank took a huge bite, and a blissful expression spread across his face. "That's the best thing I ever tasted." His words were muffled by the syrupy treat, and she had to smile.

"I will save mine for later, once I have some work done." She rewrapped the remaining rolls and set them on the counter.

"That reminds me why I wanted to see you this morning," Hank said. "I have to stop by the store after my classes. To get some more peanut butter." He gave that boyish grin. "I thought you might need some cleaning supplies. I'd be glad to pick anything up for you."

"That is *sehr* kind of you." She opened the cabinet where cleaning supplies were stored. "Actually, you could get me another bottle of window cleaner." She held up the half-empty bottle. "And a package of paper towels." There would be plenty of cleaning to do once she'd finished sorting and packing, and she must be sure the house was in tip-top shape before it was turned over to the historical society.

"Will do." Hank stuffed the last of the roll in his mouth and drained the glass of water. "I'll be off, then. If you're not here when I get back, I'll leave the things on the side porch."

"That will be fine." She'd probably be here, unless he was running very late, but in any event, no one would bother a grocery bag on the porch.

Sarah saw him out, carefully locking the door behind him. She'd certain sure not want to be in here without knowing the doors were locked.

A while later she was deeply engrossed in cleaning the study when the doorbell rang, setting up echoes in the empty house. Her hand jerked, sending a stack of old photographs toppling to the floor.

Foolish, she told herself, starting down the stairs. Jumping that way at an unexpected sound. It was good no one had been around to witness her reaction.

When she reached the bottom of the stairs, she could see Leo Frost through the glass in the front door. Relieved, she hurried to open it. She'd be glad to turn the extra keys over to him.

He stepped inside, scanning her face with a worried expression. "Are you all right, Sarah? I just heard about the accident with the buggy yesterday. You shouldn't have come in to work today."

"I am fine, and Jacob is, as well. We weren't hurt at all. Even Bess was only scared."

Some of the worry left his face. "I'm relieved that all three of you are safe, but it must have been very frightening."

"Ja." She didn't want to relive those moments. "I'm glad to have work to do today. It takes my mind off the accident."

"Chief Byler told me that the car was stolen." Leo shook his head. "At the risk of sounding like an old fogy, I sometimes find myself longing for the days when things like that happened in the outside world, not here." He dusted his hands together, as if wiping off the world's influence. "So tell me how the work is coming. Is there anything you need?"

"I asked Hank to pick up some window cleaner and paper towels for me. I hope that is all right."

"Of course, of course. I should have told you to go ahead and purchase any supplies you need. Just save the receipts for me."

She nodded, glad she hadn't done anything wrong by giving Hank the errand. "I finished sorting and packing the china from the dining room. I left the silverware in its chest, because I didn't know what you wanted done with it."

"Just leave it for the moment," he said, taking a tablet from his briefcase and making a note. "I'll have to arrange to have it valued."

She nodded. "And I've begun work on the study. I left any papers for you, but there are so many other things—souvenirs from trips, old Christmas cards, his photo albums. I don't know what should be done with those. It wouldn't seem right just to throw them away. You understand."

"All the bits and pieces of Richard's life," he said. "Yes, I understand, but with no family left it's hard to know what else to do. The photo albums, at least, might be of value to the historical society's collection."

"Mr. Strickland had gotten several old albums out just recently. He must have been looking through them that last day." Her throat tightened. He had been reliving his past, maybe, thinking about the people he'd loved. But he had died alone, and that wrenched at her heart.

Leo must have known something of what she was thinking, because he patted her hand. "Why don't you put things like the photo albums in a separate box? I'll stop by later today to look through them." He glanced at his watch. "I have to leave now. I have an appointment with the pastor about the memorial service for Richard. It will be on Saturday, since more people can come then."

She nodded. There would be many in Springville who would want to pay their respects.

Leo started out the door, then turned back again. "I nearly forgot. I'm making arrangements for Donald McKay, the antiques dealer, to evaluate items from the house. I'll let you know when he's coming, since someone else should be with him as he's doing the valuing."

She nodded again. Perhaps Mr. McKay had repeated his offer of help to Leo.

"Oh, and Maude Stevens has been agitating about the contents of the will." He looked faintly hunted. "If she should come here, don't let her have access to the house without me. The historical society will simply have to wait its turn." He gave a faint smile. "You'd think historians would be patient by nature, wouldn't you? Lock up behind me."

Smiling at his comment, Sarah snapped the dead bolt. It was far better that Leo deal with Mrs. Stevens, if necessary.

CHAPTER EIGHT

As SHE TRIED TO GET BACK to sorting and boxing that afternoon, Sarah found that Leo's comments about the accident had brought it back to mind a bit too vividly. Those moments when she'd known they were going to crash, the sensation of flying through the air—that should be what sent remembered fear shivering down her spine.

But it wasn't. The vivid, terrifying moments that wouldn't let go were those she'd spent frantically searching for Jacob, fearing she would find him lying on the road, looking the way Mr. Strickland had when she'd found him.

She tried to shake the feeling off, but couldn't. Maybe Jacob had felt the same thing when he'd tried to find her. Maybe... Her thoughts jumped ahead to the kiss. Perhaps that kiss had just been an expression of relief that they were both still alive. If so, the best way to handle the situation was to ignore it.

That explanation should make her happy, but for some reason it didn't.

The cuckoo clock on the study wall sounded, reminding her that it was time to quit for the day. She began stacking the photo albums in a box, along with the loose photos. The pictures must have been important to Mr. Strickland. He'd made notes on the backs of many of them, identifying people and places. Quickly, she stacked them in the box to be looked at later. Her hand paused on the album she'd seen first, the one with the picnic scene. Surely someone would want to keep that one, at least. She flipped open the album.

The picture wasn't there. She stared blankly at a photo of a school group: children lined up in front of the old elementary school, a teacher in a long skirt standing at the end of the row. Sarah turned the page, then went back again. She must be mistaken. The picnic photo had to be in another album.

She ran her finger along the inside binding, feeling the rough edges of a page that had been torn out. Her stomach seemed to twist. Maybe this *was* a different album. Maybe the page had been ripped out years ago. Maybe. But she didn't think so.

Mamm would be waiting at Aunt Mary's, wondering why she wasn't there yet. Sarah clutched the album. Was she really sure this was the same one? But how could anyone get in the house to tear out the page? And why?

She must be wrong. There was no time to go through all the albums again, searching for the missing picture. She could do that tomorrow. If the photo really wasn't there, Leo would have to be told.

Sarah hurried downstairs and double-checked the locks on the front and back doors. All was secure, so she scurried out the side door, locking it with the key.

She'd gone nearly a block before she realized she'd left her jacket behind, and would need it in the morning. Shaking her head, she turned back. One of her *grossmamm*'s favorite sayings slipped into her mind. *If you don't use your head, you'll have to use your feet.*

Grossmamm had been wonderful *gut* at having a saying for every event.

Sarah let herself in the side door quietly. The house was as she'd left it just moments before, and there was no reason to stop and listen as she reached for her jacket. No reason, but she did it anyway.

Quiet, of course. Nothing was out of place—

Her thoughts skittered to a halt when something creaked overhead.

She froze, her hand pressed to her lips to keep any sound from escaping. One breath, two—and then she heard the creak again and recognized what it was. Someone had stepped on the old floorboards at the top of the stairs.

She should do something. If she went to the phone, the person upstairs would hear her. Better to slip quietly back out, run to the neighbor...

Footsteps sounded openly in the upstairs hall. Sarah's fear eased, and she felt suddenly foolish. Surely someone who shouldn't be in the house wouldn't walk around so casually. It must be Leo, of course. He'd said he would try to come back this afternoon.

Since he was upstairs already, she might as well show him the album. Once she'd turned that question over to him, she wouldn't have to fret about it.

The back stairs leading up from the kitchen were closest. Sarah opened the door and hurried up, calling Leo's name as she reached the top and grasped the doorknob. "Leo? I'm glad I caught you." She turned the knob, pushing the door open. "I wanted—"

Something slammed against the door on the other side, forcing it shut. The movement sent her staggering backward. Unable to stop, she lost her balance and plunged down the stairs, arms flailing. Helpless, out of control, she was falling.

Her hand struck the railing and she grabbed it, arm twisting as it took the full weight of her body. Ignoring the pain, she held on tight, getting her feet beneath her, while her heart thudded so loudly she couldn't hear anything else.

She pressed her palm against her chest. She had to listen, had to think. Someone had slammed the door shut so she wouldn't see him or her. Had the person intended to make her fall?

She tensed in fear. Footsteps were heading quickly toward the front stairs. Maybe the person intended to slip out that way before Sarah could see who it was. Or maybe he or she was coming back, expecting to find her crumpled at the bottom of the staircase.

That possibility galvanized her into action. She had to get out of the house. Find help, call Leo or the police. And quickly.

Hanging on to the railing, she slithered down the rest of the steps, paused for a moment and then eased the door open at the bottom of the stairs. She listened intently, but couldn't hear anything. Maybe the person was already out of the house. Or maybe he was around the corner, waiting for her.

But she couldn't stay here, afraid to move, waiting for someone to come after her....

Murmuring a silent prayer, she dashed across the kitchen, down the hallway and out the house.

THERE WAS REALLY no good reason for Jacob to drive past the Strickland house on his way back from the hardware store. No reason, but he was doing it anyway.

Probably Sarah's mother would have picked her up by now. They'd be home ahead of him. Still, no reason why he shouldn't go this way.

He drew even with the house and knew the instinct that had sent him this way had been accurate. Both Leo Frost's car and the police car were drawn up by the side gate.

Heart pounding, he guided Bess to the verge and jumped down, running toward the side door.

He bolted into the house and followed the sound of voices to the kitchen. Sarah sat in a chair, with Leo and Chief Byler on either side of her. They all looked up at him.

He had eyes only for Sarah. "Are you all right? What happened?" He went to her, kneeling next to the chair. She seemed unhurt, but...

"I'm all right, Jacob. Truly. I..." She glanced at Leo, as if asking his permission. "I heard someone in the house."

He could tell by the strain in her face that she wasn't telling him everything. "Did he hurt you? Frighten you?"

She shook her head and then bit her lower lip. "*Ja,* frightened, maybe. I took a tumble down a couple of steps, but I didn't get hurt."

"Then why did you wince when I touched your hand?" He put his fingers lightly on her wrist, afraid to do more. "You should see a doctor."

"*Ach,* no, I've had worse helping *Daad* with the horses." She smiled, but her eyes were grave. "My arm twisted, is all. From when I caught myself."

"Sarah heard someone upstairs and thought it was me." Leo seemed to feel that a fuller explanation was needed. "She went up the back stairs. Apparently the intruder heard her coming. He…or she…slammed the door shut, causing Sarah to trip down a few steps." He held up his hand, as if anticipating Jacob's reaction. "We wanted her to see a doctor, but she insists she's all right."

"Did you catch him? Do you know who it was?" Jacob appreciated that Leo would be cautious in making accusations. He was a lawyer, after all. But it surely must have been a man.

Chief Byler shook his head. "He was gone by the time we got here. Sarah was very sensible. She ran outside and stopped a passing car. The motorist called us on his cell phone. But no one seems to have seen the intruder, whoever it was."

Sarah stirred in her chair. "I have told you everything. *Mamm* will be worried. I was supposed to meet her at my aunt's."

"Just a few more minutes, Sarah." Chief Byler picked up a small notebook from the table in front of him. "Tell me again about the photograph."

She nodded, but Jacob could feel her tension mounting. "Yesterday I looked in the photo albums Mr. Strickland had out in the study." She frowned. "He must have gotten them out the afternoon or evening of the day he died, because they weren't there when I tidied the room in the morning. Anyway, the first picture in the album I picked up was of him when he was about my age, at a picnic with other young people. Remember, Jacob, I told you about it on the way home?"

He nodded. "I remember. But what—"

"It is missing, that's what. I realized this afternoon when I was putting the albums in a box. It looked as if a page had been torn out."

Chief Byler stood. "Let's go up and have a quick look at it, Sarah. Then I promise you can leave."

They went upstairs, with Jacob following right behind her. He hoped Chief Byler wouldn't tell him to leave, because he would hate to argue with the law. But nothing was said. The police chief seemed to think that what Sarah knew, Jacob knew, as well.

"This is where I was putting the albums." Sarah reached for a box on the desk. "There are some loose photos as well, and— " She stopped, staring into the box. "The album. It's gone."

"You're sure?" Chief Byler scanned the remaining albums. "These all look pretty much alike to me."

Sarah shook her head, lifting them out and setting them on the desk one by one. "It was the only dark blue one with gold lettering. It's missing."

Leo's forehead wrinkled. "I don't understand. What value would an old photo have to anyone?"

Chief Byler frowned in turn. "You'd think the only person who might be interested would be a relative."

"Maude Stevens," Leo said slowly. "Her late husband was a distant cousin. And Hank Mitchell, who also claims to be a cousin."

"Claims?" The chief was on to that in an instant.

Leo's lips tightened. "I thought Richard was foolish to offer the young man the garage apartment on nothing more than his word and a letter from an elderly cousin. But Richard was sure he knew best."

"I think it's time I had a talk with Hank Mitchell," Chief Byler said. He smiled at Sarah. "Now, as I promised, you can leave. I hope your mother isn't fretting too much."

"Just one thing." Leo still looked worried. "I don't think Sarah should be alone in the house anymore."

"She won't be." Jacob said the words firmly, willing her not to argue. This was not the time for stubbornness. "I will be with her."

"Good enough," Leo said. "I'll be glad of your help, Jacob. Get on home now."

Jacob held Sarah's arm as they went down the stairs, and she shook his hand off only when they stepped out onto the porch. "*Mamm's* coming," she said, nodding down the street at her mother's buggy. "Listen, Jacob—"

"Don't bother to argue. I'm bringing you tomorrow. And I'm staying."

"Not that," she said quickly. "I'll be glad enough to have you there to help me. Just don't say anything to *Mamm* about what happened, will you? I don't want her fretting any more than she already is."

He hesitated a moment and then nodded. It didn't matter whether Sarah's *mamm* was worrying about her or not. Because he was doing enough for the both of them.

CHAPTER NINE

SARAH HUGGED HER JACKET around her as she headed for town the next morning. Mist hung in the valley, but the battery-operated safety light on Daad's buggy sent out a reassuring red glow.

She glanced at Jacob. Did he feel the same edge of tension she did at driving the buggy on a day that was too reminiscent of the accident? Usually she could read his every thought, but this morning his stoic expression defied her. It was almost like looking at a stranger, and that edged her stress up another notch.

"What...what does Levi King say about your buggy?" Levi, the local carriage maker, had hauled the remains of Jacob's vehicle away after the accident.

"He says I should learn to avoid traffic." Jacob grinned, and he was himself again, the Jacob she'd known all her life. "It will have to be totally rebuilt, for sure. If anyone can do it, Levi can."

"If you hadn't been driving me home—" she began.

"*Ach,* don't talk foolish," Jacob said quickly. "What happens is what happens. It is God's will."

She nodded, but wasn't quite convinced. Silence fell between them again, and it wasn't the comfortable silence she was used to. It seemed to vibrate with things unsaid.

Jacob's hands tightened on the lines, and Bess tossed her head slightly, as if in protest. He cleared his throat.

He was going to say something—something that might change things between them forever. Panic set her nerves jangling.

"I wonder if Chief Byler found Hank." She blurted the words out—anything to head off whatever Jacob planned to say. "It's hard to believe he would take the photo album. Why would he?"

Jacob's lips firmed for a moment. Then he shrugged. "Why would anyone? Unless he wanted it for the sake of family memories."

"But why take it?" They were on safe ground again, and her voice sounded more normal to her. "He could have asked Leo Frost. I wouldn't think he'd mind."

Jacob frowned. "I don't know. I just know I won't be easy in my mind until you're finished with this job."

"It's only a few more days, I'd guess." And then what would she do? She'd been too busy to even think about looking around for another job. Still, maybe Leo would have some suggestions. "Mr. McKay is coming this afternoon to put a price on the antiques."

"Are you supposed to be there to help him?" They were getting into traffic as they reached the outskirts of town, and Jacob's gaze was focused on the road.

"*Ja,* Leo asked me to. He doesn't want anyone left alone in the house."

"I guess we will stay, then." He drew into the alley that ran along the Strickland house, bringing the mare to a stop at the gate.

Sarah climbed down a bit more slowly than usual, mindful of the bruises that had developed after the buggy accident and then that tumble on the stairs. "I'll go and check on the boxes for the charity truck while you unharness, *ja?* The truck should be here early."

She didn't wait for Jacob's agreement, but hurried up the walk. The sooner they got to work, the better. Maybe then this strangeness between them would go away.

She went in, taking her jacket off as she did and hanging it on the hook. She'd check those boxes first and see if there was enough space for Jacob to move them out to the porch for pickup.

She walked into the sunroom and stopped dead. Hank Mitchell stood by the table next to Mr. Strickland's chair. He had an envelope in his hand.

Maybe her alarm showed in her face, because he gave her a quick, disarming smile. "Hi, Sarah. Sorry if I startled you."

"I didn't expect to see you so early." *And how did you get in?*

Hank held up the envelope. "I just wanted to pick up something of mine. I guess I should have waited until you got here, but I have to get going."

"Going where?"

He shrugged. "No point in hanging around here, is there? Cousin Richard was my only connection to this place, and he's gone."

"But what about your classes at the college? You have to have a placc to live."

"Yeah, well, maybe I can get an apartment in Lancaster." He shoved the envelope into the pocket of his windbreaker.

"What is that?" She eased back a step. It wasn't that she was afraid of Hank. But why didn't Jacob come?

"It's just the letter my grandmother wrote to introduce me to Cousin Richard." His usually cheerful expression shifted to sorrow. "I don't have much from her now, so I wanted to keep the letter."

"Is that why you took the photo from the album, too?" The words were out before it occurred to her that it might not be wise to confront Hank.

For a moment the sorrow lingered on his face, as if he'd forgotten to change his expression. Then his features hardened, making him look older. Tougher.

"So you figured that out, did you? I should have known you would, a smart girl like you. Strickland had a habit of writing on the backs of photos, unfortunately. He must have been getting suspicious of me, since he went looking for a photo of my supposed grandmother."

Her anger flared at the derogatory note in his voice, but she said nothing. There was no sense in antagonizing Hank even more.

"So you know I wasn't the person he thought. It doesn't matter now. Strickland died before I could get anything out of him."

"What did you do to him?" The anger boiled over at the memory of Mr. Strickland lying on the stairs.

"Nothing, nothing." Hank held up both hands in a gesture of innocence. "Trust me, he's no good to me dead. As long as he was alive and thinking I was his long-lost cousin, I had a chance to cash in on that. Now—well, now it's time for me to disappear." He patted the pocket with the letter. "It just makes good sense not to leave anything behind to make the police curious."

A shiver slid down her spine. Did he mean her?

He grinned, his mobile face once again youthful and harmless. "Relax, Sarah. I'm a con man, not a killer, if you even know what that means. I'm just going to walk outside, jump in my car and drive away. If you have a soft spot for me, you might delay calling the cops until I'm out of town."

Before she could say a word, he'd darted past her and out the door. A moment later she heard the roar of his car's engine.

Footsteps pounded and Jacob rushed in. "Was he in the house? What's going on? Are you all right?"

"I'm fine." She put up her hand at the volley of questions. "I have to call Chief Byler. I'll tell both of you at once."

JACOB HAD NO INTEREST in sitting in a police station, even with someone as friendly and understanding as Chief Byler. But Sarah had to be here, so he was, as well.

The police chief had said he wanted to record her statement about Hank Mitchell, so that was why they were in his office. Leo Frost had arrived, looking flustered, and exclaiming over Sarah's story as she told it.

Once she'd finished, Chief Byler took the recording to the secretary in the outer office, and they could hear the murmur of voices from there. Jacob had hoped that they'd be able to leave once the story was told, but apparently not. He balanced his hat on his knees and prepared to wait.

At least Sarah seemed calm about this. Oddly enough, he didn't think she'd been afraid of Hank, although she was certainly disturbed by what had happened.

Leo shook his head. "I never thought taking that young man in was a good idea, but Richard wasn't one to listen once he'd made up his mind."

"I don't think you could have changed anything."

Sarah's voice was filled with sympathy. "Mr. Strickland said to me once that whether he liked and trusted Hank or not, family was family. He couldn't turn him away."

"He didn't even know that Hank wasn't related to him." Leo drummed his fingers on the edge of the chief's desk. "I should have investigated his background myself, even if Richard didn't want me to."

"You probably wouldn't have found anything." Chief Byler came back into the room. "Not unless you had access to police files." He sat at his desk and pulled the computer keyboard toward him.

"You mean he had a police record?" Leo looked about ready to explode.

"My office staff started a search for him yesterday, after Sarah told us about the album disappearing." He clicked a few keys on the computer and then turned it so they could see the photo displayed on the screen.

"That's Hank Mitchell, all right," Leo said.

"Hank Mitchell, Jason Davids, James Randall, and probably some other names, as well. He's a con artist. His specialty is duping wealthy elderly people, but he has a somewhat unique method. He uses genealogy files to identify distant relatives of his mark, and then claims to be a descendant. It's surprising how many people took him at his word, only to wake up one morning and find their valuables gone."

So Mitchell was a thief. Jacob would like to think that was why he'd disliked the man, but the truth was he'd been afraid Sarah was noticing him too much.

"So the letter that Mr. Strickland's cousin supposedly wrote..." Sarah said slowly.

"Was a fake," Chief Byler stated. "The woman in

question actually died many years ago, when she was only twenty."

Sarah's blue eyes darkened. "What a wicked thing, to lie to Mr. Strickland that way. But I don't understand about the photo. Why did he take it? That's what made you suspect him."

"He was put in an uncomfortable position by Richard Strickland's death," the chief said. "If he disappeared right away, that would have made us suspicious. He wanted to get rid of anything that might expose him for what he was. I can't be sure about the photo, but I had a look at the others in the album. Strickland was apparently meticulous about recording information on the backs of pictures. There must have been something written there that would have given the masquerade away."

"He had just gotten those photos out," Sarah murmured. "Something must have made him think Hank was lying to him. The girl in the photo was probably the cousin. Hank did say something about Mr. Strickland writing on the back."

Leo nodded. "I think you have it right, Sarah. At least now we know who was to blame for the odd things that have happened at the house."

Jacob stirred. "What about the accident? Do you think he was driving the car that hit us?"

"That's one of the questions we'll be asking once we catch up with him. Along with some questions about how Richard Strickland died." Chief Byler's face set in hard lines.

"Surely he didn't harm Richard," Leo said. "He had nothing to gain and everything to lose by his death."

"Unless Richard realized he was being duped, and

threatened to have Mitchell arrested." Chief Byler stopped when his phone buzzed. His face didn't reveal a thing as he listened. When he hung up, he turned back to them. "Maybe now we'll get some answers. The state police picked up Mitchell on Interstate 80, heading for New Jersey."

He was gone in a moment, leaving the three of them to stare silently at each other.

"Well," Leo said finally. "At least now we don't have to worry about your safety, Sarah. But if you want to take the rest of the day off after all of this, I certainly can't argue."

"*Gut* idea," Jacob began, but Sarah was already shaking her head.

"Mr. McKay is coming to do the evaluation. I don't want to make him change his schedule. I'll be fine."

Jacob shifted in his chair, uneasy. Sarah was probably right, but he still didn't like it.

CHAPTER TEN

THE STRICKLAND HOUSE seemed emptier than ever when Sarah returned there after getting a sandwich at the tea shop. Oddly enough, she didn't mind. Now that the truth was out, she no longer had the sensation of something threatening in the house.

The place was just melancholy—that was the word. A resting place for Richard Strickland's memories, but he didn't need them any longer, any more than he needed the cushioned ottoman he liked to rest his feet on, or the dozens of figurines he'd collected.

Now that Hank was under arrest, there was nothing to fear in this place. She'd finally even convinced Jacob he didn't need to stay. He'd argued, but had agreed to go and run a few errands for the shop and pick up more packing boxes for her.

She couldn't really work on anything else until Mr. McKay came to do the inventory, so Sarah started a pot of coffee. It had no sooner perked than she heard the front doorbell ring.

Walking quickly to answer it, Sarah realized she no longer felt uncomfortable when she passed the stairs. The image of Mr. Strickland lying there dead was being replaced by countless images of him alive. She recognized the feeling. It had been the same when *Gross-*

mamm died. After the first sorrow, she'd been able to think of the happy memories rather than the end.

She opened the door to Donald McKay. The antiques dealer had a legal tablet, a couple of books and a clipboard in his arm, and he'd been glancing down the street in the direction of police headquarters. He stepped inside, smoothing his thinning, white-blond hair back where the wind had disarranged it.

"Is it true what they're saying?" He dropped his armload onto the hall table. "That you fought off Hank Mitchell single-handed and captured him, and that he murdered Richard?"

She might have been upset had the words come from anyone else, but the whole town knew of Donald's extravagant style of speaking. She just smiled.

"Amish don't do battle or arrest criminals, as you well know. The state police caught him trying to run away."

"That doesn't make nearly as exciting a story." McKay's eyes twinkled. "So young Mitchell was a con artist, trying to bilk Richard of his money. That just goes to show that you never know about other people. I wouldn't have thought Richard could be taken in by a smooth talker."

"He thought Hank was a relative," she said, moved to defend Mr. Strickland. "Hank actually had a letter from one of Mr. Strickland's cousins. Or at least Mr. Strickland believed it came from a cousin."

"Apparently there's a downside to all that genealogy research people do. Besides the risk of discovering that your great-great-grandfather was a horse thief."

"I know who my great-great-grandfather was," Sarah

said, playing into his joking. "He's listed right on the family tree."

"The Amish do it right," he said. "Keep those records in the family Bible, not on the internet."

Sarah nodded toward the kitchen. "Would you like some coffee before we begin?"

"Let's put in an hour of work first," McKay said, consulting his watch. "Then we'll be ready for a break. Where shall we start?"

"I know Mr. Frost wanted your opinion of the silverware. And I'd be glad to have it out of the house. I didn't think it should be here in an unlocked cabinet."

"People often overestimate the value of silver flatware." He led the way into the dining room. "But with the price of silver today, Richard's is bound to be worth quite a bit."

They took the silverware chests out of the bottom of the china cabinet, laying the contents on the table. Some of the spoons were worn paper-thin, but all the silver glowed with recent cleaning. Mr. McKay handed her the clipboard and a pen.

"It will be fastest if you write down the item in this column, how many there are of each item here, and my comments about the value in the last column. There will be some I have doubts about. I'll have to do research on those pieces."

She took the clipboard and they began to work. It was easier than Sarah initially expected, and Mr. McKay seemed to know his business. He chatted amiably about the history of the different pieces as they went along. He was nearly as interesting as Mr. Strickland had been.

They finished the silverware in little more than half an hour, and Sarah was impressed at the figures she'd entered in the column for the values of the items. Mr. Strickland had often said the silver was worth taking good care of, and he'd been right.

"Why don't we go upstairs next?" McKay headed for the staircase. "I know Richard kept a lot of his collectibles on the study shelves. Many of them are objects I acquired for him, so this won't be difficult. I'll already have records at the shop of how much he paid for them."

Sarah nodded, leading the way. Soon the house would be stripped of the things that reminded her of her late employer. She probably wouldn't be in it again once the historical society took over.

Working in the study was bittersweet. This was the place she associated most with Richard Strickland. He had often come in while she was cleaning this room, talking and telling her stories about each object, much as Mr. McKay was doing now.

"Mr. Strickland always liked talking about his pieces," she said, bending over the drop leaf table that held the collection of silver military figures. "I can almost smell the scent of his pipe tobacco. He'd lean back in his chair, smoking, with some favorite object in his hand."

Odd that even though his vision was very poor, he'd know each one by touch. It wasn't part of the Amish tradition to collect things just because they were pretty, but she could understand that to Richard they had been part of his heritage—a reminder of family.

Mr. McKay studied the figures. "The Revolutionary War soldiers, of course. I often looked for more to add to his collection, but they were hard to find—at least ones that suited his requirements."

He began picking them up, describing each one as

she made notes. In the back of her mind, Mr. Strickland still seemed to be telling his stories.

"That's all of them," McKay said. "An even dozen for the historical society's collection."

"A dozen?" she repeated, looking at him blankly while memory came to her. *A baker's dozen,* Mr. Strickland had always said. He had a baker's dozen of the figures—thirteen.

"Something wrong, Sarah?" McKay's gaze was intent on her face.

"No, nothing," she said quickly, but her thoughts tumbled and spun as if caught in a whirligig. There weren't a dozen of the figures. There were thirteen. She should know; she'd polished them often enough. They tarnished so, and Mr. Strickland had wanted them to gleam, even if he couldn't see enough to appreciate the fact.

She straightened slowly, holding the clipboard in front of her, trying to understand what this meant.

"Something is wrong," he said. "I can see it in your face."

"I don't understand," she said slowly. "There should be thirteen of the figures." She picked one up, running her fingers over the piece. "There were thirteen the last time I cleaned them. I remember that..." She stopped, recalling a chance comment from Mr. Strickland.

"What do you remember, Sarah?" McKay's voice was urgent. "Hank Mitchell must have stolen one of them. That's it, of course. He probably stole it and Richard found out. They quarreled, and he pushed Richard down the stairs." The antiques dealer took a step toward the door. "Come on. We'll go down to the phone and call Chief Byler. He'll want to know."

She stared at him, shaking her head slowly. "Mr. Strickland wasn't worried about one being missing. They were all here then. All thirteen."

McKay grasped her arm, urging her toward the door. She planted her feet, resisting.

"Well, he must have stolen it later then," he insisted. "Come on."

"Mr. Strickland was puzzled." She could see it as clearly as if it were moments ago. He'd leaned forward in his chair, holding one of the figures up to the light from the window, running his fingers over it. "One of them was wrong."

"What do you mean, wrong?" McKay's voice cracked with tension.

"He said it wasn't the right piece. That he'd have to talk to you about it." She strained, trying to remember anything else Mr. Strickland had said, but he'd turned away then, looking puzzled and distressed, murmuring something to himself.

She thought she knew what had happened, and she looked at McKay, unable to prevent the horror she felt from showing in her eyes. "It was you."

"Come now," he said, smiling. "You're confused, Sarah. I watched for pieces that would interest him, yes, but that was my only involvement. I didn't..."

His voice trailed off and his expression changed. Hardened. His smile turned into a grimace.

"It's no good, is it? You'll repeat this to the police, and they'll get an independent valuation of everything in the house. I know, because that's what Richard said he would do." His features darkened, distorted by the depth of his emotions. "Half-blind old fool, sitting here alone and gloating over his treasures. What difference did it make to him if a piece here and there was replaced with an imitation? He couldn't see them, anyway."

"He knew," she said, struggling to find her voice. "He loved them, so he knew."

"That's what he said to me that night." McKay's hand tightened on her upper arm, and he pulled her toward the door. "Standing out here, shaking his fist at me, saying he'd call the police."

She didn't have the strength to resist him. He shoved her and she stumbled, fighting to keep her feet under her. If she couldn't break free and run—

"He was off balance, waving his cane around like a crazy person." McKay pushed her toward the top of the stairs. "All I did was grab the cane to keep him from breaking something. But he stumbled. Went right over the top of the stairs. Like you will."

They'd nearly reached the staircase. She struggled to plant her feet, but the rug was sliding under her. Her free arm flailed, and she tried to grab something, anything to hang on to, but he was forcing her over—

"Sarah!" The shout came from below, Jacob's voice, Jacob's feet pounding on the steps.

McKay twisted at the sound, losing his footing. Her hand struck the railing, grabbed, held, but McKay was falling, dragging her with him. They'd both go down to the tile floor below....

McKay's grip slid from her. He screamed as he fell down the stairs, the momentum sending her over the railing. She clung there, her legs swinging in the air, but she couldn't hold on—

"I have you, Sarah." Jacob's strong hands gripped her wrists. He tried to pull her up, and she felt his muscles strain.

"You can't," she gasped. "I'll drag you over, too."

"We can do it together," he said, holding her tightly. "Swing your leg up, just like climbing the apple tree in the backyard. You were always *sehr gut* at climbing, *ja?* You can do this."

He was so calm, so sure. And he was right. They could do this together. With Jacob's powerful grip steadying her, she lifted her knee over the railing. He pulled, and they both tumbled to the rug, his arms holding her close.

CHAPTER ELEVEN

THE HOUSE SEEMED FULL of police, just as it had on the morning Sarah had discovered Mr. Strickland's body. But it wasn't the same, of course. She sat on the living room sofa, comforted by Jacob's presence next to her, and stared down at her clasped hands.

From the hallway, she could hear as the paramedics maneuvered the stretcher carrying Donald McKay out the door. He was alternately moaning and screaming at them to leave him alone. He had two broken legs, so they said. Sarah tried to close her ears to the sounds.

The outer door closed behind the stretcher, and Chief Byler could be heard giving someone instructions to stay with McKay at all times.

Jacob stirred slightly. "I know we must forgive him," he murmured in Pennsylvania Dutch, the dialect comforting. "But I think it will take me a while. When I saw you —"

Sarah put her hand over his, stopping him. "I'm safe now. It's all right. We will forget." Usually it was Jacob's job to keep her calm. They seemed to have changed places.

"Ja." His low voice was husky, his hand warm in her grasp. "Sarah..."

"I wouldn't have believed it." Leo Frost came in,

shaking his head. "Donald McKay, of all people. What possessed him to do such a thing?"

Sarah could only shake her head, as well. She had no answer to that question.

"I suspect his tastes were more expensive than his income." Chief Byler stood in the doorway. "He started off saying he didn't mean to do it. That it was an accident. Then he backed up and said that he didn't do anything wrong and had no idea that anything was missing from Strickland's house."

"But that's not true." She shouldn't be surprised, she supposed. A man who would do what McKay had wouldn't hesitate to lie about it.

"We know that, Sarah," Leo said. "If it comes to testifying at a trial, all you have to do is tell what happened. Jacob saw McKay trying to push you, as well. No one will doubt you."

"A trial." She couldn't help it if she sounded horrified at the thought.

Jacob squeezed her hand. "I will be there, too, don't forget."

"*Ja.*" The fear slid away when she met his steady gaze. Jacob would be with her.

"I've sent for a state police team to look into McKay's shop and check out his business records," the police chief said. "I suspect they'll come up with enough evidence to convict him a couple of times over." He shook his head. "I'm afraid the historical society will have to delay their plans for the property. The state police will want access until their investigation is complete, and I'll have to insist that nothing be touched until the investigation into Richard's death is finished. And then there are the charges against Hank Mitchell. Two bad guys caught in as many days, thanks to you, Sarah."

"Not me," she said quickly. "I didn't do anything." A question stirred in her mind. "But I still don't understand about how Hank got into the house even after Jacob put the dead bolts on."

"Somehow he'd gotten hold of the new key. It was found on him when he was caught." The chief looked at her quizzically.

Sarah felt her cheeks grow red. "That morning when he was going to stop at the store for me, he came in the house. I had put the new keys on the shelf in the back hall. If he was quick enough, he could have taken one while my back was turned."

"I'm sure he was an expert at that kind of thing," the chief said. "Don't blame yourself, Sarah."

Maybe not for the keys, but she did feel ashamed of having let Hank's innocent face and friendly smile deceive her.

"What about the car that hit us?" Jacob was frowning, as if he found it hard to believe so much wrongdoing.

"Neither is admitting to it, but now that we're fairly sure it was one of them, trying to keep you away from the house for a while, we'll find someone who saw them where they shouldn't have been that day. It will just take time." Chief Byler looked from her to Jacob. "I think you've both had as much of this as you can stand for now. I'll have someone drive you home."

"*Danki,* Chief, but I have Bess and the buggy," Jacob said, rising.

"Take a look outside." Chief Byler jerked his head toward the window. "There's a crowd of the curious out there. You don't want to go through that. I'll have the horse taken care of and returned to you this evening, once the curiosity has died down."

Sarah glanced out the window. People crowded along the wrought-iron fence, many with cameras. One man even had a pair of binoculars trained on the house. She drew back, shuddering.

Jacob nodded. "We will get Sarah's jacket, and then we'll be ready. We are grateful for your kindness."

For once Sarah was glad to let Jacob speak for both of them. She hurried toward the hallway, relieved to be away from the prying gazes.

Jacob took the jacket from its peg before she could reach for it. He helped her slip it on and then paused, his hands on her shoulders and his face very close to hers.

"Thank the good Lord that you are safe. When I saw you hanging from that railing…" His voice choked. "If you had fallen, I don't know how I could have gone on."

She couldn't bear the pain in his eyes. "It's all right." She touched his face, the movement tentative. His skin was warm and alive, reassuring her. "I knew you were there. I knew you would not let me fall."

His gaze was so intense it was as if he was stroking her. "Sarah, I cannot wait any longer to say this to you. I don't want to be your big brother anymore. I love you with all my heart. I want to be your husband."

She hesitated a moment, wondering at herself. All her doubts seemed to have vanished, all her thoughts of independence seeming foolish now. Loving someone was about depending on each other, and that was surely a better way to live.

"I love you, too," she said, knowing it was true deep

in her heart. "And I stopped thinking of you as a brother the moment you kissed me."

A smile lit Jacob's face, and love shone in his eyes. "My Sarah," he said gently, and then he kissed her again.

They stood together in the privacy of the small space, and Sarah wanted this moment to go on forever. But it couldn't, she knew. The chief would come, they'd be rushed away from those who would question them, and when they reached home, there would be more questions waiting. But at least now the truth had come out.

She rested her cheek against Jacob's chest and listened to the steady beating of his heart. "Poor Mr. Strickland," she said softly. "Two people he trusted were out to harm him. They could only do that because he was so alone, with no one to love and protect him."

"*Ja*. But he is at peace now, and you must let that comfort you." Jacob dropped a kiss on the top of her head, and his arms tightened around her. "That will never happen to us, Sarah. We will have each other."

She nodded, knowing what he said was true. That sort of loneliness didn't happen in the close-knit Amish community, even to someone as fussy and cantankerous as Richard Strickland had been.

As Jacob said, the man was at peace now. And she was ready to move on to a new life with Jacob. She smiled. *Mamm* would say she'd been right all along.

EPILOGUE

SARAH SAT AT THE KITCHEN table in the Strickland house, a tablet open in front of her. Soon she would stop thinking of it as Richard Strickland's house, she supposed. It belonged to the historical society now, and they would start moving things in next week. The police had finished their investigation; all the sorting and clearing had been done. Some items had gone to the historical society, according to Mr. Strickland's will, while others had been sold.

To her astonishment, the will had provided a money gift for her. She'd been reluctant to accept, but Leo said that it had made Mr. Strickland happy to leave it to her. And *Daad,* always practical, said the money would help her and Jacob to build a house of their own.

So now she waited, hearing the tramp of feet upstairs as the last few pieces of furniture for the auction house were carried out. Once the men were finished, she was to check the house, lock the doors and turn the keys over to Leo. Then her job would be done, and Jacob would be waiting for her.

In the meantime, she had a letter to write to her dear friends, with news that would surprise them.

"Dear Abby and Lena," she wrote. "I am sure you

will not believe this, but Jacob and I are going to be married. I know I always said he was like a brother to me, but it seems I was wrong...."

* * * * *

This book is dedicated to
my dear departed husband. Thanks, honey,
for a lifetime of deer-hunting adventures.

OUTSIDE THE CIRCLE

Patricia Davids

CHAPTER ONE

LENA TROYER SPOTTED the man with a rifle seconds after the magnificent deer she called Goliath stepped from the cover of the dense woods. Three smaller bucks had entered the hay meadow to graze a good ten minutes before Goliath followed them. The wily old buck never came into the open first.

From her vantage point in the cramped bell tower of her Amish school, Lena had a perfect view of the fields below. She held her breath, praying the deer would spot the hunter and flee before it was too late.

She had sketched many animals from this spot, but Goliath was her favorite subject. She'd once watched the stately buck completely lose his dignity when he slipped on a patch of ice. He'd floundered wildly for several minutes before regaining his feet. Then he'd glanced around as if to see who might have witnessed his ignoble fall. She couldn't help but laugh at his expression.

From the size of his massive antlers, she knew Goliath had eluded hunters for a dozen or more years, but he was oblivious to the danger standing fifty yards away behind the fencerow. He put his head down to graze. It was the hunter's perfect opportunity.

She expected a shot to ring out any second. Deer season didn't open for another month, but few hunters would ever have their sights on a buck the size of Goliath. Even if the season were open, the animals stood on land that belonged to Wilfred Cummings. He never allowed hunting on his property.

The hunter wore Amish clothing, a dark coat, dark trousers and a wide-brimmed black hat, but she didn't recognize him. Tall and broad-shouldered, he appeared to be a giant of a man. She was sure she'd never met him. He wasn't a member of her church district. She knew everyone in the twenty-three families that made up her Amish congregation. She wished she could see his face. The sun had gone down twenty minutes before and twilight was quickly fading to darkness.

Slowly, he raised his gun and steadied it on the fence post. Leaning forward, he sighted through his scope. A stand of low shrubs hid him from the deer. She had to do something.

Thinking quickly, Lena waved her sketchbook in the air. To her chagrin, one of the loose pages fluttered out into the evening air, but her tactic worked. Catching the flash of movement, the bucks bounded into the forest with amazing speed, their white tails held high, signaling danger to others of their kind. In a second, they were gone, and safe. Lena grinned with relief.

After all, it was illegal to hunt deer out of season. The Amish hunters she knew were law-abiding men. Her father and brothers frequently hunted wild game in the woods and fields surrounding their farms. She'd helped her older sister can venison, wild pig, quail and rabbit many times, but her family hunted only in season and only after purchasing their licenses and deer permits as required by the state. They never took more than their limit, and almost nothing from the animals went to waste.

The hunter below Lena straightened and looked in her direction. She ducked below the edge of the railing that framed the bottom of the bell tower, not wanting him to know she had spoiled his shot. The sound of his footsteps approaching the building made her cringe.

"Is someone there?" His deep voice matched his big size and sent a chill skittering over Lena's skin. She didn't answer.

It suddenly occurred to her that he might be hunting meat for his family's table. Had his sights been on one of the smaller deer? Had she taken food from his children's mouths because of a silly, sentimental attachment to a wild animal? She bit the corner of her lip as she considered the harm she might have inadvertently caused.

After a few moments of silence, Lena rose to look over the wooden railing. To her dismay, the stranger stood right below her. He bent to pick up something from the ground. She sucked in a quick breath when she saw he held her sketchbook page.

He glanced up and she drew back quickly. Had he seen her? She held still and hoped he didn't notice her shadow behind the thick pickets. Would he come inside the school to investigate? She closed her eyes and prayed he would move on. How embarrassed she would be if he found her standing in the attic with her head and shoulders poking through the trapdoor in the bell tower like some unruly child. She was a grown woman of twenty-four, not a schoolgirl. What made her behavior worse was the fact that she was the teacher. She itched to go back downstairs, but was afraid she would make too much noise and give herself away.

When the hunter's footsteps moved off, she breathed a sigh of relief. God had surely smiled on her plight. Waiting a full five minutes more, she quietly left her cramped quarters, taking her binoculars and the forbidden romance novel she'd been reading until the deer appeared. She closed the trapdoor, making sure not to disturb the bell, and descended the wooden ladder to the attic.

After taking down the ladder, she left the book in her hiding place and made her way past dusty old desks, benches and stacks of miscellaneous items stored there to the narrow flight of stairs at the opposite end of the building.

Down in the schoolroom, she grabbed her bonnet from the hook and placed it over her black prayer *kapp,* grateful to cover her chilly ears. The October days were growing cooler, but it was downright cold tonight.

She opened the front door and checked the schoolyard. There was no one in sight. Once more thankful that she had escaped detection by the foiled hunter, she rushed down the narrow track that led to a covered bridge over the creek. A stone's throw past the bridge, the school lane intersected with a paved road. Going north would take her to the village of Mount Hope. Her father's farm lay the other way. She hurried along the narrow blacktop as it wound through the woods. It was fully dark now. Her family would start to worry soon.

She'd gone only a quarter of a mile when a bright light blossomed in the woods off to one side. Surprised, she stopped in her tracks. What on earth? A loud shot rang out, followed by thrashing, then silence. The light went out.

With her heart hammering in her chest, Lena ran the rest of the way home.

ISAAC BOWMAN KEPT his face carefully blank as he offered his hand to his ten-year-old daughter. Ruby ignored him and jumped down from the buggy. She moved quickly away and stood waiting with her eyes downcast, holding her erasable board clutched in front of her like a shield.

He couldn't suppress the sigh that escaped him. Would she ever look him in the eyes? Would she ever speak to him? A simple smile would be enough.

She looked so much like her mother with her red-gold hair pulled back beneath a white prayer *kapp*. She had the same sky-blue eyes, delicate arched eyebrows, even her mother's stubborn chin. He would forever see his first love in their daughter's face.

Today, Ruby wore her best Sunday dress and new shoes. It wasn't her normal school attire, but he hadn't objected when she came down from her room. He'd gently reminded her the shoes weren't broken in and would likely hurt her feet before the day was through. When she sat at the kitchen table without changing, he decided they would drive instead of walk the mile and a half to Forestview School.

As usual, he pretended her indifference didn't hurt. "First day at a new school, eh, Ruby? What do you think of it? It's bigger than your last schoolhouse, isn't it?"

She glanced at the building and nodded.

Isaac had so many hopes pinned on this change. Pulling up roots to leave his family and his community in Indiana went against the very fiber of his Amish being. A new home, a new job, a new school for his child, all his sacrifices in coming to Mount Hope, Ohio, would be worth it if only she would smile at him.

He shook off his somber thoughts. It was best not to dwell on what might come to pass. It was better to trust that the Lord would care for them both.

Smoke rose from the chimney of the tall, narrow schoolhouse. No horses or buggies stood at the hitching rails, but there were a dozen or more children playing outside. A small barn sat behind the school. Since he planned to spend the entire day at school, he decided to let his mare spend the day in relative comfort. He unhitched his horse and led her inside, to find a brown pony munching hay in one stall. Isaac placed his mare inside the other stall. The pair whinnied a greeting and sniffed noses over the stall divider. When Isaac came out, Ruby was exactly where he'd left her.

"Let's go in and meet your new teacher." He approached the door and held it open for Ruby. She didn't move.

He motioned with his head. "Come on. It won't get any easier standing out here in the cold."

Ruby reluctantly entered the building. Isaac gave silent thanks for one hurdle overcome as he followed her.

Inside, the school was much the same as the one he'd attended in his youth. The floor was plain wood planking, worn but clean. One window had a broken pane covered with cardboard. It would need fixing before the snow started. On the ceiling above it had a water stain that proved the roof had leaked at one time. Had it been repaired? As a new parent in the district, he would do his share to see that the building was kept in good condition.

A large blackboard covered the top two-thirds of the front wall. Below it hung numerous pictures drawn by childish hands. Squarely at the front sat a large, box-like wooden desk covered with books and papers. Four rows of wooden children's desks faced it. If every desk was filled, the school had twenty-three students. Tall windows on both sides of the room let in light, revealing the young woman adding wood to the firebox of a cast-iron stove.

His daughter's new teacher was small in stature. He

doubted the top of her head would come to his chin. Her brown hair was neatly tucked beneath a black prayer *kapp,* and the dress she wore was dark blue. A white apron was tied snugly around her tiny waist and reached the bottom of her hem.

She didn't glance up from her task. "I need the blackboard cleaned."

After closing the firebox door, she looked up with a bright smile that instantly vanished. She took a step back. "Oh."

Isaac removed his hat. "*Guder mariye.* I am Isaac Bowman."

"Good morning to you, too. I…I thought you were one of my students."

He indicated Ruby hiding behind him. "This is my daughter, Ruby. I've come to enroll her in school."

"I wasn't aware I was getting a new student."

"I wrote to my cousin, John Miller, the president of your school board. He told me it wouldn't be a problem. We didn't expect to arrive until next month, but we were able to get away sooner."

"I see." She looked flustered, and Isaac had to wonder why. It was rare for Amish children to change schools, but it did happen.

"There is a school board meeting a week from Friday night," she said. "Perhaps John planned to inform me then."

Isaac stepped forward and withdrew a thick envelope from his pocket. She took another step back, as if afraid of him. His size often intimidated people; he was used to it. He extended the papers. "These are Ruby's records from her old school outside of Shipshewana, Indiana."

The young woman seemed to recover herself and took the folder from him. "I am Lena Troyer, the schoolteacher here, as I'm sure you have guessed." She managed a tentative smile for his daughter. "What grade are you in, Ruby?"

She held up four fingers.

Lena's smile brightened. The sparkle in her green eyes triggered a burst of interest that caught him by surprise. She was a very pretty woman, and single.

He forced that fleeting notion from his mind and thought of his wife. Ada Mae had been kind and loving as well as pretty. Her death lay heavy on his conscience. He had no business showing interest in another woman.

Lena said, "Fourth grade? That's excellent, Ruby. That means I'll have two boys and two girls in your class now. I'll look at your records later, but can you tell me what subjects you enjoy?"

Isaac said, "Ruby doesn't speak. She hasn't spoken since her mother died three years ago."

Lena's eyes darkened with sympathy. "How sad for both of you."

She dropped to her knees, bringing her to Ruby's level. "I'm sorry to hear your mother has gone to heaven. I know you must miss her terribly. My mother has gone to heaven, too. I know she is happy with God, but I miss her every day."

Ruby tipped her head to the side as if surprised by her teacher's admission.

Lena Troyer understood his daughter's grief. Isaac studied her with growing respect.

Rising to her feet, Lena said, "You're in luck, Ruby. Today we're having a field trip. We are going into the woods to collect nuts from the shagbark hickory trees. Does that sound like fun?"

To Isaac's amazement, Ruby nodded vigorously. He

glanced at her new shoes and hoped she wouldn't have to walk far.

Lena folded her arms tightly across her middle as she faced him. "Ruby will be fine with us. I'll make sure the children understand that she doesn't speak and that she isn't to be treated differently because of it. She will be making friends in no time. I'll be happy to give you a report of her progress in a few days."

"I will stay today and see for myself how she does."

Lena pondered his statement and then nodded. "That will be fine. Excuse me, I must go and ring the bell."

He moved to the back of the room and sat down on a wooden bench. Ruby sat beside him. The door opened and the boys walked in together and took their seats on one side of the room. Next, groups of girls filed in. Their giggling stopped when they spotted him. They walked meekly to their desks, casting frequent looks in his direction. Lena went to the front of the room. "Good morning, children."

"Good morning, Lena," they replied in unison.

Lena's age might be closer to twenty-five than twenty, Isaac decided as he studied her openly. He had to wonder how much longer she would remain a teacher, since only unmarried Amish women held the position. Surely, those pretty green eyes hadn't gone unnoticed by the single men in her community. If they had, it was a shame.

LENA STRUGGLED TO KEEP her composure. She was painfully aware of Isaac Bowman's scrutiny. Her new student's father was the hunter whose shot she had spoiled the night before last. She hadn't gotten a good look at his face, but his size and his gravelly voice were unmistakable. Would he be angry if he discovered she was the culprit?

Of course, he had to be related to the president of the school board. How was that for rotten luck?

John Miller was a strict, pious man who often chided her for being too lenient with her students. Fortunately, the families of the community supported her teaching methods, but she could easily be replaced with a young woman who met John's standards if he wished to make trouble for her. Until this moment, she hadn't realized how much she wanted to keep her job.

It would be best if Isaac Bowman didn't learn she was responsible for chasing away his game.

Turning to the blackboard, she wrote out the date and the arithmetic assignments for each of the classes. All the while, she was acutely aware of Isaac's gaze. This promised to be a very long day.

She finished at the blackboard and picked up her Bible. Each day she chose a passage to read. This morning she'd selected Matthew 5. When she finished reading the Sermon on the Mount, the students all rose, clasped their hands together and repeated the Lord's Prayer in unison. It was the only religious part of the day, for Lena, like all Amish, believed that faith must be taught at home and in church, not at school.

After everyone took their seats, she said, "Children, we have a new student joining us."

She beckoned for Ruby to come forward. Slowly, the girl walked to the front with her eyes downcast. Taking her by the shoulders, Lena gently turned her to face the class. "This is Ruby Bowman. She's a fourth grader. She and her father have just moved to Mount Hope from Shipshewana, Indiana."

Lena knew a moment of envy as she thought about

the adventure of traveling to a new place, meeting new people, seeing new things. Her life was so very dull, except for the children she taught. Teaching a mute child would be a challenge. Was she up to it? With God's help, she would be.

Directing her attention to the classroom once more, she said, "I want everyone to pay close attention. Ruby is mute. That means she can't speak."

Fannie, a first grader in the front row, whispered, "Can you hear?"

Ruby nodded.

Lena said, "I want each of you to think about what it would be like if you couldn't talk or see or walk. God gives many people such lives, but he expects us to live and work to the best of our ability."

A hand went up in the back of the room. Twelve-year-old David said, "My *onkel* Henry was born deaf, but he learned to talk with his hands."

Lena smiled at him, then looked at the girl beside her. "David's uncle uses sign language. Ruby, do you sign?"

From the back, Ruby's father spoke up. "She writes on her erasable board when she has something she wants to say."

Lena would rather that he let Ruby answer, but could understand his anxiety at having his daughter in a new school. She was nervous, too, knowing Ruby's father was watching her every move. She looked over her students. "Does anyone else know someone who lives with special circumstances?"

Mary, a little blond second grader, said, "My sister Rebecca can't walk."

Some of the children giggled. Mary looked at them with a scowl. Keeping her own grin in check, Lena said, "She's only six months old, Mary. I'm sure she'll be walking one day soon."

"I hope so," Mary declared. "She's really heavy to tote."

A number of other children shared their stories about relatives with special needs. When they were through, Lena sent the two oldest boys to bring down a desk for Ruby. She said, "Be sure and take the one closest to the stairs."

When that was done, she said, "All right, it's time to start our wildcrafting morning."

Cheers met her announcement. Lena's cousin, Abigail Baughman, was a wildcrafter. Abby often shared her knowledge of plants with Lena in the circle letters they exchanged. Lena sometimes took her students on wildcrafting trips so that they could learn to identify helpful and harmful plants and mushrooms in the woodlands around their homes. Her students loved the outings. It was a much-anticipated break from their normal schoolwork.

Lena had the older girls hand out baskets, and soon everyone was ready to go. As they headed for the door, Ruby hung back, staying close to Lena. Taking her hand, Lena smiled and winked.

Isaac fell into step beside them. "I hope this isn't a long hike."

Surprised by his comment, she said, "You are welcome to wait for us in the school. We'll be back by noon."

He shook his head in silence. When the children crossed the bridge and turned off the road into the dense woods, he spoke again. "I passed a grove of shagbark on the way here. Surely, staying on the road would make easier walking."

Lena couldn't help wondering why he was so concerned about their path. "This is a shortcut to the grove. The children know their way around these woods. It's not far."

After a twenty-minute hike through the dense forest, Lena noticed the trees were thinning. She waited as all the children walked out into a small clearing. The grove of shagbark trees stood on the other side of it. A quick count of her students as they walked past proved she hadn't lost anyone.

Suddenly, a flock of crows took flight out of the clearing, cawing and screeching in displeasure. She heard a gasp from several of the students ahead of her.

The children had stopped walking and were huddled around something on the ground. Unable to see what had upset them, Lena let go of Ruby's hand and pushed through the ring of students.

They were gathered around the body of a dead deer. She saw at once that it hadn't died of natural causes. Its head was missing.

CHAPTER TWO

SARAH, ONE OF LENA'S eighth-grade students, broke the stunned silence. "Who would do such a thing?"

Lena knew the girl wasn't upset about the death of the deer. Like all her classmates, she lived on a farm where animals were slaughtered for food on a regular basis. It was a part of everyday life. She was appalled at the wanton waste of meat. Only the head of the deer had been taken. The rest of the animal had been left to rot.

"It must have been a poacher," David declared, disgust thick in his voice.

"But why?" Little Fannie clearly didn't understand.

Isaac said, "Because the head of a buck with big antlers is worth a lot of money."

Lena looked at him in surprise. "Who pays money for such a thing?"

"*Englische* who want to hang the heads on their walls," he answered. *Englische* or English, was the Amish term for anyone not of their faith.

Lena crouched to examine the animal. From the size of the deer she feared it was Goliath. When she saw a deep scar across the animal's shoulder, she knew it wasn't. It was one of his rivals, a buck she called Snagglehead for his unusually thick antlers that grew downward instead of up. She had sketched him a few times and noticed the scar then.

David's younger brother, Reuben, said, "I've seen

pictures in the hunting magazines of heads for sale, but deer season doesn't open for another month."

Isaac glanced around the woods. "I reckon this fellow didn't want to wait. We should go on in case he comes back."

Fannie asked, "Why would he? The meat's no good now."

He looked at the child. "The man or men who did this are criminals. They may come back to hide the evidence of their crime."

David's and Reuben's eyes lit with eagerness. "Will the *Englische* sheriff arrest them?" David asked.

Isaac shrugged. "Perhaps. The local game warden will surely investigate if he hears of this. We should leave now. It may not be safe."

Lena looked at him in disbelief. "You think we are in danger?"

"I think this is bad *Englische* business and none of ours."

A chill of fright spread through Lena at his tone. She said, "Let's go back, children. We will save our nut gathering for another day."

She took the lead and kept a sharp lookout as they retraced their steps. Before they had gone two dozen yards, a glint of sunlight reflected off something beside the trail. She held up one hand. "Children, wait here."

She moved to look more closely at the object. It was a camouflaged box secured to the trunk of a tree. Isaac came to her side. She glanced at him. "Do you know what this is?"

He stroked his reddish-brown beard with one hand. She noticed for the first time that his eyes were hazel and rimmed with thick lashes. At the moment, they brimmed with worry. He said, "It's a camera."

"Strapped to a tree in the middle of the woods? Why?"

He bent to examine it. "Hunters use them to photograph wildlife, especially deer. When something walks down this trail it triggers the camera to snap a photograph."

"Did it take our pictures?"

His lips thinned to a narrow line. "I reckon so. Who owns this land?"

"An *Englische* fellow named Wilfred Cummings. I can't see him tramping through the woods to put up a camera. He's ninety-five if he's a day. He recently had a stroke and his granddaughter has come to look after him. I do know he would never allow hunting on his property. He's fond of the deer and doesn't let anyone hunt them, for my father has asked him several times."

Isaac rose to his feet. "Might be the poacher used this to find where and when the deer are moving. There may be cameras on other game trails."

Lena stepped away from the box. She had a bad feeling about this. If the camera had taken their pictures, then the person who killed Snagglehead would know they had seen the body.

She slanted a quick glance at Isaac. Then again, she could be talking to the poacher right now. It went against her Amish upbringing to suspect any man of wrongdoing, but so many things pointed in that direction.

She'd seen Isaac with a gun less than half an hour before she'd seen the bright light and heard the shot two nights ago. He knew a lot about poachers and their equipment. He'd even objected to them walking this way, and had tried to get her to stick to the roadway. Was that because he knew what they might find?

He leaned close and said quietly, "I think it best we don't mention this to your students. We don't want them coming back to investigate after school and walking into trouble."

A shiver ran up her spine. Suddenly, the woods no longer felt friendly and welcoming, but dark and ominous. She walked quickly back to the children.

Isaac picked up Ruby and carried her. The child pushed at him to put her down, but he ignored her. Lena noticed he kept scanning the forest around them. He was as uneasy as she was. A sign of guilt...or worry for their safety? He motioned to her with his head. "Come, let us return to school."

The normally cheerful children followed him quietly. Did they sense the unease that made the hair on the back of Lena's neck prickle? She brought up the rear of the group to make sure no one fell behind or wandered off. When they reached the road she felt better, but she didn't feel completely safe until all her students were back inside the school.

The children took their seats and waited for her instructions. Isaac put Ruby down and moved to the back of the room. This time he took a spot by the window, where he could look outside and watch the lane leading to the school.

Lena addressed the classes. "Since our field trip was cut short, let's do some singing."

Songs were a normal part of each school day. The children filed to the front of the room and lined up in their assigned places. Ruby stood to one side, not knowing where to go. Lena beckoned to her. Slowly, she came forward, walking as if her feet were sticking to the floor. Lena's heart went out to her. If the child couldn't talk, she certainly couldn't join in the singing.

Slipping her arm over Ruby's shoulders, Lena leaned close and offered her the *Unpartheyisches Gesang-Buch,* their German songbook. "It's Monday and we sing German songs on Monday. How would you like to pick our songs today? Do you have a favorite?"

Ruby took the book and turned the pages carefully. She stopped and pointed to a song. Lena smiled. *"'Kinder, woltt ihr Jesus lieben.'* I like that one, too. We will sing 'Children Want to Love You, Jesus.'"

Singing without accompaniment, the children blended their voices in a sweet rendition of the chosen work. When the hymn was done, Ruby selected two more songs. After they finished singing, the students went back to their seats and began working on their mathematics without urging from Lena.

She was pleased to see Ruby had a good grasp of her basics and needed no special help. With the upper grades quietly engaged, Lena gathered the first graders in a small group beside her desk where they could practice their oral reading skills.

Like all Amish children, they came to school speaking only Pennsylvania *Deitsh,* a German dialect outsiders often called Pennsylvania Dutch. English was the language of business and life outside the Amish home. It was essential that children learn to speak and write it. To that end, only English was spoken at school. Lena reverted to speaking German only when a pupil didn't understand what she was saying.

She tried to listen to each child intently, but it was impossible to ignore Isaac Bowman at the back of her classroom. His size alone made him conspicuous, and her gaze was constantly drawn in his direction.

Lena raised one eyebrow in query now, and he shook

his head. Nothing out of the ordinary was going on outside.

As the morning progressed, she began to relax. Isaac was right. The poaching was bad *Englische* business, but it had nothing to do with them. The poacher had his prize. It was sad, but there was nothing to be done about it.

Still, Lena couldn't quell the part of her that hoped the wrongdoer would be punished for his crime. It would be unwise on her part to get involved. She certainly couldn't go in person, but a letter to the authorities detailing what she'd seen might spur them to investigate. Should she write such a letter?

What if the poacher wasn't *Englische,* but Amish? If that was the case, and her letter brought trouble for someone of her faith, the church elders would surely chastise her, perhaps even shun her if she didn't admit that she'd done wrong.

Was it a risk she was willing to take? Snagglehead didn't deserve to have his life ended in such a meaningless fashion. More of the animals she loved might die for the same reason if she didn't speak out. She nibbled at her lower lip as she considered what she would do.

When noon arrived, she dismissed the children for lunch and recess. She sat down to grade some papers, assuming Isaac would follow his daughter outside. When she looked up from stacking the first-grade reading books in a neat pile on her desk, he was standing in front of her. How did he move so quietly, a man his size?

"You did well with Ruby this morning. *Danki.*" The deep quality of his voice sent tingles over her skin. He smelled of fresh cut wood and linseed oil, with a subtle underlying masculine scent all his own.

She looked down and carefully aligned the edges of

the books. "All students have special needs and special gifts given to them by our Father in heaven. I simply try to uncover those gifts and fulfill those needs."

"I can see your gift is teaching children."

She felt a blush rising at his compliment. "I'd like to think so."

"How long have you been a teacher?"

"This is my fourth year." She met his gaze and lifted her chin. She wasn't new or untried at the task, if that was what he was thinking.

"Ah." A small grin twitched at the corner of his mouth. "Reckon that means you'll be giving it up soon to raise children of your own."

"If God wills it."

Lena saw a shadow of sadness fill his eyes. "Yes, we must all accept what God wills. Spoken like a devout Amish *maidel*."

A maiden, yes, but not so devout as she should be. While it was true that Amish teachers were normally young unmarried women who left the job when they wed, she didn't have to worry about that. There were no young men wanting to court her. At least, none she would consider marrying. The men she knew were all so boring. One thing she didn't want out of life was a humdrum husband.

She dreamed of romance and adventure, like the heroines in the books she kept hidden in the school attic. Like the stories her cousins Abby Baughman and Sarah Weaver shared in the circle letters the three of them exchanged.

The women, Lena's second cousins, lived in distant parts of Ohio and Pennsylvania. When the three of them met at a wedding in Union County, Pennsylvania, they became fast friends. Since that time, they'd kept circle letters going between them.

Lena's letter went to Abby, who added her news and sent both letters on to Sarah. Sarah, in turn, added her letter and mailed all three to Lena. After catching up on what was happening with her cousins, each reader would discard her old letter and add a new one before sending it on, so that all read the exact same news. Her cousins' letters were full of excitement.

Last fall, Abby had helped a man newly returned to the faith clear his name following a jewelry theft. Her last letter had been full of comments about Ben Kline.

Then last spring, her cousin Sarah had discovered the dead body of her *Englische* employer at the foot of his staircase. While everyone believed it was an accidental death, Sarah hadn't been convinced. With the help of her longtime friend Jacob Mast she'd proved it was murder and uncovered the killer's identity. To Lena's surprise, Sarah's last letter spoke of wedding plans with Jacob. It seemed that their friendship had matured into love. Everything her cousins wrote about was thrilling.

Lena knew her own life was dull in comparison. At least she would have this morning's events to include in her next letter. Discovering there was a poacher in the area wasn't as thrilling as solving a murder, but it was more excitement than she had known in her whole life.

Lena glanced up at Isaac. He believed she was a proper Amish maiden, the kind of woman he wanted teaching his daughter. But she could feel the weight of the Amish romance novels she had stashed in the school attic pressing down on her conscience. She made up her mind to return them to her English friend Clara as soon as possible.

It was time she made a real commitment to her faith

and paid more attention to the teachings of Bishop Abram and to the *Ordnung,* the rules of her church.

Isaac Bowman appeared to be a devoted Amish father. Judging from his daughter's clothing and shoes, he was a man of some means. Was he a craftsman, a prosperous farmer or a poacher?

How had his wife died? Why were his eyes full of sadness when they rested on his daughter? Was it because she didn't speak or was it something else? Why had he chosen this community?

There were a great many things Lena wanted to know about the stranger who stood on the other side of her desk. Such as why her insides fluttered wildly when he came close, and why she suddenly felt compelled to live up to the expectations of what an Amish maiden should be.

But what if he *was* a poacher? She couldn't possibly be attracted to a man like that.

Not that I am attracted to him. Nay, I am not.

Lena rejected the idea and called upon her common sense. How could such a thing be possible? She'd only just met the man. Yet for some reason he set her pulse racing when he drew near. Like now.

Lena realized with a start that she had spent far too much time alone with Isaac. She shot to her feet. "I must go and check on the children."

She rushed toward the front door, wondering how she was going to get through the rest of the day knowing he was watching her every move.

Outside, the younger children were at play on the swings, while the older ones had divided themselves up into teams for a softball game. Ruby was sitting by herself, leaning against the side of the small barn across the schoolyard. Lena's heart went out to the little girl, who seemed so alone and withdrawn.

Lena's students were siblings and cousins from a close-knit community, but she expected them to include Ruby in their play. It was the right thing to do, and the children knew it. She beckoned to Katie Gingerich, another of her eighth-grade students.

"Katie, I'm surprised at you. Why is Ruby sitting by herself?"

"We all asked her to join us. Sarah even sat with her for a while, but Ruby wrote 'go away' on her board."

Lena frowned. Getting the girl to feel comfortable in her new school was going to be more difficult than she'd thought. "I'm sorry for doubting you, Katie. I should've known you had more Christian charity in your heart. I will speak with Ruby and see if I can find out what's wrong."

ISAAC WATCHED LENA SIT beside his daughter as he came down the front steps of the school. The new teacher seemed to have Ruby's best interests at heart, unlike her last one.

Instead of encouraging Ruby, her former teacher had often punished her for refusing to read aloud or sing with the other children. She didn't stop them from teasing Ruby or making fun of her, and had defended her actions by saying Ruby needed to be shamed out of her silence. Her attitude was the last straw that finally convinced him he needed to take his daughter somewhere new.

Someplace where people didn't know the story of her mother's death.

He was fortunate that his cousin had found them a house to rent outside the village. John had even offered to let Isaac continue his craft as a wood-carver in John's furniture business. Isaac wasn't overly fond of his stoic older cousin, but the man had a shrewd head for business and a firm belief that family was second only to God in his life. His help was a blessing Isaac couldn't afford to turn down.

Since Lena was occupied with Ruby, Isaac crossed the schoolyard and entered the barn to feed his horse. Sophie was standing patiently in her stall with her head down and her eyes half-closed. Her ears perked up when Isaac held out the feedbag, and she quickly buried her nose in the oats. As Sophie munched, Isaac realized he could hear Lena's voice through the open window.

"Ruby, can you tell me why you won't play with the other children? I know that they asked you to join their ball game."

There was silence as Ruby wrote out her answer. After a minute, Lena spoke again, "'They don't like me.' Is that what you think? You think none of these children like you. *Nay,* I think it is the other way around. I think you don't like them."

Isaac frowned. It wasn't what he'd expected Lena to say.

CHAPTER THREE

LENA REMAINED QUIET, and Isaac assumed his daughter was writing a reply to her comment. A few seconds later, the teacher said, "So, you agree that you don't like any of the children here. Not any?"

What would the young woman make of that? He leaned closer to hear what she had to say.

"You must have a reason to dislike someone. Why do you dislike Mary?"

Lena gave a deep sigh. "*Nay*, Ruby, a shrug of the shoulders is not an answer. You must explain to me why you don't like each child here at school. You may think about it and write about it tonight. Tomorrow, I will read your reasons. If they are sound, I will accept that you don't like anyone here, and no one will ask you to play with them again. If your reasons aren't sound, we will talk about it."

Again there was silence. Had Lena walked away? He frowned. He wasn't sure he approved of this. He was about to leave the barn when he heard Lena speak again. "You don't like Mary because she has a baby sister and you don't."

Isaac hadn't realized Ruby wanted sisters and brothers. He had been content with her as his only child. He hadn't stopped to think how she might feel about his failure to remarry.

Lena said, "The fact that Mary has a sister and you

don't is a true statement, but she can't help that. You are mistaken when you say you don't like her because of that. You are jealous of her because she has something you don't."

After a few moments of quiet, Lena added, "Jealousy and dislike are two different things. Birds can fly and I can't. I wish I could. It would make getting home easier. I may be jealous that they have the gift of flight and I don't, but I don't dislike birds because I must walk. They're beautiful creatures. Do you understand? No? All right, why do you dislike David?"

After a second, Lena laughed. "You're thinking. I imagine you do a lot of that, Ruby Bowman. Think about it after school, because now it's time to go back to class."

Isaac came out of the barn to see Lena headed toward the bell rope that would sound the end of recess. Ruby was still sitting beside the barn. She looked at him and then at Lena. Leaning over, Ruby wrote on her board and held it up to him. It said, "I like her."

A heavy weight lifted from his heart. It wasn't much, but it was a start. He said, "I like her, too."

He held out his hand to help his daughter up. Ruby pointedly ignored his offer and jumped to her feet. She ran to the schoolhouse, where Lena stood watching them.

So he wasn't forgiven. He wiped at the sudden moisture in his eyes. Why did his daughter reject him at every turn?

Isaac took small comfort from the fact that he'd seen the first crack in the wall Ruby had built between them. Perhaps his brother had been right about this move. Perhaps a new start was exactly what she needed.

When Isaac regained his composure, he followed

the children into the school. Lena again glanced in his direction. He pretended to be studying the ceiling so she wouldn't see the tears that weren't quite dry. When she came toward him, he gestured upward. "Has anyone been up in the attic recently?"

Her eyes grew round. She blushed a fierce shade of red and stammered, "Wh-why do you ask?"

LENA KNEW HER FACE was beet-red, but she couldn't help it. She laced her fingers together and squeezed until they ached. It seemed she must confess her interference with his hunting, after all—and in front of her students.

Before she gathered enough nerve to speak, he said, "I ask because I see a water stain on your ceiling. Has anyone checked out the leak or repaired it?"

She folded her arms tightly and stared at her shoes. "To my knowledge, no one has been up there to look for water damage recently."

"I'll go up after school. No point in letting it get worse."

"That won't be necessary," she said quickly. "I intend to bring it to John Miller's attention at the board meeting next Friday night. He likes to stay informed about the school's needs. I'm sure he'll be okay with you making a repair, but I feel he should make that decision. If you'll excuse me, I have classes to teach." Lena rushed away, hoping Isaac hadn't noticed her odd reaction to his question.

Three-thirty finally arrived, and Lena dismissed her students. She watched from the steps of the building as Isaac and Ruby drove away. The daughter was an endearing if challenging special child, but the father was a different story.

Isaac Bowman was disturbing yet attractive. Lena

didn't know what to make of him or her reaction to him. She'd never experienced such a jumble of emotions in a man's company.

When their buggy entered the covered bridge and was lost from sight, Lena rushed back inside and up the narrow stairwell to the attic. She gathered her favorite romance novels from inside one of the unused school desks. She would return them to her friend Clara Jenkins on the way home. Clara and her husband lived on the farm across the road from her home.

Lena's guilty conscience prompted her to make sure no one was about before she went downstairs. She paused to peer out the small dusty window that provided the attic's only light. All the children were gone and there was no sign of Isaac's buggy. She'd started to turn away when a movement at the edge of the forest caught her eye.

Two men in camouflaged clothing rose from their hiding place behind a clump of bushes and disappeared into the woods.

Gooseflesh broke out on Lena's arms. She quickly pulled away from the window. Why was someone watching the school? Was it the poachers? Did they mean her harm?

Cowering in the gloom, she sought strength as her father had taught her to do from the time she was small. She whispered Psalm 27:1 aloud. "The Lord is my light and my salvation; whom shall I fear? The Lord is the strength of my life; of whom shall I be afraid?"

Slowly, her fear subsided and her common sense returned. If they wished her harm, they would come to the school, for it must be obvious she was alone. Instead, they'd merely watched from a distance and left.

Perhaps they hadn't been watching the school at all.

Perhaps they had merely been resting, and only happened to stand up while she was looking.

Reassured by her logical explanations, Lena gathered her courage and went downstairs. She grabbed her cloak, wrapped herself in it and hurried down the path to the covered bridge. When she reached the far side, she paused in the shadows to check the edge of the woods. Nothing moved. She left the safety of the bridge and hurried along the road, but couldn't help glancing over her shoulder numerous times until she reached Clara's farm. Only then did she feel safe.

Clara Jenkins was a teacher in the township's public school. Sometimes Lena envied the fact that Clara had only one grade to teach instead of eight. Clara's husband had worked at a local sawmill, but he, like many others, had been laid off when the mill went bankrupt. For now, the couple was scraping by on Clara's salary. Lena helped her friends by bringing them fresh produce from the garden and fresh baked goodies from her kitchen. When she refused to take any money, Clara began loaning her books.

"Honey, what's the matter?" Clara was standing in the yard shaking out a throw rug.

Lena stopped and drew a deep breath. She held out the books. "Nothing's wrong. I'm just in a rush to get home, and I wanted to drop these by first."

Her friend smiled and came to the white rail fence that bordered her yard. "Did you finish them already? They aren't due back to the library until next week."

"I finished one of them, but I decided to return them all. You know my church does not allow us to read such books."

Clara's smile faded. Deep concern filled her dark

eyes. "Did someone catch you with them? I'm so sorry if I got you in trouble."

Shaking her head, Lena said, "No one saw them. I realized that it's important to follow all the rules of my faith rather than just the ones that are easy for me."

"But you haven't been baptized. You aren't bound by those rules yet."

"I will be baptized one day soon. I need to know in my heart that I'm ready to accept the path God asks me to travel."

"When you say it like that, I see your point. However, I'm going to miss discussing them with you."

Lena grasped Clara's hand. "We will find new things to talk about. You are not my friend *only* because you loan me books. Has Brad found a job yet?"

She shook her head. "He's been everywhere within a fifty-mile radius and hasn't had any luck. Lately, I'm starting to worry. It's like he's given up. All he's doing this week is hanging out with some high school friends who've been laid off, too. I guess everyone is struggling."

"God will smile on Brad's efforts, I'm sure of it."

"I hope you're right. Let's not talk about our hard luck. What's new with you?"

Lena considered telling her about the dead deer and the men watching the school, but decided against it. Clara was her friend, but still an outsider. It was better to talk about ordinary things. "I have a new student. Her name is Ruby Bowman and she is mute. She and her father recently moved here."

"Mute, but not deaf?"

"*Ja*. Her hearing is fine. Her father said she hasn't spoken since her mother died. I'm afraid she's going to be a handful to teach."

Clara playfully punched Lena's shoulder. "You're up to the task. You're a natural-born teacher. So the father is a widower. How interesting. Is he good-looking?"

Lena folded her arms and managed a mock glare. "That has nothing to do with his daughter's ability to learn."

"He *is* good-looking! Ah, I smell romance in the air." Smiling brightly, Clara rubbed her hands together.

"Don't be ridiculous. You've been reading too many of those books. I only met the man today."

"Love can happen in a single glance. I knew the first time I saw Brad that he was the one."

Lena took a step closer and lowered her voice. "Did you? How could you be so sure without knowing what kind of man he was?"

"People will say it's crazy, but I knew because when he looked at me...I went all jittery inside."

"Like nervous butterflies in your stomach, only worse?"

"Yes!"

Lena shook her head. "It has to be more than that. Love can only come after knowing a man for many months, even years."

Clara smiled. "Oh, I agree that love must grow over the years in order to be the real thing, but sometimes it starts with a sparkling glance. So what's his name?"

"Who?" Lena pretended ignorance.

"Don't give me that. You know who I mean. The man that makes you jittery inside when he looks at you."

"I don't know anyone like that."

"Play coy, it won't matter. Let me rephrase my question. What is Ruby's father's name?"

"Isaac. Isaac Bowman." The name rolled off Lena's tongue easily and brought a tiny smile to her lips. She quickly suppressed it. Clearly, she was the one who'd been reading too many books. No wonder her church discouraged such things.

Isaac Bowman might also be a poacher. Taking two steps back, she said, "I should get home. Goodbye, Clara."

Leaving was the only way to avoid further questions from her friend.

On her way home, Lena looked back only once to see if she was being followed, and saw no one. Still, she couldn't shake the feeling that she was being watched.

CHAPTER FOUR

TWO DAYS LATER, Isaac stood in the doorway of John Miller's office located at the back of his furniture store and factory. The familiar odors of fresh cut wood, varnish and lemon-scented wax filled Isaac with a desire to pick up his tools and get to work.

John sat behind a large metal desk with a heavy ledger open in front of him. Isaac was surprised by how much his cousin had aged in the few years since they had seen each other. Worry lines creased his forehead and frown lines bracketed his mouth.

"Am I interrupting?" Isaac asked.

John looked up from his accounts. "Isaac! I wasn't expecting you until next month."

"When the landlord you found for me wrote to say the house was ready, I decided to come early."

John closed the ledger, slipped it into the drawer and rose to his feet. He extended his hand. "It's mighty *gut* to see you, early or not."

Returning his hearty handshake, Isaac grinned. "I was wondering if I might set up shop today? I don't need much room. Just enough for my tools and a workbench."

"I have more than enough room for you here. We are not so busy as we once were before the local mill closed. Now we must get our wood from farther away. The price of shipping goes up and my profits go down."

Isaac frowned. "I hope my being here won't make things harder for you."

John shook his head. "You are family. There is no hardship in helping someone in need, especially if they are family. Besides, your mother tells me your skill as a master wood-carver has brought you much business. I'm hoping the folks who come to buy your work will also buy some of mine."

Isaac smiled. "That is my hope, as well."

John sat down at his desk again. "Make yourself at home and start work as soon as you want."

"*Gut.* I have orders for two fireplace mantels and four corbels that need to be shipped by early next week. How does the bishop here feel about using the internet for our businesses?"

"I have an *Englische* woman who takes our phone and internet orders and posts pictures of our pieces to a website that she runs for me. The bishop has no objection as long as it is handled by her and not by my Amish employees. Where is Ruby?"

"At school."

"Is she better? Your wife's death was sad business."

Isaac's throat tightened. Even now he found it hard to talk about the tragedy. "Ruby still doesn't speak, but I think she will do well in her new school. The teacher seems to have a gift for helping her fit in."

"You've met Lena Troyer?"

"*Ja,* I took Ruby to school the day before yesterday and spent the day there."

John crossed his arms over his chest. "I haven't had a chance to tell Lena you were coming. Was she upset?"

"She was surprised, but she took it in stride." Isaac

was pleased with the way she had handled his daughter. He felt comfortable knowing Ruby would be under her care.

John's scowl deepened. "Lena was not my first choice for our teacher. She is much too lax with the children. They need discipline at school as well as at home. Let me know if you feel she isn't doing her job. I have someone else in mind for the position, if need be."

Isaac kept silent. If Lena lost her job, it wouldn't be from something he said.

The outside door of the shop opened just then and two men in suits entered. John's face paled when he saw them.

Isaac sensed his cousin's alarm. "John, who are they?"

"Moneylenders come for their pound of flesh."

Shocked, Isaac asked, "Is your business in such dire straits?"

He pulled himself up straight. "It was, but I have collected some outstanding debts, and I will be fine now. Excuse me, cousin. I must speak to these men privately."

Isaac left John with his unwelcome visitors and went outside for his tools. A group of tourists were busy snapping pictures of his horse and buggy tied up in front of the store. He kept his face turned away and held up his hand to signal that he didn't want them taking his photograph. The group immediately lowered their cameras and moved off.

A voice behind Isaac said, "They're a polite bunch for outsiders. Don't turn around, brother. I'd rather we aren't seen together."

Surprised by the odd request from someone he wasn't expecting to see, Isaac pulled his tool chest from the back of the buggy without looking at his youngest brother. "I didn't know you planned to be in Mount Hope, Samuel."

"I didn't. When I suggested that you move here, I had no idea I'd be coming, too. But I go where the action is, and right now the action is here. How's Ruby?"

After glancing about to see who was near, Isaac moved to his horse and lifted her front foot as if to check her shoe. "Ruby is much the same. I take it this is not a social visit?"

"Nope. Just business."

"It is dangerous business you do, Samuel. You must take care." Isaac lowered his mare's foot and patted her shoulder.

"Always."

Isaac glanced toward their cousin's business. "Does John know you are in town?"

"No. I doubt he'd recognize me, but I'd rather he didn't know. The fewer people who do, the safer I'll be."

Isaac adjusted a strap on Sophie's headstall. "I understand, but I don't like it."

"I don't like it, either, but this is the way it has to be for now. Don't go out late at night, big brother. I wouldn't want you to get hurt."

Isaac heard a door open, followed by the musical chime of a bell that belonged to the hardware store next to John's business. A cigarette butt was flung between Isaac's boots, followed by harsh laughter. The sound of footsteps faded away. He stepped on the butt to put out the smoldering end. Only then did he look to see where his brother had gone.

Samuel had joined two other men Isaac had never seen before. His brother was right about one thing. Isaac doubted John would recognize him. Samuel was dressed in faded jeans and a gray corduroy jacket, his hair long and shaggy beneath a red ball cap. A short dark beard and mustache altered the look of his face. If Isaac hadn't heard Samuel speak, he might not have recognized him, either.

The three men got into a late-model pickup and drove out of town. Isaac watched them leave with a heavy heart. Samuel had left the Amish faith instead of choosing to be baptized. His decision had shocked and saddened the family. What had he gotten himself into now?

"TEACHER, TEACHER, my brother and me seen another deer with its head cut off." Eli Miller's breathless announcement made everyone in the school turn to look in his direction.

It was the third such occurrence in the past week. When would it end? When the last buck had been slaughtered? Lena had no idea if Goliath was still among the living. She hadn't seen him since the poaching started, and she still didn't know who was responsible. Was it Isaac?

Eli ran up the center aisle with his twin brother, Marvin, close on his heels. They were seventh-grade students and overly eager to be done with schooling. Lena scowled at them. "That is not how we enter the school building. Take your seats. You are both tardy."

"We had to stop and check if the poachers were still about," Marvin declared.

"Did you see them?" Katie asked. "I heard shooting again last night. That's the third time this week. I don't know how anyone can hunt in the dark."

Eli slid into his seat. "My dad works with Isaac Bowman in John Miller's shop. Isaac told my dad that they use spotlights. The deer just freeze when a bright light hits them, and it's like shooting fish in a barrel."

Lena remembered the bright light in the woods and the sound of gunfire the first night she'd seen Isaac. Once again she thought it was odd how much Ruby's father knew about poaching. Was it merely a coincidence that his arrival had coincided with the start of these activities?

Daily, he'd been bringing Ruby to school and staying briefly to chat. Lena wasn't sure what to make of his behavior. Surely he could see Ruby was settling in.

She glanced at the child. Like the rest of the students, Ruby was staring at Eli and hanging on his every word. Did she know anything about her father's activities at night? Lena tried to think of a way to phrase the question without having it sound like an accusation, but nothing came to her.

If Isaac was involved in something illegal, Lena realized there was little she could do about it. Her only acceptable option would be to tell the bishop of her suspicions. But suspicions were not proof of wrongdoing. If she had proof, that would be another story. Even then, nothing was likely to be done. Isaac had not yet joined their church. The bishop had no authority over him.

To go outside of the church and inform the local *Englische* authorities would only get her in hot water with her family and the bishop. Such a thing was not done unless the church elders made the decision. Lena couldn't see them putting the lives of a few deer ahead of the deeply held Amish belief that they must live separate from the world.

If these crimes were to be reported, it would have to be by someone from outside the Amish community.

There were only a few *Englische* families in this rural and predominately Amish part of Ohio. Most of them lived in the nearby towns. Lena considered telling Clara about the poaching and asking her to report it, but decided against confiding in her friend. Clara had enough troubles of her own. The last thing Lena wanted to do was add to them.

The obvious choice was to speak with Wilfred Cummings about what she had seen. It was on his land that deer were being poached. It seemed strange that a man who disliked hunting of any kind would ignore gunfire on his property at night, but maybe his advanced age or his recent stroke had robbed him of his hearing. Perhaps he had already informed the authorities and an investigation was under way. She prayed it was so.

Eli gave a huge sigh. "I hope the poachers leave some deer for my *daad* to hunt. *Mamm* makes wonderful venison stew."

Marvin folded his arms tightly. "If I see them, I'm going to tell them to go hunt someplace else."

Lena immediately dismissed her concerns about reporting the crimes, and focused on her responsibilities to the children. "If you see them, Marvin, you are not to speak to them. I want all of you to be especially careful coming to and from school. I don't want anyone taking shortcuts through the woods, and I certainly don't want anyone going to look for these men. They may be dangerous."

The obstinate set of Marvin's chin drooped. "You sound like my *mamm*."

Lena leveled a stern look in his direction. "Your mother is a wise woman, and is to be obeyed. Shall I mention this conversation to her?"

Marvin sank a little lower in his seat. "No."

"All right, enough about poachers. It's time for school to begin."

Lena opened her Bible and began the day as always.

When she was finished reading and prayers were over, the students filed to the front of the room and lined up to sing some of their favorite English songs. Ruby stood with the other children in her class and mouthed the words, but no sound emerged from her throat. After the singing, the classes began to work quietly on their assignments.

While they did, Lena had a few free minutes to prepare for the school board meeting to be held that night. Other than the leak in the roof and the broken windowpane, the building itself didn't need much work. The barn was another story.

The hayloft door had broken free of a hinge and now threatened to fall from the remaining one. It posed a threat to animals and students alike. Several shingles had come loose, too. With the arrival of Ruby, Lena was now short of textbooks. Ruby was sharing with another fourth-grade girl, but it would be better if she had her own books.

None of the children were discipline problems. If it weren't for the poaching, Lena would consider this to be her easiest year. The school board meeting might not be the best place to discuss the subject of poaching, but the three men on the board were also fathers and grandfathers of the children. Two were church elders. The meetings were always well attended by the children's parents. The women of the community couldn't hold positions on the board, but they made their voices heard at home and in such meetings. It might be good to plant the seed of concern, for these men would be the ones to sanction any action.

During the last period of the day, Lena set the students to tidying up the school for the upcoming meeting. The windows were washed inside and out by the eighth-grade girls. The boys cleaned up the grounds and raked the leaves that had piled against the sides of the building. Ruby and several of the other girls washed and dried the blackboard, while the twins took the erasers outside and clapped them together until they were free of chalk dust.

When the school was as clean as they could make it, Lena allowed the students to leave a few minutes early. As they cheerfully headed home, she came to a decision. Tonight, she would mention what she'd seen in the woods, and voice her concern for the children's welfare.

Outside, she paused on the steps to scan the edge of the forest, as she had done frequently during the past weeks. Nothing moved, nothing seemed out of place. If anyone was watching the school, he remained well hidden.

Walking quickly, she crossed the covered bridge. On the far side, she discovered Ruby sitting on the bank of the creek. The child was bent over her writing board, hard at work on something.

"Ruby, what are you doing here?" Lena said.

She instantly hid her board behind her back and shook her head.

Lena gathered her skirt and sat beside the child. "May I see what you're working on?"

Ruby slowly brought out her board. On it, she had drawn the outline of a small rabbit sitting among the weeds beside the bridge. The drawing was crude, but Lena saw some underlying skill in its composition.

"This is very nice."

Ruby shook her head and immediately smeared the picture with her hands.

"Oh, don't spoil it." Lena held the board out of the child's reach. "Let me have your marker."

Reluctantly, Ruby handed it over. With careful strokes, Lena repaired the missing ears and added a happy expression to the bunny's face. "There, I've fixed him."

Taking back the board and marker, Ruby wrote under the drawing, "It's a girl."

Lena smiled. "Sorry. I didn't know. Let me have the pen again." Taking the board and marker, Lena scooted around to hide her effort until she was finished. Then she said, "Now, all can tell it's a girl."

She held the picture up. The rabbit wore an Amish bonnet with the ribbons tied in a bow under her neck. Her ears protruded through holes on the top.

Ruby smothered a giggle, with her hand over her mouth. It was the first sound Lena had heard her make.

"Do you like it?" she asked, and Ruby nodded.

Returning to the board, Lena sketched a somber rabbit in a black hat with a pained expression above his bushy beard. "Frau Rabbit must have a husband. The poor fellow suffers from a sour stomach."

Ruby took the board from Lena and studied it. After a few seconds, she wrote beneath the picture, "How do you do that?"

"How do I give them expressions? It's easy." She drew five circles along the bottom of the board. In the first one, she added eyes, nose and a mouth with a small smile. In the second, she placed eyes that were slightly narrowed with a crease between them, and a flat mouth that turned down at the ends.

Handing the board to Ruby, she said, "You make a sad face in the next circle."

The girl bent over the sketch with fierce concentration. She tried several times to make a sad face, but was unhappy with each attempt and rubbed all of them out. On the board, she wrote, "I can't do it."

"It takes practice. No one bakes a perfect pie on their first try. I'll draw some examples and you can practice copying them." Soon Lena had filled in the remaining circles with an astonished face and a sad one.

The next hour flew by as the two sat side by side drawing artwork that included flowers, grass and the schoolhouse on the hill. It wasn't until a buggy turned off the roadway and came toward them that Lena realized how late it was getting.

The buggy came to a stop beside them. Isaac held the lines with a look of intense worry on his face. "Ruby, you should have been home long ago. What are you doing? I cannot waste time looking for you. I have work to do."

Lena scrambled to her feet. "It's my fault, Isaac. I was showing her how to draw and the time got away from me. Don't be harsh with her."

He wiped a hand across his face. Slowly, his expression relaxed. "Reckon I can't scold her for listening to her teacher."

Ruby hopped to her feet and climbed into the buggy. Isaac looked at Lena. "Would you like a lift home? We go right past your father's farm."

The lengthening shadows told her she was going to be late if she didn't accept his offer, but still she hesitated. She didn't know him that well, but to refuse would make her appear ungrateful and stuck-up.

She had been curious to know more about Isaac Bowman. Wasn't this her chance? With his daughter in the buggy, this might be the perfect opportunity to find out how he felt about the poaching. If he was involved, he might reveal that, too. Should she risk questioning him?

He held out his hand. "What harm can come from a simple buggy ride?"

CHAPTER FIVE

ISAAC WAITED FOR LENA to make up her mind. Did she realize how expressive her pretty face was? What caused her indecision? Was she leery of accepting a ride from a man outside the circle of her family and friends, even one of her faith? Did she have a special fellow she didn't want to upset by accepting a ride from an unmarried man?

Isaac normally didn't think of himself as unmarried. He'd promised to love and care for one woman all the days of his life. Now that Ada Mae was gone, his vow had become meaningless in the eyes of others, but not in his own mind. Yet here he was, hoping Lena would accept a ride from him.

That he liked spending time with her and enjoyed her company was something of a puzzle to him. Over the past week he'd made a point to stop and visit briefly when he brought Ruby to school each morning. Lena was always polite, but never overly friendly. She certainly hadn't given him the impression that she was interested in him as anything other than her pupil's parent.

Each day, he found himself wanting to spend more time with her. He'd never expected to feel this way with another woman. It should feel wrong, but it didn't. Perhaps her refusal was a good thing. He shrugged his shoulders. "Suit yourself."

If she wanted to walk, that was her business. Grasping the reins, he started to turn his horse around. Ruby grasped his arm and shook her head. She beckoned to Lena and patted the seat beside her.

Lena smiled at his daughter. "I would be glad of a ride if it is not too much trouble."

Pleased at her change of heart, he said, "No trouble at all."

Lena climbed onto the front seat, sandwiching Ruby tightly between them. "If you go by our farm, you must be renting the old Stoltz place."

"Only the house and stable. I understand a young Amish couple is renting the fields."

"That must be Caleb and Betty Beachy. Father mentioned Caleb was expanding his produce farm. With their third baby on the way, he needs more land, and good earth is hard to come by."

"I don't know many people in the area yet. Ada Mae, my wife, was the outgoing one. She was always interested in the goings-on of the community. She liked meeting new people."

Isaac stopped speaking in surprise. He never talked about Ada Mae if he could help it. He glanced at Ruby. She didn't appear upset at the mention of her mother. She was drawing on her board and showing her creations to Lena.

"That is very good, Ruby. Is that your dog?"

Ruby sucked in her breath and glared at her teacher.

Isaac took a second look at his daughter's sketch. It was clearly a horse. He glanced at Lena and noticed a distinct twinkle in her eyes. She winked at him, inviting him to play along.

His heart gave an odd little leap. He stifled a grin and said, "It looks just like Grandpa Bowman's dog, Henry. Only Henry's tail curls up over his back."

Ruby wrote, "It's a horse" in big letters across the top of her board.

Lena studied the sketch, turning her head one way and then the other. "A horse? I kind of see that now."

Isaac chuckled. Ruby stared at him wide-eyed and then glanced at Lena. On her board, she wrote, "Are you teasing me?"

Lena laughed out loud and patted her head. *"Ja,* child, your papa and I are teasing you."

A sheepish grin curved the girl's lips. She glanced at her papa. He grinned at her and said, "Your papa can play a joke, too. Have you forgotten that?"

Ruby's smile widened as she happily returned to her work and began a new sketch. Lena offered encouragement and suggestions. As the horse trotted briskly along the blacktop, Isaac forgot about his worries and sadness. It was wonderful to see Ruby enjoying herself, even smiling. It had been ages since he'd seen her happy.

After a few moments, he felt Lena's gaze on him. He glanced at her and caught a speculative glint in her eye. He wondered what she was thinking. He didn't have to wonder long.

"The poaching in this area is really getting out of hand. It's hard to believe no one knows who is doing it."

"I suppose it is," he replied.

"It certainly is a shame. I hope the men killing our deer realize how wrong it is and stop."

"They will stop when the big deer are gone."

"You seem to know a lot about poachers and their ways."

Should he tell her about Samuel? Would she understand his *Englische* brother's strange job? Isaac found himself wanting to confide in Lena, but he didn't dare. To reveal Samuel's presence in the area might put his brother in jeopardy. Instead, he said, "I have read a lot about poaching."

"Reading is a good thing. Do you like to hunt?" She posed the question with an indifferent tone, but she was watching him intently.

"I reckon I like it as much as the next man. Hunting fills the larder and stretches the money I must spend for food."

"But you don't enjoy hunting for the sake of hunting?"

He didn't understand where her questions were leading. "Are you asking if I enjoy killing animals?"

She shrugged. "I guess I am."

"*Nay,* I do not enjoy it."

An ATV roared out of the woods on Isaac's side of the buggy and swerved past them. Isaac's mare threw up her head in panic. The driver, dressed in camouflaged clothing, barely managed to keep from hitting them. The horse scrambled backward and the buggy's rear wheel dropped into the steep ditch on Lena's side.

Frightened further by the tipping vehicle, Sophie bucked, lashing out with her back feet. Ruby screamed as Lena tumbled from her seat and fell out the door. Isaac had only a glimpse of her rolling into the ditch before his horse bolted down the highway.

Fear took the breath from his body as he fought to bring the panicked animal under control. He was hampered by Ruby's death grip on his arm. When he glanced back at last, he couldn't see Lena. Was she hurt? After a few tense moments, he was finally able to bring a wide-eyed Sophie to a standstill.

"Easy, girl, easy," he said, hoping to calm the mare and his daughter. "Ruby, *liebchen,* let go. I need my arm to drive. We must see if Lena is all right."

She lifted a tearstained face to look at him. He wanted to pull her close and reassure her, but didn't dare let go of the reins. Ruby released him, jumped out of the buggy and raced back toward her teacher.

Isaac turned the mare around and drove to where Lena sat at the side of the road. Though her *kapp* was missing and her hair had tumbled down her back, she seemed in one piece. Grass and weeds clung to her coat. Ruby was trying to help her up.

When Isaac was sure his horse was calm, he jumped from the buggy and hurried to Lena's side. "Don't move. Are you injured?"

Lena blushed as she stared up at him. "My dignity is sorely bruised, but that's all."

He quickly checked her arms and legs for signs of injury. He saw only a scratch on her cheek. "Thanks be to God. Your dignity will mend faster than a broken bone. Are you sure you aren't hurt?"

"I'm fine," she insisted.

He helped her to her feet, keeping a firm arm around her lest she fall. "Take it easy. Does anything hurt now?"

Ruby threw her arms around Lena's waist and buried her face against her. Lena hugged the child. "I'm fine. I jerked away when the horse kicked out, and lost my balance. The thick grass in the ditch padded my fall."

The memory of his wife's pale, limp form sent a chill over Isaac's skin. It could have been so much worse. "It was lucky you didn't land on the roadway."

Unwrapping Ruby's arms, Lena took the child's face in her hands. "I'm okay. Don't be scared. It's all over now. Let's go home, shall we?"

Ruby nodded. She ran down the road a few feet and came back with Lena's *kapp*. Lena stepped away from Isaac and he let his arm fall to his side. At the buggy, he climbed in, then reached out to help her. Her hand trembled in his grasp, and anger at the careless fool who'd caused the accident roared to life in him.

"Did you recognize the man on that insane machine?"

"I did not. It happened too fast." She settled on the seat beside him.

He fought the urge to gather her into his arms and hold her close. He didn't have the right to comfort her in such a manner. Ruby had no such qualms. She sat on the other side of Lena and kept one arm around her waist.

Lena repaired her bun with the ease of long practice and secured it. When she'd settled her *kapp* on her head, she gave a heavy sigh. "I shall think twice about riding with you again, Isaac Bowman. 'What harm can come of a simple buggy ride?' you said, and then I land on my...dignity in a ditch."

Few women could come out of such an experience with their sense of humor intact. His anger evaporated and a chuckle escaped him.

She rounded on him. "Are you laughing at me?"

"Not at all," he lied. He turned the buggy around on the narrow road and proceeded toward her home. With each bump and jolt of the wagon he could feel her body pressing against his hip and side. Her nearness made it hard to concentrate on his driving, but the trip was over much too quickly.

When they drew close to Lena's farm, an *Englische* woman from the house across the road came out to wave them down. Isaac stopped the buggy beside her. "Lena, can I speak to you for a few minutes?" she asked.

"Certainly." Lena glanced at him and said, "I will walk from here."

He shook his head. "I'll wait for you."

"Nonsense. Take Ruby home. I'm fine. Are you coming to the school board meeting tonight?"

"I plan on it."

"I will see you then." She got out and patted Ruby's hand. "Keep practicing your art. God has given you a measure of talent. It is up to you to put it to good use."

Short of hauling her back into his vehicle, Isaac had no choice but to leave Lena with her friend. As he drove away, he missed her warmth and softness beside him, so much that he had to admit he was coming to care a great deal for Ruby's new teacher.

LENA GAZED AFTER Isaac and Ruby as they continued down the road. She wished she was still with them. Seated beside Isaac's large frame, she'd felt safe, secure and oddly happy in spite of her ignoble fall. Surely she couldn't have such feelings if he was killing the deer she loved simply for money.

None of her probing had answered that question to her satisfaction. If she listened to her head, she would steer clear of Isaac Bowman. If she listened to her heart, she would be thinking about being courted by him.

She shook her head at such silliness. Her fall must have rattled her more than she knew. She turned to her friend. "What's wrong?"

Clara asked, "Is that him? Goodness, he is a big man."

"Did you want something?" Lena had no intention of getting into a discussion about Isaac. Her feelings were much too disjointed for her to make sense of them.

Curiosity faded from Clara's face, to be replaced with a look of deep concern. "I didn't need anything special. I was...I was just wondering if you had seen my husband today."

"Nay, I have not. I've been at school all day."

Clara's eyes suddenly filled with tears. "When I saw you in the buggy I thought perhaps you'd been to town. I'm so worried about Brad. He hasn't been himself since he lost his job. Lately, he's taken to staying out until all hours of the night. He won't tell me what he's doing. He says I have to trust him. I do trust him, only it's hard when he shuts me out."

Lena drew her friend into a comforting hug. "Brad is a good man. If he says you must trust him, then that is what you must do. That doesn't mean you have to turn a blind eye to his behavior. Don't stew in silence. Make sure he knows how much you worry about him."

"What if he's seeing another woman?"

"What man would want another woman when he already has the best? Brad knows how lucky he is to have you. Stop this foolish worry."

"But what if he is? Something is going on."

"Shall I speak to him for you?"

"Right! Like he's going to tell my Amish friend if he's being unfaithful."

"You are letting your imagination poison your heart. Pray for wisdom and guidance. God will answer you." There was little else Lena could do or say to comfort her friend. The couple would have to work through their problems together.

Clara pulled away and wiped her eyes with the heels of her hands. "Thank you for listening to me. I don't know what I would do without your friendship."

Lena glanced past Clara to the highway. Isaac's buggy was already out of sight. She hadn't recognized the driver that spooked Isaac's horse, but she had recognized the machine. "Clara, does Brad still have his green four-wheeler?"

"No, he told me he sold it last week. Why do you ask?"

"I thought I saw it in the woods today. Do you know who he sold it to?"

"I don't, but I can ask him."

"Would you? Wait, isn't that Brad's truck coming this way?"

Clara turned to look and her tense body sagged with relief. "It is. That man is going to get a piece of my mind for worrying me so."

"I've heard Papa tell my sister not to scold her husband when he has an empty stomach. Papa says a man is much more amenable when he is well fed."

Clara managed a watery smile. "I'll keep that in mind."

Lena waved as Brad turned into the drive. He gave a friendly wave in return and pulled to a stop. Clara walked to his side of the truck as he rolled down his window.

"Where have you been?" she demanded.

"Out looking for work, as if you have to ask," he muttered. He sent Lena an apologetic glance.

She knew it was best to leave the couple to sort out their troubles, but she wanted to know who'd been driving Brad's old hunting vehicle through Wilfred Cummings's woods. "Brad, who bought your four-wheeler?"

"A guy by the name of Samuel Bow."

"Is he a local?" Lena didn't recognize the name.

"No, he said he was from Canton. He paid cash, so I didn't ask any questions. Why?"

"I thought I saw it today."

"That could be. He said he wanted it for hunting wild pigs."

So it wasn't someone she knew. Was Samuel Bow

hunting deer instead of pigs? "Have you heard shooting at night?"

"Yeah."

She looked at him in surprise. "Aren't you concerned that it's illegal hunting?"

"There are a lot of people out of work around here, Lena. I can't blame a few of them for taking a deer or pig by spotlight at night. I just hope they leave a nice buck for me when the season opens."

Clara scowled at him. "Like we can afford the license and tag fees."

"I'm going hunting, Clara, and that's the end of it. I've given up everything else."

It was clear to Lena that there was an argument brewing. She said a quick goodbye and started for home, mulling over what Brad had told her. In spite of what he thought, she knew there was more to the poaching than a few locals filling empty freezers. When she walked in her front door, her sister, Anna, was setting the table for supper.

Anna, the oldest of the Troyer children, was a widow and nearly twenty years older than Lena. After her husband passed away, Anna had returned home to run her father's house. Her arrival left Lena free to take up the teaching post and earn some much-needed extra income.

"Forgive me for being late," Lena took off her coat and hung it on a peg by the front door. Her father's hat already rested in its usual place.

Anna laid the last plate and turned back to the stove. "You will have to hurry if you arc to get back to the school in time for the board meeting."

Their father walked in from the living room. A short man with a ready smile and bowed legs, Micah Troyer was well loved in the community. "Take the buggy. That will make your trip shorter."

"*Danki,* Papa."

Settling in his place at the head of the table, he fastened his gaze on Lena. "What took you so long getting home tonight?"

She decided not to tell him about her tumble. It was over and she was fine. "I was giving drawing lessons to one of my students and the time got away from us. Isaac Bowman gave me a ride home, but I stopped to talk to Clara for a bit."

"More of your sketching is not a good thing, Lena. There is work to be done here at home."

Her father tolerated her pastime but didn't encourage it. He didn't see how it could be useful to an Amish housewife. Lena decided to change the subject. "I'm going to let the board know I'm concerned about the poaching in the woods around the school."

He frowned. "For what reason?"

Lena raised her chin. "I thought the elders might want to notify the authorities to put a stop to it."

Her father ran a hand over his beard as he often did when he was contemplating what to say. "I know you have a tender place in your heart for the deer. This poaching is a bad thing. The *Englische* law is to be obeyed when it does not conflict with the laws given to us by God and our church. But I don't see how it is any of your business to try to stop it, Lena."

Her hopes that her father would support her were instantly dashed. Briefly, she wondered how Sarah and Abby would handle the situation. Knowing the strength of character it took for both of them to solve crimes in their own communities bolstered Lena's resolve. This was something she would have to do by herself. She would speak out at the meeting tonight, even without her father's blessing.

ISAAC SAT AT THE BACK OF the schoolroom on one of the benches that had been set up for the men. The women, including Lena, sat across the aisle. She didn't appear to be suffering any ill effects from her fall.

Throughout the meeting, his gaze was constantly drawn to her face. She had something on her mind; he could tell by the way she nibbled at the corner of her mouth. When had he come to know her so well?

"Do we have any other business?" John's eyes scanned the room.

The elder sitting beside him bent toward him and spoke softly. John nodded and said, "The building is in need of a few repairs. If you can help, raise your hand."

A number of hands went up. Isaac raised his. John wrote down the names and assigned each man a task. Looking at Isaac, he asked, "Can you fix the barn's hayloft door and see to any other repairs that are needed on the building?"

Nodding once, Isaac signaled his consent, and John wrote something briefly beside his name. When all the repairs were covered, he glanced around the room. "Is there anything else?"

Lena raised her hand; John nodded for her to speak. She rose to her feet, her hands clasped tightly in front of her. "As many of you know, the children have reported seeing dead deer in the area and hearing shooting. It is clearly the work of poachers. It may be one man, it may be more. I bring it to your attention because I feel it is an issue that needs to be addressed."

Isaac glanced at his cousin to find a deep scowl

forming on his face. "I don't see that this has anything to do with the school board," John said. "Is there any other school business?"

Lena didn't sit down. Isaac had to admire her courage in facing John's ire. She said, "I believe it is school business when the children are being exposed to danger."

Behind her, one of the mothers asked, "Why do you believe our *kinder* are in danger?"

"Many of you have heard the shooting late at night. It goes on during daylight, too. Early in the morning and late in the evening, times when the deer are most active and the children are walking to and from school. I've seen men in hunting gear watching the school."

A murmur moved through the crowd as the parents discussed Lena's statement among themselves. John's scowl deepened. He rose to his feet. "I see no need to create panic, Lena. A careful hunter will not mistake a child for a deer."

"But we don't know that these men are careful," she insisted.

"What would you have us do? Suspend classes until the hunting stops?" he scoffed.

Lena blanched, but didn't back down. "I feel this activity should be reported to the sheriff or the game warden."

"We do not concern ourselves with the actions of outsiders and we do not bring outsiders in to solve our problems. You know this, Lena. Have you forgotten the teaching of our faith to remain separate from the world?"

"Of course not."

"*Gut,* then the matter is closed." John sat down.

"But what if the hunter is one of us?" Lena added quickly.

Isaac could tell his cousin had reached the limit of his patience as he rose and addressed the crowd. "Does anyone here know who is hunting deer out of season? Are any of you to blame?"

Stark silence followed his question.

John focused a stern glare on Lena. "Are you satisfied that it is not one of us?"

Isaac read displeasure on many of the faces around him. Lena had made a mistake by suggesting the poacher might be one of them.

He saw that she realized her error, too. She lowered her gaze. Bright spots of color stained her cheeks.

John glared at her. "Your job is to teach the children, Lena Troyer, not to question your elders or seek to involve the *Englische* in our lives. I have made that point before. I will not repeat it again."

Lena sat down. John's threat was clear. Leave the subject alone or risk losing her job.

LENA FELT THE EYES of everyone on her as she struggled to bear her humiliation with dignity. Most of these parents had supported her in the past, but she had foolishly suggested one of them, or a member of their family, might be poaching. She wasn't sure they would speak up for her again if John Miller decided to replace her.

She cringed at the thought of her father hearing about this. He would, she was sure of that. It was best that he hear it from her and not from someone else. She waited in growing discomfort for the meeting to end.

The moment the group was dismissed, she scurried out the door to her waiting buggy. She wasn't fast enough, because Isaac was there a second later.

"For what it's worth, I appreciate your concern for my daughter's welfare," he said quietly.

Would a poacher offer kind words of comfort? If only she knew for certain that he wasn't involved. "But you think John is right and I shouldn't go to outsiders."

"You have done all you can without incurring the ire of many." After unhooking her mare from the hitching post, he stood beside her buggy.

She slipped past him, climbed into the front seat and held out her hands. "I can't stand by and do nothing."

He didn't give her the reins. "Be careful, Lena. John is not a man to trifle with. You could lose your job over this."

She had only the starlight overhead to help her read his face. It wasn't enough. She wanted to know what was in his eyes. Was he truly concerned for her? Or did he want her to stop pressing the issue for his own self-ish reasons? She wished she could tell. How could she be attracted to a man she wasn't sure she could trust?

"I didn't know I loved teaching until all this began to happen," she said. "But I won't let that love be used against me. There is evil in our woods. Turning a blind eye to it only allows it to grow."

More people were coming out of the school. She didn't want to speak to anyone else. "I must get home."

Isaac hesitated, as if he wanted to say something more, but in the end handed over the reins. "Good night, Lena Troyer. May God travel with you."

CHAPTER SIX

LENA'S FATHER WAS UPSET and made no bones about it when she told him about the board meeting. She endured a long, stern lecture about respecting her elders. At the following Sunday service, only two of her friends spoke to her before the preaching. After the bishop's fiery sermon on living apart from the world, avoiding worldly involvement and showing those who advocated such the error of their ways, no one spoke to her at all.

She'd been given a small taste of what it would be like to be shunned. She didn't care for the feeling.

On Monday, all her students were subdued. None of them talked about the poaching. Even the twins kept silent on their favorite subject in spite of the fact that Lena had heard gunfire over the weekend and knew some of the children must have, too.

Classes went smoothly during the day, but she had a hard time keeping her mind on her work. It was a huge relief when it was finally time to dismiss everyone.

She stepped out of the school after the last student was gone, and pulled the door closed. Once more she had a choice to make. She could go home and keep silent, or she could try again to stop the poaching. Her family and her church had made it clear which path she should choose.

After crossing the bridge, Lena reached the highway and turned toward home, but she had one stop to make first.

Wilfred Cummings lived a half mile from the school in an old, two-story stone house set back in the woods. He loved the wildlife that flourished in his forest and enjoyed seeing the sketches Lena drew. She hadn't been to visit him since his stroke, and that was remiss of her. She considered the elderly man a friend.

It had been Wilfred who'd showed her the trapdoor in the bell tower. The school building had originally belonged to his family and he'd been a teacher there. When Lena told him she'd taken the teaching position, he'd driven her to the school and pointed out the hidden opening.

He admitted that he'd rigged the trapdoor in the roof so that he might watch for a special girl coming home in the evenings. She'd worked at her father's store in town and he'd objected to her seeing Wilfred. Her father often walked home with her, but if she was alone, Wilfred would hurry out to meet her. His eyes had misted over when he'd told the story, and Lena knew he was talking about the woman who'd become his wife, a woman who'd died long before Lena knew him.

When she came within sight of Wilfred's house, she saw that the yard was overgrown and untrimmed. A gray car and a black, mud-splattered truck sat in the gravel driveway. Lena spotted a curtain moving in an upper-story window, so it looked as if someone was home. She drew a deep breath to firm her resolve, then approached the front door and knocked.

Instead of the stooped figure of Mr. Cummings, a woman in her mid-forties answered the door. She looked Lena up and down with a faint scowl. "May I help you?"

This had to be his granddaughter. Lena smiled.

"Hello. I'm Lena Troyer. I live nearby. I was hoping to speak to Mr. Cummings about an important matter."

"Mr. Cummings is sleeping. If you have come hoping to convert my grandfather to your religion, you are wasting your time."

Stunned at her assumption, Lena shook her head. "Oh, no. The Amish do not seek to convert anyone to our ways. Each person's path to God is their personal journey to make."

The woman relaxed a fraction. "I apologize for jumping to conclusions. I'm Glenda Carter. Wilfred is my grandfather."

"You are forgiven. Many people have misconceptions about our faith. When do you think it would be possible for me to see your grandfather?"

"It's hard to say. He's very elderly."

"*Ja,* I've known him since I was a child. My grandmother told me that he donated the land and the building for our school when she was a young girl."

"How odd, since he isn't Amish."

"Odd perhaps, but very generous. I am the teacher at the school."

The frost returned to Glenda's eyes. "If you're looking for a donation, I'll give him the message. However, I warn you, he isn't likely to part with any of his money. He's become a real Scrooge in his old age."

"I'm not here to raise money. I merely wanted to let Wilfred know that someone has been poaching deer on his property."

Glenda frowned. "Are you sure?"

"I've seen one of the dead animals myself. My students have seen others. We have heard shooting late at night and seen the bright lights the poachers are using. Have you not heard them?"

"I'm a sound sleeper. That's so sad. Grandfather is abnormally fond of the deer. He plans to leave all his land to the state to be made into a wildlife refuge. Have you told the authorities about this?"

Lena shook her head. "It is not our way to involve outsiders. By coming here, I am pushing the boundary of what is permitted. But like your grandfather, I have a special place in my heart for the deer. They are some of God's most beautiful creatures. Are you sure I can't speak to Wilfred? I saw the curtain move at his bedroom window. I know he's awake."

A man a few years older than Glenda moved to stand behind her. He placed a hand on her shoulder. "That was me looking out the window. Grandpa is asleep."

"Miss Troyer, this is my husband, Chuck. Miss Troyer was just telling me she thinks someone is hunting deer at night in our woods. Have you heard shooting?"

"I have, but I thought it was some of the Amish getting a jump on the hunting season. They don't believe they have to obey our laws."

Lena pressed a hand to her chest. "I can't speak for every Amish person, but my family and all the families in my church recognize and obey the law of the land."

Glenda looked over her shoulder at him. "She wants us to notify the authorities because she says the Amish won't."

"I've heard they don't involve the law. Don't you pray for and forgive wrongdoers?"

"We forgive others as Christ forgave us."

Chuck scratched his neck. "I don't mind letting the game warden know we think something is going on, but I don't expect they'll do anything about it."

Glenda turned back to Lena. "Thank you for your

concern. I'm afraid telling Grandfather about this may upset him unduly. His health is very fragile. You understand, don't you?"

Lena nodded. "Of course. Will you contact the authorities?"

Chuck smiled. "We'll be happy to pass along what you've told us."

"*Danki.* That is all I can ask. Let me know if there is anything I can do for you or for your grandfather. I've always been fond of him. My sister makes an excellent tonic from natural herbs. I'll bring some by tomorrow."

"That won't be necessary. I'm sorry, but I don't put much faith in folk remedies. We're doing everything our doctor has suggested. Grandfather mainly requires rest. I should be getting back to him." Glenda smiled and closed the door in Lena's face.

Left standing on the stoop, she had no choice but to go home. She had done all she could do.

On her way back to the highway, she was startled when a man emerged from the dense woods in front of her. Her foolish heart raced faster when she recognized Isaac. In his hand, he held a game camera exactly like the one they had found together during the class outing.

"Lena. What are you doing out this way?"

A shiver raced over her at the sound of his deep voice. She wasn't sure if it was fear or attraction that triggered it. Finally, she managed to say, "I stopped in to see how Mr. Cummings was getting along."

She focused her gaze on the camera in Isaac's hand. Here was the proof she needed. He was in league with the poachers. Her foolish heart had been wrong about him. Gathering her courage, she asked, "What are you doing here?"

He held out his hand. "Ruby told me that the twins

found three more slaughtered deer out this way. I wanted to check on the situation."

She folded her arms tightly across her chest. He was lying. "They didn't mention it to me."

His eyebrows shot up. "Are you surprised? I'm sure their parents have told them to keep quiet about it."

That could well be true. "Why do you have a camera?"

"After a little searching, I found the carcasses, and this camera nearby. These poachers aren't taking the trouble to hide their work. One of the deer was a doe. They left her to rot. The bucks had their heads taken."

A slight smile softened his stoic face as he hefted the camera in his hand. "When I saw this, I thought it was much too valuable an item to be left in the woods. I removed it for safekeeping. I'll put an ad in the paper that I found it, although I doubt anyone will report it missing. Perhaps the deer can move about in safety for a few nights."

Was he telling the truth? Or had she happened upon him while he was getting ready to set the camera in a new location? She wanted to believe Isaac, but did she dare? So much pointed in his direction.

The trouble had started after he came to town. No one knew much about him, but he seemed to know everything about the poaching trade. She'd seen him aiming a gun at Goliath. If she hadn't scared the deer away, would the buck's head be hanging on a wall somewhere right this minute?

Part of her wanted to demand that Isaac tell her the truth about his activities. Was he poaching for the quick money it brought in?

Another part of her didn't want to ask, and that frightened her more than anything. If Isaac believed she thought he was poaching, and he wasn't, where would that leave the relationship she sensed was growing between them? Not in a good place.

ISAAC WISHED HE KNEW what Lena was thinking. He expected her to be pleased that he had removed the camera. Instead, her expression grew more guarded. She didn't return his smile. He wasn't sure why, but he wanted her to.

Maybe it was because the gentle smiles she gave her students reminded him of the way his wife used to look at him. Thinking of Ada Mae brought back the feelings of guilt he couldn't shake. He did his best not to remember.

Tipping his head toward the road, he said, "Come, I will walk you home." The words came out sounding more like a command than an invitation.

Her chin came up. "I'm perfectly capable of seeing myself home."

He softened his tone. "I didn't mean to suggest you weren't. I'm going in that direction. We might as well go together—unless you object to walking with me. Are you afraid our names will be linked by gossip if we are seen together?"

Her mouth opened and then snapped closed on whatever she intended to say. Without a word, she began walking at a brisk pace.

He had no trouble adjusting his stride to match hers. After a few hundred feet, he finally asked, "Have I done something to upset you?"

Pausing, she stared at him intently. "Have you?"

That wasn't the answer he expected. "If I have, I'm sorry. I don't know what I did or said that offended you. Enlighten me."

She chewed her bottom lip as she considered her reply. After a moment, she shook her head and started walking again.

Totally confused, he followed after her. "Does this mean I have not offended you?"

Stopping, she faced him once more. Her cheeks were red from the exertion and the cold weather. The wind played with her bonnet ribbons and a few strands of hair that had come loose. She was pretty; he admitted that. But pretty alone wasn't enough to hold his interest the way Lena Troyer did.

As if she suddenly became aware that she was staring at him, she glanced down and became the perfect image of a demure Amish woman. It was a look that didn't ring true. He had a feeling Lena was anything but demure.

She said, "Nothing you have done or said has caused me distress. I'm sorry if I gave that impression."

Whatever had upset her, she clearly wasn't willing to discuss it. Why, he wondered, was it so important for him to keep on her good side? Was it because she was Ruby's teacher?

No, this had nothing to do with his child. He wanted Lena to like him because he liked her. The last thing he'd expected to find in Mount Hope was a woman who stirred his interest, but Lena did just that.

He didn't want to care for anyone the way he'd cared for Ada Mae. She had been the best part of his life, and he'd let her down. He wouldn't allow himself to be put in such a position again.

He cleared his throat. "It will be dark soon. We should go."

Silently, they walked along the narrow lane. They had nearly reached the highway when the sound of a truck behind them made them step aside. The man at the wheel passed them with a scowl on his face. He turned his vehicle toward town and disappeared.

Isaac glanced at Lena. "Do you know that man?"

"He is Chuck Carter, the husband of Mr. Cummings's granddaughter."

"He didn't look happy."

Lena didn't reply.

Isaac said, "Ruby seems to like school. How is she doing in her studies?"

"Well."

"That's *gut* news." His daughter was a safe topic of conversation.

He caught the glance Lena slanted in his direction. "She still isn't making friends. Has she always been a loner?"

"*Nay,* only since her mother passed away."

"If you don't mind my asking, how did your wife die?"

He did mind. What would she say if he admitted as much? She would politely accept that he didn't wish to talk about Ada Mae's death, but she would still wonder what had happened. Perhaps it was best to admit the truth now.

"My wife died of a punctured lung after she was kicked in the chest by one of our horses."

His throat closed around the words he wanted to say: that it had been his fault. He knew Ada Mae didn't trust the young gelding he had been so proud to own. It had been his pride, in more ways than one, that had resulted in his wife's death and his daughter's affliction.

"I am sorry for your loss. Was Ruby with your wife when the accident happened?"

"Why do you ask?" He didn't like this prying. He wasn't ready to discuss what had happened.

"I want to understand why Ruby stopped speaking."

"Only Ruby and God know why she remains silent." Isaac hoped his tone conveyed that he didn't wish to talk about it.

Lena took the hint and fell silent. An air of tension simmered between them and that, too, was his fault.

He shouldn't spend any more time alone with Ruby's new teacher. Emotions he didn't want to face seemed to surface whenever she was near. Not seeing her was the best plan. He was becoming much too interested in Lena Troyer, not as a teacher, but as a woman.

IN THE DAYS FOLLOWING Lena's visit to Wilfred's house, the sounds of gunfire in the woods stopped. The Carters must have followed through and notified the law. Lena began to breathe easier knowing that the deer were safe, at least until the legal hunting season opened in a few more weeks. Even though she climbed to the bell tower every evening, she still hadn't seen Goliath. She began to fear he had been killed, and she mourned his loss.

She saw Glenda Carter once more, when she went to town on Monday evening. The woman was coming out of John Miller's store, and Lena stopped to thank her for helping. Glenda assured her she was glad to do it, but couldn't stay and talk because Wilfred needed his medicine. As Lena watched her drive away, she was glad her friend had such a devoted granddaughter to care for him.

On Wednesday afternoon, when the children finished their lunches, Lena read them a story about a young man who loved to draw, and how he turned his gift into a business by painting wooden boxes to sell to tourists so he could help support his aging parents.

When she closed the book, Lena looked over the young faces so intent on her words. "Art for art's sake is worldly and unacceptable to us. Art must have a purpose. God has already made a beautiful world and nothing we make can add to that beauty. What are some of the ways we can use art?" Lena still didn't know how her own art could be used to better someone's life.

Katie held up her hand. "The quilts we make are pretty and useful."

Lena nodded. "That's right."

She pointed to David when he raised his hand.

"I sent a picture of my new horse to my cousin so he would know I have a better horse than he does."

"That is prideful, David. Can you think of a nicer reason?"

The boy scrunched up his face and then said slowly, "No."

Ruby held up her hand. Lena walked to her desk to read what she wrote. "Ruby says her father uses art by carving furniture to sell. Very good, Ruby."

Lena moved to the front of the room. "Today, I'd like you to use your art to show me one kind of animal that lives on your farm. It can be any animal you want."

An hour later, she had pictures of horses, cats, dogs, pigs and an owl. One by one, she hung them around the room so that everyone could see. It wasn't until after school was out that she realized Ruby hadn't turned in a picture.

When Lena left the school that afternoon, she caught sight of someone peeking around the edge of the barn. The fleeting glimpse of a black prayer *kapp* and red-gold hair was enough to tell her who it was.

CHAPTER SEVEN

LENA CALLED OUT, "Ruby, won't your father be worried if you don't come home on time?"

The child stepped out from behind the building and came forward with lagging steps. Lena descended the stairs and waited for her. Ruby stopped in front of her and began writing. She held her board up for Lena to see. "He doesn't care."

"I find that hard to believe. Your father is very concerned about you. Why didn't you go home with the other children?"

Ruby scribbled her answer: "I wanted to walk home with you."

Lena was secretly pleased. Not only was it good to find someone who enjoyed her company, but she'd grown quite fond of Ruby. "All right then, let's go."

Walking side by side, they followed the dirt road down the short hill and through the covered bridge. Lena resisted an overwhelming urge to check the woods for watchers, and kept a one-sided conversation going until they reached the lane leading to her father's house.

Looking down at Ruby, she smiled. "I appreciate you keeping me company. I will see you tomorrow at school."

The girl wrote a question on her board and held it up for Lena to see. "Can you teach me to draw as well as you do?"

"I don't see why not. God has bestowed consider-
able talent upon you. If you are sure your father doesn't
mind, come up to the house with me."

After introducing Ruby to Anna, Lena led the child
upstairs to her room. From a cupboard in the corner,
she withdrew a tattered book. "This book has easy-to-
follow lessons for developing your talent. If your father
agrees, you can keep it if you want."

Ruby's bright smile told Lena she'd made a friend for
life. She wrote on her board, "Will you ask him for me?"

Lena nodded. Staring at the child's happy face, she
prayed Isaac wouldn't object.

Ruby jotted another note and held it up. "Please?"

After getting the child's hopes up, how could she refuse? "Is he at work?"

Ruby shook her head and pointed to the floor. Lena
took that to mean he was at home. He must be worried
that Ruby wasn't home yet. They should hurry. At least
the walk to the old Stoltz farm was closer than walking into town.

"Come," Ruby whispered, excitement glowing in
her eyes. She took Lena's hand and tugged her toward
the door.

Lena stood rooted to the spot. "Ruby, you spoke!"

The girl gave her a funny look and shook her head.

"You did. You spoke. You said, 'Come.'"

Shaking her head again, Ruby scrawled, "No, I
didn't" on her board.

Lena leaned close to examine the writing. "What
does this say?"

Rolling her eyes, Rudy whispered, "No." Then her
eyes grew wide and she snapped her mouth shut.

Lena dropped to her knees and hugged the child.
"Ruby, this is wonderful. God is so good!"

Holding her at arm's length, she coaxed, "Say something else. You can do it."

Ruby opened and closed her mouth. No words came out. Finally, she cupped Lena's face between her hands. In a tiny whisper, she pleaded, "Don't tell Papa."

ISAAC HAD FINISHED the wash and was hanging the wet clothes on the line when he heard a muffled laugh behind him. Turning around, he saw Samuel standing by the back door of the house. His brother looked tired and worn, but he was smiling.

"What are you laughing at, little brother?"

"The sight of you doing woman's work."

Isaac secured one of Ruby's dresses to the clothesline with wooden pins. "At least I know how to wash clothes. You look like you could use a lesson or two."

Samuel brushed at the front of his jacket. "My current companions don't value cleanliness."

"What do they value?"

"Money, guns, drugs and the money to buy more drugs."

"It is no joking matter, Samuel. Do you know what you're doing?"

"Don't worry about me, Isaac."

Crossing to where his brother stood, Isaac laid a hand on his shoulder. "How can I not?"

"I shouldn't be here. I don't know why I came."

"I'm glad you did." Isaac gazed into Samuel's eyes and saw the affection they'd always shared.

"Is your little teacher all right? I'm sorry I spooked your horse. I never saw you until it was too late."

Isaac frowned. "That was you?"

"I said I'm sorry. You were just in the wrong place at the wrong time."

"Lena was not harmed, but you frightened us half to death. What were you thinking?"

"I had only a short window of time to make contact with my supervisor. We had arranged to meet each week over in the next town. That day I had trouble getting away. If I didn't show, I knew the department would come looking for me with guns drawn. I didn't want them rushing to my rescue and having all my work go down the drain. Not yet. I don't have enough to make a case that will stick."

"This undercover work is too dangerous, Samuel. Why must you do it?"

"Because I believe it's important. The Department of Wildlife has invested a lot of manpower and money into shutting down poaching rings, but these people are careful. They confiscated my cell phone and search my stuff all the time. I haven't met the ringleader yet. We want the brains behind this operation, not the small fry."

"God is the judge of all men. Can you not leave justice to him?"

"Spoken like the good Amish fellow you are."

"Do not mock me, Samuel."

His brother gave him a wry smile. "I don't. I wish I had your faith that everything turns out the way it should in the end. I, on the other hand, like to see justice done before the crooks die of old age."

"I pray for you every day, as do all in our family."

"While you're praying, you might add a request for a new wife. Ruby needs a woman in her life and so do you. You're getting dishpan hands, bro." With a jaunty salute, Samuel strode away and vanished into a narrow neck of woods at the back of the barn.

Pray for a new wife? Isaac shook his head. His

brother had developed an odd sense of humor in his years among the *Englische*.

Isaac tried to dismiss the idea, but it wouldn't leave him alone. What kind of woman would he pray for if he did such a thing?

Someone kind, who shared his love of God and his Amish faith, for certain. But what else?

She would have to love his daughter as her own. It didn't matter if she was pretty or not, but a pleasant face would be nice. Lena's delicate features came to mind. She was everything he needed.

He was being foolish. Isaac went back to hanging up the laundry. He tossed a sheet over the line and spread it evenly before pinning it in place. He was content with his life as it was. Pray for a wife—why would he do that?

"If two people are meant for each other, God will bring them together." He ducked under the sheet and came face-to-face with Lena.

She took a quick step back and looked around. "Who are you talking to?"

Isaac was looking at her with the strangest expression on his face. Lena wasn't sure what to make of it. "Isaac, are you all right?"

He blinked hard. *"Ja,* I'm fine. What are you doing here? Is Ruby okay?"

"Ruby is fine," she quickly assured him. "She has gone to do her chores."

"Gut." He spun around, walked into the clothesline and struggled to keep his balance for a second before whipping the sheet out of his way and picking up an empty laundry basket.

Not knowing what to do, she reached for the basket. "Can I help you?"

"*Nay,* I have said I'm fine, and I am," he bellowed.

She took two steps back. "Forgive me. I can see you would rather not have company at the moment."

He visibly gathered himself and said in a moderate tone, "I'm sorry. I was distracted. Ruby's teacher is always welcome in our home. What can I do for you?"

Lena caught sight of the girl standing behind him. Ruby shook her head and folded her hands together in a pleading gesture.

Clearly, this might not be the best time to broach the subject of her newfound speech. Lena said, "I would like to give Ruby a book of drawing instructions, but I wanted to check with you first."

The child sagged with relief and smiled.

Isaac continued toward the house. Lena had to rush to keep up with him. He asked, "Do you think it a suitable book for her?"

"I do, but I'm not her parent."

"Then I'm sure it is fine." He paused at the back door. "Thank you for stopping by." A second later, he was in the house and the door was closed in her face.

What on earth was he trying to hide?

Ruby ran forward and threw her arms around Lena's waist in a fierce hug. Lena patted her back. "You will have to tell him soon, Ruby. If you don't, I must."

Looking up at her, Ruby shook her head in denial.

Lena cupped the child's face. "He has prayed for this day, I know it in my heart. You do him a great disservice by staying silent now. He will rejoice. I know he will."

Ruby relinquished her hold on her and slowly walked into the house. Lena had no idea if she intended to tell her father the good news or not. Nor did she have any idea why the child would want to stay silent. There was so much here she didn't understand.

Lena left Isaac's house and walked home. The evening air had turned chilly. She pulled her coat collar up around her neck to block the wind. When she arrived, her father was sitting at the table even though supper wasn't ready.

She glanced at Anna. Her sister wore a worried expression, and kept clasping and unclasping her hands. Something was wrong.

Her father stood. "John Miller and the school board members stopped by this evening. Since you were not home and no one knew where you had gone, he asked that you come to his home tomorrow night at six o'clock for a special meeting of the board."

Lena braced herself to hear the worst. "Did he say what the meeting was about?"

"*Nay,* he did not, but he warned me that you may face a shunning if you do not appear. What have you done to shame us, Lena?"

CHAPTER EIGHT

ON THE WAY to John Miller's house, Lena passed his furniture shop. The Closed sign hung in the window, but the door stood open slightly. She saw Isaac Bowman inside.

Seated on a tall stool in front of a workbench, he was bent over something she couldn't see, concentrating intently. It was late and there was no one else about. Unobserved, she watched as he used a mallet and chisel with meticulous care. What was he making?

Curiosity, and a burning desire to put off her meeting with the school board, prompted her to step through the open door. As she did, Isaac held up his project. It was the lid of a chest, with a beautifully carved bouquet of roses inside an oval frame.

She knew from her conversations with Ruby that Isaac was a wood-carver, but Lena had had no idea he possessed such skill. Could a man capable of creating such beauty also be capable of illegally slaughtering deer?

The time had come for her to ask him outright. Did she possess enough courage? Would he understand her suspicions and forgive her if she was wrong, or would she ruin the friendship growing between them?

He must have sensed her presence for he suddenly turned in her direction. His eyes widened in surprise.

"*Gut-n-owed*, Lena."

"Good evening to you, too, Isaac."

"If you are looking for John, he has gone home."

Lena knew she should leave, but something made her step closer. "*Danki.* I will seek him there. You seem to be hard at work."

"Happily so. My orders are piling up fast."

"I see why. Your work is exceptional."

Like a moth to the light of a lantern, she felt irresistibly drawn to this man for reasons she didn't understand.

Isaac ran his hand across the surface of the carving. "My grandfather was a master wood-carver. He taught me to respect the wood and to try to understand it."

Lena moved across the space until she stood at his elbow. She gazed in wonder at the intricately carved flowers and leaves. "What did he mean when he said you had to understand the wood?"

"Grandfather believed God has placed a story inside each piece of wood and it is up to the carver to find that story."

She ran her fingers over the crisp edges of the carving. "How do you go about finding it?"

"Most of the time, I stare at a piece for a long while. I run my hands over it to feel the grain and texture, and then it occurs to me what the wood might like to say."

Few people would have guessed that there was a sensitive and intuitive soul inside Isaac's big burly frame. She looked at him in a new light and with new respect. "How did this piece tell you it held a bouquet of roses?"

He laughed. "The woman who ordered this chest wanted a bouquet of roses on the lid. I talked it over with the wood and the wood agreed. Would you like to see some of my other pieces?"

Lena grinned and nodded. "I'd love to."

He led the way to the back of the shop, where furniture in all stages of completion was stacked in neat rows. Isaac pulled out a large headboard. The finials had been carved to resemble pinecones, while crossed pine branches were etched into the center of the piece.

Impressed with his skill, Lena said, "I see now where Ruby gets her talent for drawing."

"She tells me that you are an artist, too."

Lena looked at him with joy. "She spoke to you?"

"Of course not. She wrote that you enjoy sketching."

Disappointed, Lena shrugged. "I enjoy sketching, but my gift is a small one."

He studied her face intently. She realized they were alone together inside the deserted building, and her pulse quickened. He stood close enough that she could smell his masculine scent over the aroma of fresh cut wood. His eyes darkened as he gazed at her. She had the oddest sensation that he wanted to kiss her. Would she let him?

He suddenly stepped back. "Over here is a fireplace mantel I finished yesterday. I knew as soon as I saw this piece of wood that it needed a leaping buck on each end."

Isaac opened a cardboard box and pulled aside the packing material.

Lena stared at the mantel, stunned. It was a beautifully carved piece of oak. She wasn't shocked by the skill displayed; she was shocked to recognize the animal he had etched into the wood. It was Snagglehead.

There was no mistaking the buck's unusual, downturned, twisted antlers. The rendition was amazingly accurate. Isaac would have needed more than a fleeting glimpse of the buck to portray him so well.

Lena glanced from the mantel to Isaac, who stood

waiting for her to comment. Snagglehead had been killed right after Isaac came to town. If he had poached the deer and taken the head, he would have had ample opportunity to study the animal's unique horns.

Her stomach churned with anxiety. Did she really want to know if he was one of the poachers?

Isaac's smile vanished. "Is something wrong?"

"Lena, there you are." John Miller stood in the doorway to the shop, an expression of displeasure on his face. "Come along, I'd like to get this meeting over with as soon as possible."

She came back to the present with a painful thump. She had been called to answer to the board for her actions, but she didn't know why. Had John discovered she'd gone behind his back by contacting Wilfred's family? That was the most likely reason. She mentally prepared herself to beg the board's forgiveness and admit her sin as she followed John to his front door.

ISAAC PUZZLED OVER Lena's reaction to his mantel. He was particularly pleased with this piece. It had taken all his skill to convey an animal in motion. Lena seemed to like his other work.

Maybe she didn't approve of carving animals in general. Some might consider he was creating graven images by doing so. Perhaps the bishop of this district forbid such things. Surely John would have mentioned it if that were the case. Isaac would have to confer with the bishop before he joined this new congregation. It might not be the church for him.

A half hour later he was still working, but kept an eye out for Lena's return. Suddenly he saw her rush past the door with her hands covering her face. The sound of broken sobs reached him.

Dropping his tools, he raced out the door after her. "Lena, what is wrong?"

He caught up with her beneath a streetlight near the shop. She stopped and dropped her hands to her sides. "I've been fired."

"What?" He gaped at her in stunned surprise.

"I've been fired. I'm to finish out the week, which is only tomorrow, and then a new teacher will take over. All because I told Wilfred Cummings's granddaughter about the poaching even though I knew John wanted me to ignore it. I don't know how he found out." Her eyes suddenly flashed with anger. "Unless you told him."

"Me? Why would I tell him?"

"To make sure I didn't report it to anyone else."

He didn't know how to respond. She took a step closer and jabbed a finger into his chest. "Did you tell John? Did you kill Snagglehead and Goliath and who knows how many other deer? Tell me!"

She was like a spitting kitten attacking a bear. He took two steps back, but still she advanced. "I want the truth, Isaac!"

He held his hands up. "Lena, calm down."

"I am calm, and I want to know how you could carve Snagglehead so exactly without staring at his severed head!"

This couldn't be happening. The woman was unbalanced. He grabbed her arms. "You are not making any sense. Who is Shaggyhead?"

Her eyes narrowed. "He's the deer we found dead in the woods the first day you came to my school. The one you carved so beautifully into that fireplace mantel in John's workshop. You couldn't portray him so exactly from a glimpse of him in the wild. What do you have to say for yourself?"

Isaac's anger rose to match hers. She believed he was a poacher! And to think he was beginning to fall for her. He gripped her hand and pulled her along after him. "Come with me."

"Let me go."

He didn't slow down. A kitten was really no match for an angry bear. "Not until you've seen what I have to show you."

"Do you have a mantel with Goliath's head etched in it, too?"

He didn't reply until he was inside the shop by his workbench. Releasing her, he pulled open a drawer and shook a piece of paper under her nose. "This is how I knew what Bumblehead looked like."

"Snagglehead." She snatched the paper from his hand.

Lena didn't want to give Isaac the satisfaction of looking at the paper he shoved at her, but her angry outburst was beginning to wane and her common sense had started to creep back in. For a guilty man, he looked very indignant.

She opened the paper and stared at it. Her stomach dropped to the level of her shoes. It was one of her sketches, one that she'd done of Snagglehead last year.

Biting her lip, she looked up into Isaac's smoldering eyes. "Where did you get this?"

"I found it on the ground near the school."

Lena folded her arms. "On the day you had in your sights the biggest buck you'd ever seen? What luck that something scared him away."

"How could you know that?" Isaac folded his arms to mimic her stance. He looked much more imposing than she did.

"I was there. I was in the bell tower of the school. I saw it all."

"You scared the deer away?"

She raised her chin. "I did. You were hunting illegally."

"Is that so?" He arched an eyebrow.

He looked so sure of himself, her confidence began to seep away. "From my vantage point, it looked as if you were."

"But from your vantage point you could not see the legal wild boar permit and tag in my pocket."

"Wild boar? There weren't any wild boar in the field that day." She'd seen feral pigs numerous times in the past and knew what a nuisance they presented, but she hadn't noticed any when she'd seen Isaac for the first time.

"No, they weren't in the field. They were just beyond the trees and moving toward a cornfield where I have permission to hunt."

She wiped at the moisture on her face and sniffed once. "So you weren't aiming at the deer?"

"I was scouting the area. I saw your big deer and I did put my sights on him, but he wasn't what I was after. However..."

"When the deer spooked, the pigs did, too," she finished for him.

"There's no sausage in my larder this fall."

Lena pressed her hands to her forehead. "Oh, you must think I'm *ab im kopp*."

He unfolded his arms and took her hands between his big callused ones. "I don't think you're crazy. I think you are a woman who cares for all God's creatures. I'm so sorry my cousin fired you."

"If you didn't tell him I went to see Wilfred, who did?"

"I don't know. It could have been anyone."

"Isaac, can you forgive me for thinking such terrible things about you?"

"In time—if I can see more of your sketches."

"My drawings? Why?"

"The one I have was easy for me to copy in wood. There might be others I could use. I would pay you for any I chose."

"I will think about it."

"Fair enough. It's getting late. You should be getting home. Where is your buggy?"

"Papa dropped me off."

Isaac let go of her hands. She missed the strength and warmth of his touch instantly. "Is he coming back for you?"

"Nay." She hated to admit it. "Papa said a long walk to think over my sins would do my soul good."

"Then I shall join you on your trek."

Quickly, she shook her head. "You don't have to do that."

"But I do. I walked to work this morning, so I'm afoot, too. I will get a lantern for us."

"Is Ruby home alone?"

"Nay, she is spending the night with a friend from school."

"I am glad she is making friends here."

LENA WAS GRATEFUL for Isaac's large, reassuring presence as they walked along the verge of the highway. The night air was cold on her face, but there was no wind to make it biting. Isaac's lantern illuminated a small circle of the ground before them, but didn't reach into the dense forest that pressed close to the roadway. Only a sliver of moon hung in the sky.

Until the poaching started, Lena wouldn't have thought twice about walking home alone in the dark. Now, that sense of safety was gone. She wasn't sure it would ever return. Her quiet, uneventful corner of the world had been invaded by an evil presence.

She glanced at the tall man walking beside her. She was so glad he wasn't involved in the poaching.

As if he sensed her scrutiny, he looked her way. "My Ruby is happier now than I have seen her in many, many months. I have you to thank for that. You have been good for her in a way I could not be."

Should she tell him that his daughter spoke? Lena had promised her she wouldn't. If only she knew why Ruby didn't want her father to know. "Ruby is a special girl. There is nothing I want more than to help her."

"I see that about you. I wish I had your gift for making her happy."

Lena shoved her hands deeper into her coat pockets. Was this the time to ask about his wife? She was certain her death held the key to understanding Ruby's silence.

Knowing it might shatter the tenuous relationship she sensed growing between them, she hesitated, but finally said, "Isaac, can you tell me about the day your wife died?"

Seeing the sadness that came over his face touched Lena deeply. She wanted more than anything to comfort him, but wasn't sure how to do that. She laid her hand on his arm.

His lips pressed into a hard line. For a moment, she thought she had gone too far, pried too deeply.

He gave a deep sigh. "I reckon you are bound to hear

the story sooner or later. It is said that a man's pride goes before his fall. So it was with me, only it was my wife and child who suffered because of my sin."

CHAPTER NINE

ISAAC'S VOICE SHOOK with raw pain. Lena wanted to wrap her arms around him and hold him close, but she sensed he would reject her comfort. Instead, she said, "Tell me what happened."

"My carving was much in demand in the little community where we lived. Many *Englische* tourists came to our town and they paid well for Amish crafted furniture. Instead of giving more of my earnings to the church, I spent far too much to buy a high-stepping, spirited horse and a new buggy, the kind I always wanted when I was a boy."

He fell silent. Lena didn't press him. He had to find his own way to tell the story.

After drawing a deep breath, he said, "Ada Mae disliked our new horse. She didn't trust him. I told her she was being foolish. One day, she wanted to go visit her sister, who was ill. I promised I would close the shop at noon and take her, because I knew how much she hated to drive that horse."

Isaac stopped walking. Lena stood beside him. They were alone in the world, cocooned in the lantern light, with only the moon and the stars to see them.

After a short while Isaac began speaking again. "As I was closing up my shop, a man came in. He owned a store in New York City. He wanted to feature some of my work there. I was flattered by the offer and greedy at the thought of the money to be made. To my shame, I forgot that Ada Mae and Ruby were waiting for me."

"You are only human, Isaac. We all forget things."

"You are kind to say that, but it was my pride that made me forget them. When I came home an hour later, I found my wife lying in the barn. Ruby was with her. Ada Mae had grown tired of waiting for me and decided to drive herself. I wish she had simply come to the shop, but I imagine she was upset with me. She did have a temper at times.

"When she tried to harness the horse, he kicked her in the chest. The doctor said a broken rib punctured her lung. She lay dying for more than an hour as I discussed money with a man whose name I can't remember now."

"Oh, Isaac, how terrible."

"Terrible for me, yes, but worse for Ruby. She was with her mother the whole time. My workshop was less than two hundred yards away. I don't know why Ruby didn't come get me. If only she had."

He stopped as his voice broke with emotion. After a moment, he recovered enough to continue. "I managed to get Ada Mae to the doctor, but it was too late. She died in the hospital emergency room. If only Ruby had come to me as soon as it happened, Ada Mae might have been saved. I try to accept it was God's will, but I can't stop thinking that I could have saved her."

"Why *didn't* Ruby get you?"

"I don't know. I've asked her that a hundred times. Ada Mae's parents and her sisters, our bishop, my family, we all asked Ruby the same thing. She has never answered any of us. She's never spoken since that day."

"The poor child." The answer to Ruby's silence lay in the time she'd spent with her dying mother. Somehow, Lena needed to learn from Ruby herself what had happened that day.

She and Isaac walked along in silence until he said, "I don't know if she forgave me."

"Ruby?"

"My wife. I don't know if she forgave me or not. I pleaded for her forgiveness, but she never woke up. Now I will never know."

Lena grasped his arm, forcing him to stop and face her. "Isaac, was your wife a devout woman and true to her faith?"

"She was."

"Did she often neglect her Christian duty?"

He shook his head. "Never."

"You say that with great certainty."

"Ada Mae loved God. She lived her life to please him."

Lena wanted to shake him. "Why then do you think her faith failed her at the end?"

His brows drew together in a frown. "I never said she lost her faith."

"Is not forgiveness the cornerstone of all the Lord has taught us?"

"You know it is."

"Then *believe* that she forgave you, Isaac. To doubt that she did is to say her faith meant nothing to her."

"You are right," he admitted in a bemused voice.

"Frequently." She tugged on his arm. "Come, it's late and I have lessons to prepare for the morning."

The woods receded on one side as their route skirted the creek near the school. They were almost at the school lane when the sound of raised voices reached them, coming from near the covered bridge.

Isaac said, "Stay here. I will see what is going on."

"Nay, don't go." Lena grabbed his hand.

He squeezed her fingers. "Someone may need our help."

She was being silly. The woods weren't populated with bogeymen. She nodded. "You're right."

"Occasionally," he said, with a smile that set her insides whirling.

She grinned in return, but quickly sobered. "Be careful, Isaac."

A chill wind swept over her skin, making her shiver as she watched him walk toward the bridge. He held the lantern high and called out, "Is everything all right? Do you need help?"

A flash of light, followed by the report of a gun, made her jump. The lantern in Isaac's hand exploded and went dark. A second later, she was knocked to the ground by a hurtling force that carried her off the edge of the road and down the creek bank.

A hand clamped over her mouth. She struggled to get free until Isaac whispered in her ear, "Quiet."

Reeds poked Lena's back and scratched her neck. She lay panting under his weight, listening for the sound of another shot or the burning pain of a bullet. Silently, she prayed as she'd never prayed before.

Nearby, she heard a man's voice growing closer. "Are you crazy? No one cares about a few dead deer. If you kill a man, the law will be crawling all over us in no time."

"Quit your whining. I aimed for the light. I just wanted to scare him."

"How do you know you didn't scare him to death?" The sound of footsteps stopped on the road above. Lena squeezed her eyes closed. *Lord, deliver us from evil.*

"The Amish are tougher than that. Mind your own

business after this, farmer." An engine roared to life and a vehicle rumbled closer, then moved past, the noise fading into the distance. Gradually, the night sounds of the forest returned.

Lena realized her arms were pinned to her sides by Isaac's strong embrace. His face was mere inches from hers. He was listening intently. After a few minutes, he fastened his gaze on her face.

She whispered, "Are they gone?"

"I think so. Are you hurt?"

"I'm not sure, but I don't believe so." She was shaking from head to foot. She tried to sit up but his weight prevented it. She wiggled beneath him.

"Be still, woman." His voice held an odd quality that made her freeze.

"Isaac, let me up."

"Not yet. Lena Troyer, I'm surely going to regret this," he whispered, his breath tickling her ear and sending shivers over her skin.

"Regret what?"

"This." He lowered his face to hers and kissed her tenderly on the mouth.

It was Lena's first kiss, and so much more wonderful than she had imagined it would be. Isaac's beard prickled her skin, but in a good way, for it was softer than it looked. To her surprise, her nose didn't get in the way at all. Warmth flooded her body from the inside out. She wanted her arms free so she could wrap them around him.

As abruptly as it began, the kiss was over and Isaac was pulling her to her feet. "We should get out of here."

"Where shall we go?" she asked breathlessly. If he suggested they fly to the moon she was willing to go along with him.

He looked at her closely. "Are you sure you're okay?"

The warm, fuzzy haze brought on by his kiss was quickly being replaced by the cold reality of the situation. Gathering what dignity she could manage, she scrambled up the bank unaided. "I'm fine. I'm not the one they shot at. Are you okay?"

"My hand stings. I reckon I have a cut or two from broken glass." He climbed up after her.

She grasped his arm and held it toward the faint light of the moon. His hand was laced with black rivulets. She could smell the blood. Without a lantern it was impossible to tell how badly he was injured. "Should we go back to town?"

Isaac pulled away from her. He walked across the road and picked up his hat. After reshaping it, he settled it on his head. "They went in that direction. It's closer to go to your father's house."

"It is closer still to Clara's home. She has a phone. We can call the sheriff."

Isaac laid a hand on Lena's shoulder. "There's no need to do that. We must forgive these men and pray for them."

She nodded, embarrassed that she had so easily forgotten the teaching of her faith during her fright. "Then let us hurry home before they come back. They are surely madmen. May God protect us."

"And all those we care about," Isaac added, staring in the direction the men had gone.

THE FOLLOWING MORNING, Lena arrived at the school much later than normal. She had taken hours to fall asleep. It wasn't the fright that kept her awake, or the fact that she'd lost her job. No, it was reliving Isaac's kiss that had her staring at the ceiling of her bedroom until the wee hours.

What did it mean? Was he in love with her? How was that possible? They'd known each other only a few weeks.

She liked him. Okay, she more than liked him, but he'd not said a word about his intentions all the way to her father's house, or later, after she'd patched the cuts on his hand.

It was clear he still mourned the loss of his wife. Did Lena somehow remind him of her?

No, he kissed me! In her heart, she knew he hadn't been thinking about anyone else.

He was coming to tackle the barn repairs today. Somehow, she would find a chance to ask him what he meant by kissing her. Did he regret it, as he'd said he would?

"Please don't let that be so," she whispered.

She glanced at the clock; it was time to start classes. This would be the last time she did so. Tears stung her eyes as she rang the bell to call the children in from their play.

When everyone took their seats, she saw that Ruby and the twins were still absent. Lena glanced again at the clock on the wall. She would have to have a conversation with the twins' parents regarding their tardiness.

No, she would leave that task for the new teacher.

Suddenly, the door burst open. The twins came in, half carrying, half dragging a man between them. Blood covered the front of his clothing.

Lena rushed toward them. "What has happened?"

"We found this fellow down at the bridge. He's been shot."

The stranger's face was twisted in a grimace of pain.

His eyes opened and focused on her. "They're following me. Don't want to lead them here. Don't want to put the children in danger. Have to find Isaac."

"Isaac Bowman?"

"*Ja,* my brother." He tried to stand on his own but slumped forward. The twins kept him from falling.

Katie looked out the door. "There are two men on four-wheelers coming this way. Lena, they have guns."

"How far away are they?" she asked.

"They're at the bridge."

Lena ran down a list of possible hiding places, and discarded them all. There was no time to get the man up to the attic or out to the barn, and those were the first places the others were sure to search.

She glanced around and her gaze landed on her desk. In one of the romance novels she'd read, the heroine had hid inside the kneehole of a desk to avoid being detected. Would it work? She had no other choice.

Lena spoke to the children. "I want everyone to take his or her seat and remain silent no matter what happens. We must all pray to God to deliver us from evil this day."

She turned to the twins. "Help me hide him under my desk." The boys nodded and assisted the stranger to the front of the classroom, where he sank to the floor. Lena leaned down to speak to him. "You must remain silent. Can you do that?"

"Don't put yourself at risk for me," he managed to whisper.

"Just do as I say and be quiet." She helped push him into the space beneath her desk. He barely fit.

Quick-thinking Katie was already wiping up traces of blood from the floor with her apron. She stuffed it in her desk and sat down.

Lena spoke to the twins. "Take off your coats and give them to me. They have blood on them."

The boys did as she asked, and she used their coats to cover the wounded man. "Quickly, everyone take your seats and pray."

Lena pulled her chair up as close to the desk as she could get it. There was fear in every face looking up at her for courage. Barely a second later, the men drove up to the school. One appeared in the open doorway. The other came in the back way. Lena tensed. Both men carried rifles.

Lena stayed seated, hoping her skirt would hide the wounded man as one of the gunmen walked behind her.

"May I help you?" She was amazed at how level her voice sounded.

"We're looking for someone," the man in front of her said. Lena realized that she knew him. It was Chuck Carter, the husband of Wilfred's granddaughter.

Lena held her hands wide. "As you can see, there is no one dangerous here."

"I think we'll just have a look for ourselves." Chuck advanced into the room. His companion went to check out the window.

Lena said, "You are frightening the children with your guns. Please take them outside, then search all you want."

"Not a chance, lady. If everyone sits quietly, no one will get hurt."

Lena repeated what he had said in Pennsylvania Dutch so that the youngest children could understand. She calmly reassured them in the same language.

Chuck Carter scowled at her. "What did you just say?"

Lena rose and moved from her desk to the front row,

where Mary was starting to cry. She put her arm around the child. "Some of the students don't yet understand English. I simply told them what you said."

"Ask them if they've seen a blond man dressed in jeans and a red shirt this morning."

Lena pretended to repeat his question, but she actually told the children to all shake their heads.

The man near the window said, "Boss, someone is coming. A buggy just turned off the highway."

Chuck grabbed Lena by the elbow and pulled her toward the glass. "Who is it?"

She recognized Isaac and her heart sank. He and Ruby were driving into danger, and there was nothing she could do about it. "It is Isaac Bowman. He has come to fix the hayloft door."

Letting go of her, Chuck said, "Take your seat. Dick, check upstairs and then go bring in the Amish fellow. I'll keep an eye on him while you search the barn. Sam couldn't have gotten far."

Fear tightened Lena's throat. "Please, we mean you no harm."

"It's not you I'm worried about. Do as you're told and everything will be fine. Once we find the...poacher, we'll take him to jail." Chuck smiled at her, but his eyes remained cold. She didn't believe him. They were all in danger.

Behind him, Lena saw Ruby standing in the doorway with a look of panic on her face. Neither of the men had seen her. Speaking in Pennsylvania Dutch, Lena calmly said, "Go back to the barn and tell your father that there are men with guns here. Go very quietly. Tell him they are looking for a wounded man that I have hidden under my desk. He must go for help quickly before these men can stop him. Understand?"

Ruby nodded and backed down the steps.

Chuck's eyes narrowed. "What are you yammering about?"

"I'm praying for your soul. We are all praying for your soul." She began the Lord's Prayer in German. The children joined in.

Isaac heard a whisper behind him. He turned in astonishment when he realized it was Ruby. He stared at her mutely.

She whispered more loudly, "Papa, Lena is in trouble."

Joy sent a jolt through his heart and made it skip a beat. He dropped to his knees and grasped his child's shoulders. "Ruby, you spoke."

She nodded. "Help her, Papa."

"I don't understand. Why does Lena need my help?"

"There are men with guns in the school. You have to help Lena." Ruby's voice grew stronger.

Men with guns? Were they the ones who'd shot at him last night? He rose to his feet. He had no idea what he could do against armed men, but he wasn't leaving Lena to face them alone. "Ruby, I want you to hide in the hayloft."

She grabbed his arm. "Lena wants you to go for help. The men are looking for a wounded man. Lena is hiding him under her desk."

Isaac racked his brain for a way to help Lena and the children inside. If the men were hunting for someone, he would give them someone to chase. He might be able to draw them away from the school long enough to let the children and Lena escape.

He knelt beside his child again. "Ruby, can you run

to the nearest *Englische* house and tell them what is happening?"

She nodded. "I can."

"Can you run through the woods and stay clear of the road?"

"*Ja,* I can do it."

He had to trust her. "I am going to lead the men away from here. I want you to watch from the window. When they follow my buggy around the bend in the road and you can't see them anymore, I want you to run as fast as you can."

Drawing the men away would work for only a short time. How could Lena get everyone to safety by herself? She couldn't. He would have to help.

He looked toward the covered bridge, which sat at a slight angle to the school. If he jumped out of the buggy as it came out the other side, he might be able to get under the bridge and hide before the men went by. Or they might see him and know it was a trick.

But what choice did he have? Nothing else came to mind. His only other option was to walk up to the school and stand calmly beside Lena as they waited for God's mercy.

If his plan failed, Isaac would do just that.

He gathered Ruby in his arms. "I love you more than you will ever know. Do not fear. God will protect you."

He kissed her cheek and set her back on the floor. Then he looked out the doorway. Sophie stood calmly beside the barn with her head drooping. Her quiet demeanor didn't fool Isaac. Like many Amish-owned horses, Sophie had been a racehorse in her younger years. When she broke into a run, she could still fly like the wind.

The buggy sat between the barn and the school. He

prayed the gunmen would believe their quarry was escaping.

He glanced at Ruby. "Ready?"

She shook her head as tears streamed down her face. She hadn't gone for help for her mother and he had no idea why. Isaac prayed she would be able to do it now.

He pulled her close once more. "You can do this. I have faith in you. You can save Lena and all the children. All you have to do is run. Okay?"

"Okay," she whispered, and wiped her tears.

He wanted his daughter away and safe. He didn't know how he would live if any harm came to her.

Isaac slipped out of the barn and into the buggy. Once there, he slapped the reins against Sophie's rump. She jumped and trotted off. He slapped her again and yelled. By the time she reached the bridge she was at a full gallop.

Isaac glanced out the rear window. Two men stood on the school step. Ruby ran out and pointed toward him. Why wasn't she hiding?

He didn't have time to wonder. Sophie slowed only a little when she entered the bridge. Isaac had a second to think he was as likely to break his neck as he was to succeed in this crazy plan, then he jumped.

He hit the ground on the far side of the bridge, clipping the timber with his shoulder as he did so. Pain shot up his arm as he rolled off the road and down the creek bank. He ignored it as he scrambled to get under the bridge and out of sight.

Sophie continued on at a dead run down the school lane, and swung to the left when she hit the blacktop. She knew the way home.

The sound of engines was his first indication that his

plan was working. Within moments, two four-wheelers roared across the bridge and after Isaac's buggy.

Peering through the tall grasses, Isaac saw Sophie toss up her head as the machines bore down on her. She instantly picked up her pace. The race was on as she galloped around the bend in the road, with his buggy bumping and swaying behind her.

"Go, Sophie, go," he muttered as he climbed out of the creek bed. He flexed his arm, glad to realize nothing was broken.

It was a good thing, because Ruby came flying through the bridge and launched herself into his arms. He kissed her and put her down. "Go now, child. I'm all right."

She grinned. "I told a big lie, papa. I told those men someone was stealing your buggy."

Wonderful child. "You are forgiven," he said, "but you must never lie again. Now go."

She took off like a deer into the woods, making a beeline for Clara's farm.

LENA SHOVED THE DESK aside, folded her apron into a thick pad and pressed it against the oozing wound in the stranger's side. All the children were grouped around her. The man opened his eyes. "That hurts."

"*Gut,* that means you are still alive. We must get out of here. Those men will come back."

"I think I'm past walking." He closed his eyes again.

Lena bit her lip. How was she going to get him to safety, and the children, too? She looked at Katie. Her family's farm was the closest to the school. Could she trust Katie with the lives of so many *kinder?* What choice did she have?

"I'm putting you in charge, Katie. Take all of the

children and get into the woods as fast as you can. You older children, carry the little ones if you have to. Stick together and don't stop until you reach Katie's home."

Katie's eyes grew wide. "What are you going to do, Lena?"

"I must stay with this man."

"But those bad men may come back." Mary glanced fearfully at the door.

"As long as I know all of you are safe, I'll be fine. Go now!"

Katie quickly took charge. Picking up Fannie, she herded the rest of the children toward the door. Suddenly, it swung open. Mary screamed.

Lena jumped to her feet and stepped over the wounded man to place her body between him and his assailants. Instead of the gunmen, Isaac stood in the doorway. Lena flew down the aisle and threw her arms around him. "You're safe."

He returned her hug. "For now. We've got to get out of here. I don't know how soon they'll be back."

Lena spoke to Katie. "Take the children and do as I said."

They piled out the door, leaving Isaac and Lena alone. She looked behind him. "Where is Ruby?"

"She's gone to your friend Clara's house."

"Clara won't be there. She teaches school. But perhaps Brad will be home."

"Ruby is smart. If they are not there, she will go to your father's house."

A low moan drew their attention to the wounded man. Isaac's eyes widened in shock. He rushed toward the stranger and dropped to his knees. "Samuel, what has happened?"

"I got shot."

Lena looked from one to the other. "You know each other?"

Isaac nodded. "This is my *Englische* brother, Samuel. He works for the Department of Wildlife as an undercover agent. Who shot you, and why?"

"I came back to look for you last night...to make sure you were okay. Chuck Carter followed me. He figured out then that I wasn't who I claimed to be. We fought. Lost my gun in the shuffle. I got away, but he managed to get a shot off. I foolishly got in the way of the bullet. He and his wife are the brains behind this poaching ring."

"I can't believe Wilfred would allow them to do this," Lena said. "He loves the deer."

"The old man can't get out of bed since his last stroke, but he's no fool. He let his granddaughter know he changed his will. When he dies, she gets nothing. As long as he's alive, she has a place to stay and food to eat. She and her husband decided to make some quick money off the old man by selling illegal hunts and poaching deer on his property while he's too sick to realize what they're doing. When the deer are gone, they will be, too."

"Wilfred has been trapped in that house with such evil people?" Lena couldn't suppress a shiver.

Samuel's brows furrowed with pain. "Luckily, his attorney is also an old friend. The guy comes out from Canton once a week to check on him. I think they would have let the old guy starve to death if no one had been the wiser."

Lena pressed a hand to her heart. "Poor Wilfred."

Isaac rested a palm on Samuel's flushed face. "Why didn't you come to me?"

"I tried. After I got shot, I hid until daylight. Then

I started for your place. I guess I passed out. The next thing I knew, two boys were trying to drag me here. I'm so sorry. I didn't mean to bring those men down on a school full of kids."

Isaac quickly reassured him. "God was merciful. The children are all safe. Now we must get you out of here. Sophie cannot run forever. When they catch her, they will find my buggy is empty and they'll be back."

Isaac slipped one arm under Samuel's knees and another around his shoulders, then picked him up as easily as a child.

Samuel groaned.

Lena rushed to open the door for them. "You can't carry him all the way to town."

"Sure I can. Samuel is the runt of the litter, aren't you?"

His brother managed a half smile. "It's better than being bigger than an ox."

Outside, Lena checked the road. There wasn't any sign of the gunmen returning. "Hurry. If we can get across the bridge, we can hide in the woods beyond and make our way to town. I know a path. It's steep and rough, but shorter than staying on the highway. The children from town come that way to school. We will have to cross the road several times, for it meanders back and forth, but if we are careful, we should be able to get Samuel to a doctor without being seen."

"She's got a quick wit, Isaac. I think she might be the one you've been praying for."

"Shut up and save your breath," he growled.

Lena had little time to wonder what they were talking about. Even though he was carrying his brother, she had a hard time keeping up with Isaac's long strides. When they reached the blacktop, he said, "Lena, you don't have to stay with us. You will be safer alone."

"Nonsense. I'm not leaving you and that is that," she declared, propping her hands on her hips.

"Oh, yes, she's the one, big brother." Samuel laughed weakly, then his head rolled back and she knew he had fainted.

The three of them had gone nearly half a mile through the woods when they came to the road again. They'd started across it when Lena heard the sound of an engine. "They're coming!"

Isaac stopped. "*Nay*, that's a truck, not a four-wheeler."

No sooner had he said that than a gray pickup came barreling around the bend in front of them. It skidded to a stop and Lena saw the driver was Brad Jenkins. Ruby sat on the seat beside him.

Lena rushed to open the door. She pulled Ruby into her arms. "I'm so glad you are safe."

The girl hugged her back. "I got help."

Lena smiled at her. "I see you did. Bless you, child."

With Brad's help, Samuel was loaded into the back of the truck. Isaac sat beside him, pillowing his head on his lap as Brad headed for the hospital in Millersburg, the closest large town.

HOURS LATER, an exhausted Lena sat on a chair in the hospital waiting room. Ruby was curled up beside her. Isaac had gone to find them some coffee.

Samuel had come through surgery without complications. He was in the recovery room now and would soon be moved to a room where they could see him. Lena shifted her position on the hard seat.

Ruby woke up when Lena moved. "Are the bad men coming?"

"Nay," Lena soothed. "All the bad men have been taken to jail. We will not see them again."

"Is *Onkel* Samuel okay?"

"The doctors say he will be fine. We should be able to see him soon. I want to tell you how brave you were today, Ruby." Lena looked up to see Isaac standing in the doorway, a cup of coffee in each hand.

"Today, maybe, but not when my *mamm* died. I wasn't brave then." The girl's voice cracked and she tried to stifle her tears.

Lena stroked Ruby's cheek, but didn't take her gaze off Isaac. He said, "I'm sure you were brave that day, too, only in a different way."

Ruby looked over at him. *"Mamm* said, 'Don't leave me, Ruby. Your papa will come soon. He'll come. Don't leave me.' I should have left her. I should have gone for help. You were so mad at me for staying with her. I tried to tell you what happened, but I couldn't speak."

"Oh, *liebchen,*" Isaac said as Lena took the coffee from him. He sat beside Ruby and gathered her into his arms. "It was not your fault. God wanted your mother to come and live in joy with him. You cannot change the will of God."

"Do you still hate me, Papa?"

Isaac's voice trembled. "I've never hated you, Ruby. I have loved you every day of your life."

"I'm sorry I didn't go for help, Papa. I'm sorry I let Mama die."

He held her close, and tears welled up in his eyes. "I'm sorry I didn't come. Can you forgive me for failing you and your mother?"

Ruby cupped his face between her hands. "I forgive you, Papa. Please don't cry."

He kissed her hands and then her cheek. "Bless you, child. You will forever remind me of the love she and I shared. You are, and have always been, God's gift to me."

Lena had tears in her eyes, too. It was so good to see them repairing the damage silence and guilt had caused.

Isaac managed a watery smile for Lena. "We have had quite an adventure-filled day."

She pressed a hand to her mouth as a giggle escaped.

He gave her an odd look. "What is so funny?"

"All my life I have wanted to have adventures. I had no idea how frightening and exhausting they can be. I hope I am done with them."

"I'm sorry to hear you say that."

She cocked her head to the side. "Why?"

"I have been thinking about another sort of adventure you might like to consider."

She gave him a puzzled glance. "What kind do you mean?"

"The kind where I pick you up in my buggy and we go for rides in the evenings and after church services. Maybe even a picnic or two when the weather gets warm again."

Ruby looked from Lena to her father. "That's what courting couples do. Are you going to court Lena? 'Cause if you are, I think that's great. I like her a lot."

He smiled indulgently at his daughter. "It's up to Lena more than it's up to me."

Taking Lena's hand in his, Isaac gave her fingers a

gentle squeeze. "What about it, Lena Troyer? Are you up for another adventure?"

She smiled and squeezed his hand in return. "*Ja,* that sounds like an adventure I would love."

EPILOGUE

THE FOLLOWING WEEKS WERE busy ones for Lena. The day after the gunmen came to the school, Isaac took Lena to visit John Miller at his home. When John learned it was Lena's quick thinking and bravery that had saved his cousin's life and kept the children safe, he happily restored her position as teacher for as long as she might want it.

He called a special school board meeting for Friday evening and stood before everyone as he shared his decision. Grateful parents and grandparents came forward to thank Lena, Isaac and Ruby for their part in preventing a tragedy. Lena was overwhelmed by the gratitude of her community. The experience was truly humbling.

Her students came to school excited and happy to learn she wasn't leaving. It took far more discipline than she normally used to get the boisterous pupils to settle down and return to their lessons. Luckily, it was time to start planning for the school Christmas program. Everyone looked forward to the event and wanted to be included.

In her letter to her cousins, Lena downplayed her part in the events, but Abby and Sarah quickly wrote back asking for more details about the chilling episode and about Isaac Bowman.

Seated at her desk in the empty schoolhouse, Lena brought out the last circle letter to read again while she waited for Isaac to pick her up. She had such good news to share with him.

When the schoolhouse door opened, she looked up and knew she would never tire of seeing his large frame filling the doorway. He had won her heart and she would never let him forget how much she loved him.

He rushed inside. "Are you ready? Our driver is anxious to get going. He says the forecast is calling for snow tonight."

"Isaac Bowman, that is no way to enter the school building. First, you must come and greet me properly."

"My apologies, teacher." He strode forward, leaned over the desk and kissed her.

When he straightened, she smiled. "That is much better."

He sat on the corner of her desk. "School was never this much fun when I was young. What have you got there?" He pointed at the papers in her hand.

"A circle letter from my cousins. They wish to hear more about you."

"About me? What have you told them already?"

"That you are kind and a gifted carver and a great kisser."

He frowned. "You didn't!"

"No, silly. But I may."

Standing, he took her hand. "Leave the letter here and come along. Wilfred is expecting us."

"Poor man, he has no one else to visit him." Wilfred Cummings had been moved to a nursing home outside Millersburg. It was doubtful he would ever go home again. Lena visited him weekly, but found him saddened by the events and his family's part in them.

Lena stood, but slipped the letter in her pocket. Isaac

waited impatiently as she got her coat. When they were in the car at last and on their way, he relaxed.

Lena leaned forward to speak to the driver Isaac hired for her weekly trips. "Mr. Johnson, would you be able to drive us to Spring Township in Pennsylvania the first Thursday of December?"

"I would. What's the occasion?"

"My cousin Sarah Weaver is getting married to Jacob Mast and I'd like Isaac to meet them."

Isaac looked at Lena with a bright grin. "That's wonderful news."

"I think so. Mr. Johnson, would you be able to drive us to Homestead, Ohio, on the second Thursday in January?"

"I reckon so. Another wedding?"

"Yes, my cousin Abigail Baughman is marrying Ben Kline. I'm dying to meet the man who won her heart."

Isaac whispered in her ear. "With all these weddings in the works, it's giving me ideas."

She sat back and looked at him with wide, innocent eyes. "What ideas?"

"Why don't we follow these visits with a wedding trip of our own?"

Her mouth dropped open. "Isaac Bowman, that is no way to propose to a girl."

"I'm not proposing to a girl. I'm proposing to a sensible, loving woman who has the chance to make my life and Ruby's life complete by saying yes."

The driver suddenly slammed on his brakes. Lena had a glimpse of a deer leaping across the road in front of them as the car skidded to a halt. Mr. Johnson let out a low whistle. "Do you see the size of that buck? Where were you during hunting season, fella?"

Lena and Isaac looked toward the forest. At the edge

of the woods, Goliath stood with his head held high. A light snow was beginning to fall. He gave one shake of his majestic antlers and vanished among the trees.

Turning to Isaac, Lena leaned toward him and whispered one word in his ear. "Yes."

* * * * *